"Without Fu-Manchu we wouldn't have Dr. No, Doctor Doom or Dr. Evil. Sax Rohmer created the first truly great evil mastermind. Devious, inventive, complex, and fascinating. These novels inspired a century of great thrillers!"
Jonathan Maberry, *New York Times* bestselling author of *Assassin's Code* and *Patient Zero*

"The true king of the pulp mystery is Sax Rohmer—and the shining ruby in his crown is without a doubt his Fu-Manchu stories."
James Rollins, *New York Times* bestselling author of *The Devil Colony*

"Fu-Manchu remains the definitive diabolical mastermind of the 20th Century. Though the arch-villain is 'the Yellow Peril incarnate,' Rohmer shows an interest in other cultures and allows his protagonist a complex set of motivations and a code of honor which often make him seem a better man than his Western antagonists. At their best, these books are very superior pulp fiction... at their worst, they're still gruesomely readable."
Kim Newman, award-winning author of *Anno Dracula*

"Sax Rohmer is one of the great thriller writers of all time! Rohmer created in Fu-Manchu the model for the super-villains of James Bond, and his hero Nayland Smith and Dr. Petrie are worthy stand-ins for Holmes and Watson... though Fu-Manchu makes Professor Moriarty seem an under-achiever."
Max Allan Collins, *New York Times* bestselling author of *The Road to Perdition*

"I grew up reading Sax Rohmer's Fu-Manchu novels, in cheap paperback editions with appropriately lurid covers. They completely entranced me with their vision of a world constantly simmering with intrigue and wildly overheated ambitions. Even without all the exotic detail supplied by Rohmer's imagination, I knew full well that world wasn't the same as the one I lived in... For that alone, I'm grateful for all the hours I spent chasing around with Nayland Smith and his stalwart associates, though really my heart was always on their intimidating opponent's side."
K. W. Jeter, acclaimed author of *Infernal Devices*

THE COMPLETE FU-MANCHU SERIES
BY SAX ROHMER

Available now from Titan Books:
THE MYSTERY OF DR. FU-MANCHU
THE RETURN OF DR. FU-MANCHU
THE HAND OF DR. FU-MANCHU
DAUGHTER OF FU-MANCHU

Coming soon from Titan Books:
THE BRIDE OF FU-MANCHU
THE TRAIL OF FU-MANCHU
PRESIDENT FU-MANCHU
THE DRUMS OF FU-MANCHU
THE ISLAND OF FU-MANCHU
THE SHADOW OF FU-MANCHU
RE-ENTER FU-MANCHU
EMPEROR FU-MANCHU
THE WRATH OF FU-MANCHU

THE MASK OF FU-MANCHU

SAX ROHMER

TITAN BOOKS

THE MASK OF FU-MANCHU
Print edition ISBN: 9780857686077
E-book edition ISBN: 9780857686732

Published by Titan Books
A division of Titan Publishing Group Ltd
144 Southwark Street, London SE1 0UP

First edition: March 2013
10 9 8 7 6 5 4 3 2 1

First published as a novel in the UK by Cassell and Co. Ltd, 1933
First published as a novel in the US by Doubleday, Doran, 1932

The Authors Guild and the Society of Authors assert the moral right to be
identified as the author of this work.

Visit our website: www.titanbooks.com

Did you enjoy this book? We love to hear from our readers.
Please email us at readerfeedback@titanemail.com or write
to us at Reader Feedback at the above address.

To receive advance information, news, competitions, and exclusive offers online,
please sign up for the Titan newsletter on our website: www.titanbooks.com

Frontispiece illustration: a movie theater premium based on a design by W. T.
Benda, acclaimed mask maker from the early twentieth century, and illustrator
of the cover for the May 7, 1932 issue of *Collier's* magazine. Special thanks to Dr.
Lawrence Knapp for the illustration from "The Page of Fu Manchu," http://
www.njedge.net/~knapp/FuFrames.htm.

A CIP catalogue record for this title is available from the British Library.

Printed and bound in the United States.

This cardboard mask, handed out by theaters to promote the 1932 movie *The Mask of Fu Manchu* (starring Boris Karloff), was based on a design by artist W. T. Benda for the Rohmer serialization in *Collier's* magazine.

CHAPTER ONE

ONE NIGHT IN ISPAHAN

"Shan! Shan!"

Someone calling my name persistently. The voice was faint. I had been asleep, but dreaming hard, an evil from which ordinarily I don't suffer. The voice fitted into my dream uncannily...

I had dreamed I was asleep in my tent in that desolate spot on the Khorassan border, not a hundred yards from the valley called the Place of the Great Magician. No expedition of Sir Lionel's in which I had been employed had so completely got on my nerves as this one.

Persia was new territory for me. And the chief's sense of the dramatic, his innate showmanship (a trait which had done him endless damage in the eyes of the learned societies) had resulted in my being more or less in the dark as to the real object of our journey.

Perhaps, when names now famous are forgotten, that of Sir Lionel Barton will be remembered; he will be measured at his true stature—as the greatest Orientalist of his century. But, big, lovable, generous, I must nevertheless state quite definitely that he was next to impossible to work with.

When he made that historic discovery, when I realised what we had come for and what we had found, I experienced an attack of cold feet from which up to the moment of this queer awakening I had never wholly recovered.

It's a poor joke to dig up a Moslem saint, even if he happens to have been really a heretic. I never remembered to have welcomed anything more than Sir Lionel's decision to trek swiftly south-west to Ispahan...

"Shan! Shan!"

That voice again—and yet I could not escape from my dream. I thought that only two stretches of canvas separated me from the long green box, the iron casket containing those strange fruits of our discovery.

Sir Lionel's party was not a large one, but I felt that the Moslems were not to be relied upon. It is one thing to excavate the tombs of the Pharaohs; it is a totally different thing in the eyes of an Arab to desecrate the resting place of a true believer, or even of a near-true believer.

To Ali Mahmoud, the headman, I would have trusted my life in Mecca; but the six Egyptians, who, together with Rima, Dr. Van Berg, Sir Lionel, and myself made up the party, although staunch enough ordinarily, had occasioned me grave doubts almost from the moment we had entered Persian territory.

As for the Afghan, Amir Khan...

"Shan!"

I threw off the coil of dreams. I opened my eyes to utter darkness. My right hand automatically reached out for the torch—and in the physical movement came recognition of my true surroundings.

Khorassan? I was not in Khorassan. Nor was I under canvas—

had not been under canvas for more than a week. I was in a house in Ispahan, and someone was calling me!

I grasped the torch, pressed the button, and looked about.

A scantily furnished room, I saw, its door of unpainted teak, as were the beams supporting its ceiling. I saw a rug of very good quality upon an otherwise uncarpeted floor, a large table littered with papers, photographs, books, and other odds and ends, and, from where I lay in bed, very little else.

My dream slipped into the background. The doubtful loyalty of our Moslem Egyptian workers counted for nothing, since by now they were probably back in Egypt, having been paid off a week before.

But—the green box! The green box was in Van Berg's room, on the floor above… and the door directly facing my bed was opening!

I reached down with my left hand. A Colt repeater hung from a nail there. Sir Lionel had taught me this trick. To place a pistol openly beside one's bed is to arm the enemy; to put it under the pillow is simply stupid. In doubtful environment, the chief invariably used a nail or hook, whichever was practicable, between his bed and the wall.

Directing the ray of my torch upon the moving doors, I waited. As I did so, the door was flung open fully. Light shone upon tousled mahogany-coloured curls and wide-open, startled gray eyes; upon a slim, silk-clad figure!

"Turn the light out, Shan—quick!"

It was Rima who stood in the open doorway.

I switched off the light; but in the instant of pressing the switch I glanced at my watch. The hour was 2 A.M.

11

CHAPTER TWO

WAILING IN THE AIR

It was one of those situations to which at times I thought the dear old chief took a delight in exposing me. His humour inclined to the sardonic, and in electing, when we left Nineveh, to start off without a break or any leave east into Persia and right up to the Afghan border, he had seriously upset my plans.

Rima, his niece, and I were to have been married on our return to England after the Syrian job. Sir Lionel's change of plan had scotched that scheme. There was laughter in his twinkling eyes when he had notified me of the fact that information just received demanded our immediate presence in Khorassan.

"But what about the wedding. Chief?" I remember saying.

"Well, what about it, Greville?"

"There are plenty of padres in these parts, and the engagement has been overlong. Besides, after all, Rima and I are wandering about in camp together, from spot to spot..."

"Greville," he interrupted me, "when you marry Rima, you're going to be married from my town house. The ceremony will take place at St. Margaret's, and I shall give the bride away. I don't care a hoot about the proprieties, Greville. You ought to know that by now. We're setting out for Khorassan tomorrow morning. Rima is a brilliant photographer, and I want her to come with us. But if she prefers to go back to England—she can go."

This was the situation in which my brilliant but erratic chief had involved me. And now, at 2 A.M., Rima, with whom I was hungrily in love, had burst into my room in that queer house in Ispahan, and already in the darkness was beside me.

I wonder, indeed I have often wondered, if my make-up is different from that of other men: definitely I am no squire of dames. But, further, I have sometimes thought that although ardour has by no means been left out of me, I have inherited from somewhere an overweight of the practical; so that at any time, and however deeply my affections might be engaged, the job would come before the woman.

So it was now; for, my arm about Rima's slim, silky waist, her first whispered words in the darkness made me forget how desirable she was and how I longed for the end of this strange interlude, for the breaking down of that barrier unnaturally raised by my erratic chief.

"Shan!" She bent close to my ear. "There was a most awful cry from Dr. Van Berg's room a few minutes ago!"

I jumped up, still holding her. She was trembling slightly.

"I opened my window and listened. His room is almost right over mine, and I felt certain that was where the cry had come from. But I couldn't hear anything."

"Was the voice Van Berg's?"

"I couldn't tell, dear. It was a kind of—scream. Then, as I hurried along to wake you, I heard something else—"

She clung to me tightly.

"What, darling?"

"I don't know!" She shuddered violently. "A sort of dreadful *wailing*... Shan! I believe it came from the mosque!"

"Then you called out?"

"I didn't call out till I got right to your door and had it open."

I understood then that I had confused dreaming with reality. The distant voice, as it had seemed to me, had been that of Rima urgently calling at the opened door.

"It's the green box!" she whispered, in an even lower tone. "Shan, I'm terrified! You know what happened on Thursday night! It must have been the same sound..."

That thought was on my own mind. Van Berg had been disturbed on Thursday night by an inexplicable happening, an outstanding feature of which had been a strange moaning sound. The chief had declined to take it seriously; but I knew our American colleague for a man of sound common sense not addicted to nervous imaginings.

And the green box was in his room...

Barefooted, I stepped towards the door, releasing Rima, whom I had been holding tightly.

"Stay here, darling," I said, "unless I call you."

I crept out into the corridor. It was dimly lighted a few paces along by a high, barred window. Almost opposite in the narrow street stood a deserted mosque, its minaret, from the balcony of which no mueddin had called for many years, overlooking the roof of our temporary residence. Moonlight, reflected from the dingy yellow wall of this mosque, vaguely illuminated the passage ahead of me.

The once holy building had a horrible history, and I knew that Rima associated the sound she had heard with the legend of the mosque.

Stock still I stood for a moment, listening.

The house was silent as a vault. It possessed three floors. The rooms beneath on the ground floor contained the stored furniture—

or part of it—of the owner from whom Sir Lionel had leased the place. The ground-floor windows were heavily barred, and Ali Mahmoud slept in the lobby; so that none could enter without arousing him.

There were four rooms above, two of them unoccupied. Locked in one were a pair of Caspian kittens, beautiful little creatures with fur like finest silk, destined for the chief's private menagerie, practical zoology being one of his hobbies. In the end, or southeast, room, Dr. Van Berg was quartered. Our records, the bulk of our photographs, and other valuables were in his charge as well as the green box.

No sound disturbed the silence.

I advanced cautiously in the direction of the staircase. The widely open door of Rima's room was on my left. Moonlight poured in upon the polished uncarpeted floor. Her shutters were open.

Pausing for a moment, puzzled, I suddenly remembered that she had opened them when that cry in the night had disturbed her.

Personally, I kept mine religiously closed against the incursions of nocturnal insects, since we were near the bank of the river and no great distance from a fruit market. I had switched off my torch, the reflected light through the high window being sufficient for my purpose. I passed Rima's door—then pulled up short, my nerves jangling.

From somewhere, outside the house, and high up, came a singular sound.

It was a sort of whistle in a minor key, resembling nothing so much as a human imitation of a police whistle. It changed, passing from a moan to an indescribable wail... and dying away.

"Shan, did you hear it? That's *the sound*!" Rima's voice reached me in a quavering whisper, and:

"I heard it," I answered in a low voice. "For God's sake, stay where you are."

The chief's door was ahead of me, in comparative shadow there at the end of the passage. I could see that it was closed: a teak door, ornamented with iron scrollwork. Sir Lionel was a heavy sleeper. A narrow stair opened on the right and led down to the lobby. No sound reached me from beneath. Evidently Ali Mahmoud had not been aroused.

On my left was a stair to the floor above. I crept up.

My nerves were badly jangled, and creaking of the ancient woodwork sounded in my ears like pistol shots. I gained the top corridor. Two windows faced west, commanding a view of low, flat roofs stretching away to a distant prospect of the river. The moonlight was dazzling. In contrast to the passage below it was like stepping from midnight into high noon.

I paused again for a moment, listening intently.

A sound of scurrying movement reached my ears from beyond Van Berg's closed door. I took a step forward and paused again. Then, my hand on the clumsy native latch:

"Van Berg!" I said softly.

The only reply was a queer soft, plaintive howl.

Let me confess that this nearly unnerved me. A vague but unmistakable menace had been overhanging us from the hour of our momentous discovery in Khorassan. Now, awakened as I had been, my memory repeating over and over again that weird, wailing sound, I recognized that I was by no means at my best.

Clenching my teeth, I raised the latch…

I peered along the narrow room. It extended from the corridor to the opposite side of the house. I saw that the shutters were open in the deep, recessed window. Moonlight reflected from the wall of the mosque afforded scanty illumination.

A sickly sweet perfume hung in the air, strongly resembling that of mimosa, but having a pungency which gripped me by the throat. I pressed the button of my torch.

Some vague thing, indeterminate, streaky, leapt towards me. I shrank back, pistol levelled... And for the second time I heard *the sound*.

Perhaps I have never been nearer to true panic in my life. That moaning wail seemed to come from outside the house—and from high above. It seemed to vibrate throughout my entire nervous system. It was the most utterly damnable sound to which I had ever listened.

Only my sudden recognition of one of the facts saved me. The Caspian kittens were in the room! I remembered, and gasped in my relief, that the doctor was extremely fond of them. The little creatures, who were very tame, crouched at my feel, looking up at me with their big eyes, appealingly, as it seemed.

A vague stirring came from the depths of the house. The smell of mimosa was overpowering... Probably Rima had run down and aroused Ali Mahmoud.

These ideas, chaotically, with others too numerous to record, flashed through my mind at the same moment that, stricken motionless with horror, I stood staring down upon Dr. Van Berg, where he lay under the light of my torch.

His heavy body was huddled in so strange a position that, what with anger, regret, fear and other unnameable emotions, I could not at first realise what had happened. He was clothed in silk pajamas of an extravagant pattern which he affected, and his fair hair, which he wore long, hung down over his forehead so that it touched the floor.

He was lying across the green box.

He lay in such a way that his big body almost obscured the box from my view. But now I saw that his powerful arms were outstretched, and that his fingers were locked in a death grip upon the handles at either end.

That long moment of horrified inertia passed.

I sprang forward and dropped upon one knee. I tried to speak, but only a husky murmur came. There was blood on the lid of the box, and a pool was gathering upon the floor beside it. I put my hand under Van Berg's chin and lifted his face. Then I stood upright, feeling very ill.

What I had seen had wiped the slate of consciousness clear of all but one thing. My fingers quivered on the Colt repeater. I wanted the life of the cowardly assassin who had done Van Berg to death—big, gentle, fearless Van Berg. For here was murder—cold-blooded murder!

A sort of buzzing in my ears died away and left me perfectly cool, with just that one desire for retribution burning in my brain. I heard footsteps—muffled voices. I didn't heed them.

I was staring about the room. Staring at the open window trying to recall details of Van Berg's story of what had happened on the Thursday night. In the room there was no hiding place, and the window was thirty feet above street level. The mystery of the thing was taking hold of me.

"Greville Effendim," I heard.

I glanced back over by shoulder. Ali Mahmoud stood in the open doorway—and I saw Rima's pale face behind him.

"Don't come in, Rima!" I said hastily. "For God's sake, don't come in. Go down and wake the chief."

CHAPTER THREE

THE GREEN BOX

Upon the horror of that murder in the night, I prefer not to dwell. The mystery of Van Berg's death defied solution. As I recall the tragic event, I can recapture a sharp picture of Sir Lionel Barton arrayed in neutral-coloured pyjamas and an old dressing gown, his mane of gray hair disordered, his deep-set eyes two danger signals, standing massive, stricken, over the dead man.

The bed had been slept in—so much was evident; and about it the strange odour of mimosa clung more persistently than elsewhere.

There was no stranger on the premises. Of this we had assured ourselves. And for a thirty-foot ladder to have been reared against the window of the room and removed without our knowledge, was a sheer impossibility.

Yet Van Berg had been stabbed to the heart from behind—palpably in an attempt to defend the green box: an attempt which had been successful. But, except that his shutters were open, there was no clue to the identity of his assassin, nor to the means of the latter's entrance and exit.

"I didn't hear a sound!" I remember the chief murmuring,

looking at me haggard eyed. "I didn't hear that damnable wailing—it might have told me something. Anyhow, Greville, he died doing his job, and so he's gone wherever good men go. His death is on my conscience."

"Why, Chief?"

But he had turned away…

We conformed to the requirements of the fussy local authorities, but got no help from them; and shortly after noon, Mr. Stratton Jean, of the American Legation at Teheran, arrived by air, accompanied by Captain Woodville, a British intelligence officer.

I reflected, when they came in from the alighting ground just outside the ancient city, that the caravan route is nearly two hundred and forty miles long, and that in former days a week was allowed for the journey.

It was a strange interview, being in part an inquest upon the dead man. It took place in poor Van Berg's room, which had always served as a sort of office during the time that we had occupied this house in Ispahan.

There was a big table in the corner near the window laden with indescribable fragments, ranging from Davidian armour to portfolios of photographs and fossilised skulls. There was a rather fine scent bottle, too, of blue glass dating from the reign of Haroun-er-Raschid, and a number of good glazed tiles. A fine illuminated manuscript, very early, of part of the Diwan of Hafiz, one of Sir Lionel's more recently acquired treasures, lay still open upon the table, for Van Berg had been busy making notes upon the text up to within a few hours of his death.

The doctor's kit, his riding boots, and other intimate reminders of his genial presence lay littered about the floor; for, apart from the removal of the body, nothing had been disturbed.

That fatal green box, upon which the bloodstains had dried, stood upon the spot where I had found it. The floor was still stained...

Mr. Stratton Jean was a lean Bostonian, gray haired, sallow complexioned, and as expressionless as a Sioux Indian. Captain Woodville was a pretty typical British army officer of thirty-five or so, except for a disconcerting side-glance which I detected once or twice, and which alone revealed—to me, at least, for he had the traditional bored manner—that he was a man of very keen mind.

Mr. Stratton Jean quite definitely adopted the attitude of a coroner, and under his treatment the chief grew notably restive, striding up and down the long, narrow room in a manner reminiscent of a caged polar bear.

Rima, who sat beside me, squeezed my hand nervously, glancing alternately at the two Persian officials who were present, and at her famous uncle. She knew that a storm was brewing, and so did Captain Woodville, for twice I detected him hiding a smile. At last, in reply to some question:

"One moment, Mr. Jean," said Sir Lionel, turning and facing his interrogator. "If Van Berg was a fellow citizen of yours, he was a friend and colleague of mine. You are doing your duty, and I honour you for it. But I don't like the way you do it."

"I just want the facts," said Stratton Jean, dryly.

I saw the colour welling up into Sir Lionel's face and feared an outburst. It was avoided by the intervention of Captain Woodville.

"Thing is, Jean," he drawled lazily, "Sir Lionel isn't used to being court-martialed. He's rather outside your province. But apart from a distinguished military career, he happens to be the greatest Orientalist in Europe."

I waited with some anxiety for the American official's reaction to this rebuke, for it was nothing less than a rebuke. It took the form of a smile, but a very sad smile, breaking through the mask-like immobility of those sallow features.

"You mean, Woodville," he said, "I'm being too darned official for words?"

"Perhaps a trifle stiff, Jean, for a man of Sir Lionel's temperament."

Mr. Stratton Jean nodded, and I saw a new expression in his eyes, yellowed from long residence in the East. He looked at the chief.

"If I've ruffled you, Sir Lionel," he said, "please excuse me. This inquiry is one of the hardest things I've ever had to undertake. You see, Van Berg and I were at Harvard together. It's been a bad shock."

That was straight talking, and in two seconds the chief had Jean's hand in his bear-like grip and had hauled him out of the chair.

"Why in hell didn't you tell me?" he demanded. "We worked together for only two months, but I'd sell my last chance of salvation to get the swine who murdered him."

The air was cleared, and Rima's nervous grip upon my hand relaxed. And that which had begun so formally, was now carried on in a spirit of friendship. But when every possible witness had been called and examined, we remained at a deadlock.

It was Captain Woodville who broached the subject which I knew, sooner or later, must be brought up.

"It is quite clear. Sir Lionel," he said in his drawling way, "that your friend died in endeavouring to protect this iron box.

He pointed to the long green chest upon which the white initials L.B. were painted. Sir Lionel ground his teeth audibly together and began to pace up and down the room.

"I know," he said. That's why I told you, Greville"—turning to me—"that I was responsible for his death."

"I can't agree with you," Stratton Jean interrupted. "So far as my information goes (Captain Woodville, I believe, is better informed), you were engaged with the late Dr. Van Berg in an attempt to discover the burial place of El Mokanna, sometimes called the Veiled Prophet of Khorassan."

"Veiled Prophet," Woodville interjected, "is rather a misnomer. Actually, Mokanna wore a mask. Isn't that so. Sir Lionel?"

The chief turned and stared at the last speaker.

"That is so," he agreed. They exchanged a glance of understanding. "You know all the facts. Don't deny it!"

Captain Woodville smiled slightly, glancing aside at Stratton Jean; then:

"I know most of them," he admitted, "but the details can only be known to you. As a matter of fact, I'm here today because some tragedy of this kind had been rather foreseen. Quite frankly, although I don't suppose I'm telling you anything that you don't know already, you have stirred up a lot of trouble."

Rima squeezed my hand furtively. It was nothing new for her distinguished uncle to stir up trouble. His singular investigations had more than once imperiled international amity.

CHAPTER FOUR

THE VEILED PROPHET

"You have said, Mr. Jean," said Sir Lionel, "that my particular studies are outside your province, but my interests were shared by Dr. Van Berg. Already he occupied a chair of Oriental literature, but, if he had lived, his name would have ranked high as any. Very well."

He paced up and down in silence for a while, hands locked behind him. The two Persian officials had gone. Those queer discords characteristic of an Eastern city rose to us through the open window: cries of street hawkers, of carriage drivers; even the jangle of camel bells. And there were flies, myriads of flies…

"It was Van Berg who got the clue which set us off upon this expedition—the expedition which was to be his last. Down on the borders of Arabia he picked up a man, an Afghan, as a matter of fact, named Amir Khan. This man told him the story of the spot known locally as the Place of the Great Magician. It's in the No Man's Land between Khorassan and Afghanistan.

"Van Berg, with whom I had been in correspondence for some years, although we had never met, learned that I was in Iraq. He was a Persian scholar, and he knew parts of the country well. But of Khorassan and Afghanistan he knew nothing. He got into communication with me. He asked me to share the enterprise. I accepted—as you know, Greville—"he darted one of his quick glances in my direction—"and we moved down and joined Van Berg, who was waiting for us on the Persian border.

"I interviewed the man Amir Khan. I could talk his lingo and so get nearer to the truth than Van Berg had succeeded in doing—"

"I never trusted Amir Khan!" I broke in. "His story was true, and he did his job, but—"

"Amir Khan was a *thug*," the chief continued quietly; "I always knew it. But servants of Kali have no respect for Mohammed; therefore I was prepared to trust him with regard to the matter in hand. He advanced arguments strong enough to induce me, in conjunction with Van Berg, to proceed with a party, who had been in my employ for more than a year, northeast of Persia. In brief, gentlemen, we went to look for the burial place of El Mokanna, the Hidden One, sometimes called the Veiled Prophet, but, as Captain Woodville has pointed out, more properly the Masked Prophet…"

This was "shop" and overfamiliar. I turned my head and stared from the open window towards a corresponding, ruinous, window of the mosque opposite. The deserted building certainly had a sinister reputation, being known locally as the Ghost Mosque. If this circumstance, together with that eerie sound which had heralded poor Van Berg's death, were responsible, I cannot say. But I became the victim of a queer delusion…

"Mokanna, Mr. Jean," the chief was saying, "about 770 A.D., set himself up as an incarnation of God, and drew to his new sect many thousands of followers. He revised the Koran. His power became so great that the Caliph Al Mahdi was forced to move against him with a considerable army. Mokanna was a hideous creature. His features were so mutilated as to be horrible to see…"

Brilliant green eyes were fixed upon me from the shadow of the ruined window!…

"But he was a man. He and the whole of his staff poisoned themselves in the hour of defeat. From that day to this, no one has known where he was buried. His sword, which he wore on ceremonial occasions, and which he called the Sword of God, forged to conquer the world, his New Creed graved upon golden plates, and the mask of gold with which he concealed his mutilated features, disappeared at the time of his death and were supposed to be lost."

I shifted uneasily in my chair. The startling apparition had vanished as suddenly as it had come. Above all things I wanted to avoid alarming Rima. Already I suspected sleepless nights; I realised that she could know no peace in the shadow of the Ghost Mosque with its unholy reputation.

The apparition did not reappear, however; and I turned, looking swiftly at Rima.

She was watching the chief. Clearly, she had seen nothing.

Walking up and down while speaking, in that manner of a caged bear, Sir Lionel had paused now and was staring at the ominous green box.

"Amir Khan did not lie," he went on. "The tomb-mosque that contained the ashes of the prophet is a mere mound of dust today; what it concealed was never more than a legend. Its site, though, is strictly avoided—supposed to be haunted by *djinns* and known as the Place of the Great Magician. We camped there, and our excavations were carried out secretly. Few pass that desolate place on the edge of the desert. We found—what we had come to find."

"Is that a fact?" said Stratton Jean in an odd voice.

Sir Lionel nodded, smiling grimly.

The prophet was dust," he added; "but we found his gold mask, his New Creed engraved upon plates of gold, and his sword, a magnificent blade with a jewelled hilt. There were other fragments— but these were the most important."

He paused and pointed to the green box.

"Those two Persian birds were mighty keen to know what was in this box. I told them it contained priceless records. They pretended to be satisfied, But they weren't. It's a heavy thing to travel—but strong as a safe."

He began to pace up and down again.

"I left the Place of the Great Magician, taking the relics of El Mokanna away in that box! Van Berg and I had a conference before we left; Greville, here, was present. In spite of our precautions, there were rumours flying about, and it was becoming fairly clear that some sort of small but fanatical sect still existed who held the name of El Mokanna in reverence. The desertion of our Afghan guide, Amir Khan, was very significant—wasn't it Greville?"

"It was," I agreed.

At the chief's words I lived again in memory, instantaneously, through those days and nights in that lonely camp, with Rima's presence to add to my anxieties. I knew that we were hundreds of miles from any useful help, and I knew that in some mysterious way the influence of the Veiled Prophet lived, was active, although the Hidden One himself was dead; that if the truth should leak out, if it should become known that the sacred relics were in our possession, our lives would not be worth a grain of sand!

Almost, in those anxious days and nights, I had come to hate Van Berg, who was the instigator of the expedition, and to distrust Sir Lionel, whose zeal for knowledge had induced him to lead Rima into such peril. His scientific ardour brooked no obstacle. She was a brilliantly clever photographer, and there was a portfolio, now, on poor Van Berg's table, which in the absence of the actual relics constituted a perfect record of our discoveries.

"I improvised a bomb," Sir Lionel went on, "to which I attached a time fuse. We were headed south for Ispahan when all that remained of the tomb-mosque of El Mokanna went up in a cloud of dust."

That wild light, which was more than half mischief, leapt into his eyes as he spoke.

"Although I had covered my tracks, there were consequences which I hadn't counted on. Most of the work had been done at night, but it appears that travellers from a distance had seen our lights. The legendary site of the place was more widely known than we had realised. And when, some time after our departure, which took place after dusk, there was a great explosion and a bright glare in the sky, the result was something totally unforeseen..."

"If I may interrupt you, Sir Lionel," said Captain Woodville quietly, "from this point I can carry on the story. An outcry— 'Mokanna has arisen'—swept through Afghanistan. That was the spot at which I came into the matter. You had been even more successful than you seem to appreciate. None of the tribesmen who, as you suspect, and rightly, still hold the Mokanna tradition had any idea that you or any human influence had been concerned with the eruption which reduced a lonely ruined shrine to a dusty hollow. A certain fanatical imam took upon himself the duties of a sort of Eastern Peter the Hermit."

The speaker paused, taking a cigarette from his case and tapping it thoughtfully upon his thumb nail. I glanced swiftly over my shoulder. But the cavernous window of the mosque showed as an unbroken patch of shadow...

"He declared that the Masked Prophet had been reborn and that with the Sword of God he would carry the New Creed throughout the East, sweeping the Infidel before him. That movement is gathering strength. Sir Lionel, and I need not tell you what such a movement means to the Indian government, and what it may come to mean for Arabia, Palestine, and possibly Egypt, unless it can be checked."

There came a moment of silence, broken only by the striking of a match and the heavy footsteps of the chief as he restlessly paced up and down—up and down. At last:

"Such a movement would call for a strong leader," said Rima.

Captain Woodville extinguished the match and turned to her gravely.

"We have reason to fear, Miss Barton," he replied, "that such a leader has been found. I suspect also, Sir Lionel—" glancing at the chief—"that he wants what you have found and will stick at nothing to get it…"

CHAPTER FIVE

NAYLAND SMITH TAKES CHARGE

"Someone to see you, Greville Effendim."

I raised my eyes from the notes which I had been studying but did not look around. Through the open window in front of the table at which I had been working I could see on the opposite side of the narrow street the sun-bathed wall of that deserted mosque of unpleasant history.

A window almost on a level with that through which I was looking was heavily outlined on one side and at the top by dense shadows. Only that morning I had explored the mosque—penetrating to the gallery behind that window. What I had hoped to find I really don't know. Actually, I had found nothing.

"Show him in, Ali Mahmoud."

I pushed the notes aside and turned, as footsteps on the landing outside told me that my visitor had arrived.

Then I sprang swiftly to my feet...

Something I had vaguely prayed for, something I had not dared to expect, had actually happened! A tall, lean man, with clean-shaven face so sunbaked as to resemble that of an Arab, stood in the doorway.

"Sir Denis! Sir Denis!" I cried. This is almost *too* wonderful!"

It was Sir Denis Nayland Smith, Assistant Commissioner of Scotland Yard, one of my chief's oldest friends, and the one man in the world whom I would have chosen to be with us now. But the mystery of his appearance had knocked me sideways; and, as he grasped my hand, that lean, tired face relaxed in the boyish smile that I knew and loved; and:

"A surprise?" he snapped in his queer, staccato fashion. "It was a surprise to me too, Greville. If anybody had offered me a hundred to one, three days ago, that I should be in Ispahan now, I should have taken him."

"But..." I looked him up and down.

He wore a leather overcoat over a very dilapidated flannel suit, and, since he was hatless, I saw that his crisp, wavy hair, more heavily silvered in the interval since our last meeting, was disordered.

"But where does Scotland Yard come in?"

"It doesn't come in at all," he returned. "I resigned from Scotland Yard six months ago, Greville. I have been on a sort of secret mission to southern India. I came back via Basra intending to return overland and by air. There is no time to waste, you understand. But at Basra I had news."

"News of what?" I asked, my brain in somewhat of a whirl.

"News that changed my plans," he returned gravely, and his piercing glance fixed me for a moment. "Excuse me if I seem eccentric, but would you mind stepping around the table, Greville, and looking out of the window. I should be glad to know if there is anyone in the street."

Too surprised to reply, I did as he asked. The narrow street was empty as far as I could see it to the left. To the right, where it lay in deep shadow and climbed upward under the lee of the deserted mosque, I could not be so sure that someone, or something, a vague figure, was not lurking. However, after watching for some moments, I determined that the figure existed only in my imagination.

"Nobody," I reported.

"Ah! I hope you're right—but I doubt it."

Nayland Smith had shed his leather coat and was engaged in loading one of those large, cracked briars that I had known so well, with the peculiar cross-cut mixture which he favoured, and which he kept in a pouch at least as dilapidated as his pipe.

The room, which we used as an office, was in better order than during poor Van Berg's time. The bed in which our late colleague had slept had been removed, and I had reduced the place to something like order.

I went to a side table, pouring out a drink. Nayland Smith's eyes were more than normally bright, and his features, I thought, looked almost haggard. He had dropped into an armchair. He took the glass which I handed to him, but set it down in the arm rest, its contents untasted; and:

"Greville," he said, "the hand of destiny may clearly be seen in all this. Where is Barton?"

"I expected him back by now," I replied. "Rima is with him. Do you know what's happened, Sir Denis? Is that why you're here?"

"I know that Dr. Van Berg has been murdered," he returned grimly. "But that isn't why I'm here."

He lighted his pipe absent-mindedly, three matches being used before he was satisfied; then:

"I am here," he went on, "because there is a dangerous movement on the Afghan border and creeping south day by day. Definite orders reached me at Basra. That's why I'm here, Greville. Heaven knows we had enough trouble before, but now that the tribes are rising in response to a mad rumour that El Mokanna, the Masked Prophet, has come out of his tomb to lead them, I don't know where my duty lies."

He had picked up his glass, but he set it down again and fixed me with a steady glance of his steel-gray eyes.

"I suspect that it lies *here*!" he snapped. "Some madness of Barton's is at the bottom of this superstitious rumour, which by now has swept all over the East—Near and Far."

I sustained that stare with great difficulty, and presently:

"You are right, Sir Denis," I admitted. "The truth of the matter I don't know, and I don't think the chief knows it—but I have every reason to believe that poor Van Berg met his death at the hands of some fanatic inspired by this rumour. He died in this room. And the manner of his death remains a mystery to this present hour."

"Barton is mad," said Nayland Smith definitely. "His investigations have caused nearly as much trouble as the zeal of the most earnest missionaries."

He stood up and began to pace the long, narrow room in his restless fashion. In this trick, which betrayed the intense pent-up vitality of the man, he reminded me of the chief. Together, the pair of them emitted almost visible sparks of force.

"Be as brief as you can," he directed. "The clue to the trouble lies here—obscured by now, probably. I have Captain Woodville's report—but it omits almost every essential point. Give me your own story of the death of Van Berg." He stared at me intently. "The peace of the world, Greville, may rest upon your accuracy."

CHAPTER SIX

PERFUME OF MIMOSA

"Poor Van Berg," I explained, "slept in this room, which throughout the time that we have been in Ispahan we have used as an office. All the records are kept here, and up to the time of the tragedy the most valuable record of all: a strong iron box, which the chief almost invariably carried with him, and in which it was his custom to deposit valuable finds."

"At the time of Van Berg's death," Nayland Smith said sharply, "what did this box contain?"

"It contained," I replied, "to the best of my knowledge, fifteen plates of thin gold, upon which were engraved the articles of the New Creed; the 'Sword of God,' a very beautiful piece; and a grotesque golden mask—all that remained of El Mokanna, the prophet of Khorassan."

Nayland Smith nodded.

"Van Berg was definitely uneasy from the time that we entered into occupancy of this house. It belongs to a Persian friend of Sir Lionel's—for the chief has friends everywhere; and he arranged in some way that it should be our headquarters in Ispahan. In certain respects it suited us well enough. But, as you can see, it's in a queer district and it lies actually in the shadow of the so-called Ghost Mosque."

"Ghost Mosque!" Nayland Smith echoed. "I don't want to interrupt—but explain more fully what you mean."

"I will do my best. It appears that years ago—I am rather shaky as to dates—an imam of the mosque opposite, who happened to be related to the Grand Sherif of Ispahan, conceived a passion for the favourite wife of the then heir apparent, who formerly had a house near by. They were detected together—so the story goes—inside the gallery of the minaret. The exact details of their fate at the hands of the eunuchs are more lurid than pleasant. But the guilty pair were finally thrown from the gallery to the street below. The mosque has never been used since that day; and the death cries of the victims are supposed to be heard from time to time…"

Nayland Smith tugged at the lobe of his ear irritably, but made no comment; and:

"This circumstance, no doubt," I added, "accounts for the ease with which Sir Lionel obtained possession of so large a house at such short notice. It was shut up on our arrival, and musty from long disuse. I give these details, Sir Denis, first, because you asked for them, and, second, because they have a curious bearing on the death of Van Berg."

"I quite understand."

"The chief related this story with tremendous gusto when we took up our residence here. You know his bloodthirsty sense of humour? But the effect on Rima was dreadful. She's as fit as any man to cope with actual danger and hardship, but the bogey business got completely on her nerves. Personally, I treated it as what it really is—a piece of native superstition. I was altogether more worried about the real purpose of our long delay in Ispahan. I don't know to this present hour, why Sir Lionel hung on here. But my scepticism about the Ghost Mosque got rather a jar."

"In what way?"

"Last Thursday night—that is, two nights before his death—Van Berg aroused me. He said that he had been awakened by a sound which resembled that of a huge bird alighting upon the balcony outside his window."

"This window?" Nayland Smith interrupted, and pointed.

"This window. The shutters were closed, but not latched, and this sound, so he told me, aroused him. He sprang out of bed, switched on the electric torch which lay beside him, and ran across to the shutters. As he did so, he heard a low moaning sound which rose to a wail and then died away. When he threw the shutters open and looked out into the street, there was nobody there."

"Did he examine the woodwork?"

"He didn't say so."

Nayland Smith snapped his fingers and nodded to me to go on.

"Imagine my feelings. Sir Denis, when Rima awakened me on Saturday night saying that she had heard a cry from Van Berg's room, almost immediately above her own (that is, the room, in which we are now), followed, as she crept out of her door to awaken me, by a moaning sound outside the house, and high up in the air!"

"Where is your room?"

"At the farther end of the same corridor below."

"I must inspect this corridor. Go on."

"Rima woke me up—I had been fast asleep. I won't disguise, Sir Denis, the fact that our possession of these relics had become somewhat of a nightmare. When I learned of the disturbance in

Van Berg's room above, followed by that strange cry, which I could only suppose to be the same that he himself had heard, I feared the worst… and I was right."

"Did Rima more particularly describe this cry?" Nayland Smith asked impatiently.

"No. But I can do so."

"What?"

"I heard it later myself as I went along the corridor past her room."

"Was the moon up?"

"Yes."

"Was her door open?"

"Wide open."

"Was there any light in her room?"

"Yes—she had opened her shutters and was listening, so I understand, for further sounds from Van Berg's room above."

"Was that when she heard the sound?"

"No. She heard it as she opened her door and came along to me."

"Is there a window facing the door of her room?"

"Yes, almost immediately opposite; in fact, just below where I am standing."

"Good!" rapped Nayland Smith. "Go on."

I stared at him for a moment. I detected something like a glint of satisfaction in the steely gray eyes and began to wonder if he had already seen light where all around was darkness to the rest of us.

"I had just reached Rima's door," I went on, "when I myself heard the extraordinary sound for the first time."

"It was not the cry of a dacoit?"

"It was not."

"Give me some idea of it. Can you imitate it?"

"I fear that's impossible."

"Was it a sound made by a human being? By an animal—by some kind of musical instrument?"

"Frankly, I dare not venture to say. It began with a sort of whistling note, which rose to a shriek and died away in a kind of wail."

Nayland Smith, who had been pacing up and down throughout the whole time that I had been speaking, accelerated his step and began tugging at the lobe of his left ear, in a state of furious irritation or deep reflection—I could not determine which. Until, since I had paused:

"Go on!" he snapped.

"Quite frankly, I was scared out of my life. I called very softly to Rima to go down to the lobby and wake Ali Mahmoud, and I went on upstairs to the corridor outside this door."

"Did you hear anything?"

"Yes; a vague, scuffling sound. I stepped forward to the door and called Van Berg. The scuffling continued, but there was no reply. I opened the door."

"It was not locked, then?"

"No. Van Berg had no occasion to lock his door, since his room, so far as we knew, was inaccessible except by means of the street entrance—and Ali Mahmoud slept in the lobby. I saw that the shutters—those before you—were half open. Two Caspian kittens, pets of the chief, which are now locked in an adjoining room, were in here. Van Berg was very fond of animals, and I imagine that they had been sleeping at the foot of his bed at the time he was aroused."

"You need not tell me where he lay," said Nayland Smith grimly; "the stain is still on the floor. Where was the iron box?"

"He lay across it," I said, and my voice was rather shaky, "clutching the two handles. He had been stabbed from behind with a long, narrow blade, which had pierced right through to his heart. But there was not a soul in the room, and the street below was deserted. Apart from which this window is thirty feet above the ground."

"Did you examine the ledge and the shutters?"

"No."

"Has *anyone* examined them?"

"Not to my knowledge."

Sir Denis stood with his back to me for several moments; then, turning:

"Go on!" he cried. "You must have derived some other impressions. Had the bed definitely been slept in, for instance?"

"Yes, undoubtedly."

"Was Van Berg armed?"

"No. His revolver—a heavy service type—was on a table beside his bed. His flash lamp was still under his pillow."

"Was he a heavy drinker?"

I stared uncomprehendingly.

"On the contrary."

Nayland Smith gave me a steely glance.

"H'm!" he snapped—"amazing! A man, already apprehensive of attack, a man of some experience, wakes to the certain knowledge that there's an intruder in his room—and what does he do? He springs out of bed, unarmed, in semi-darkness—although a flash lamp and a revolver lie under his hand—and throws himself across the iron box. Really, Greville! Reconstruct the scene for yourself. Was Van Berg's behaviour, as you indicate it, *normal*?"

"No, sir Denis," I admitted. "Now that you draw my attention to the curious points, it wasn't. But—good heavens!" I raised my hand to my forehead.

"Ah!" said he—"forgotten something else?"

"Yes—I had. The perfume."

"Perfume?"

"There was a strange perfume in the room. It resembled mimosa…"

"Mimosa?"

"Extraordinarily like it."

"Where was this smell most noticeable?"

"About the bed."

He snapped his fingers and began to walk up and down again.

"Naturally," he murmured. "One small point cleared up… but—mimosa…"

I watched him in silence, overcome by unhappy recollections.

"Where is the iron box now?" he suddenly demanded.

"It's in my room!" roared a great voice—"and I'm waiting for the swine who murdered Van Berg to come and fetch it!"

Sir Denis, in his restless promenade, had reached the window—had been staring out of it, as if considering my statement that it was thirty feet above street level. He turned in a flash—so did I…

Sir Lionel Barton stood in the doorway, and Rima was beside him, a neat, delightful figure in her drill riding kit and tan boots.

If Rima was surprised to learn the identity of the tall man in shabby gray flannels who now turned and confronted her, I can only describe the chief's reaction as that of one half stunned. He fell back a pace—his deep-set eyes positively glaring; then:

"Smith!" he said huskily—"Nayland Smith! Am I dreaming?"

The grim face of Sir Denis relaxed in that ingenuous smile which stripped him of twenty years.

"By God!" roared the chief, and literally pounced upon him. "If I were anything like a decent Christian I should say that my prayers had been answered!"

CHAPTER SEVEN

RIMA AND I

Down in the little garden of the house I had a few moments alone with Rima. At some time this garden had been a charming, secluded spot. Indeed, except for a latticed window above, it was overlooked from only one point: the gallery of the minaret. But neglect had played havoc with the place.

The orange trees flourished—indeed, were in full blossom—and a perfect cloak of bougainvillea overhung the balcony below the latticed window. But the flower borders were thickets of weeds and a stone cistern in which a little fountain had long ceased to play was coated with slime and no more than a breeding place for mosquitoes.

"I don't know what it is about Sir Denis Nayland Smith," said Rima. "But I have never experienced such a sense of relief in my life as when I came into that room today and found him there."

"I know," I replied, squeezing her reassuringly: "it's the sterling quality of the man. All the same, darling, I shan't feel happy until we're clear of Ispahan."

"Nor shall I, Shan. If only uncle weren't so infernally mysterious. What on earth are we staying on here for?"

"I know no more than you do, Rima. What was the object of this afternoon's expedition? I'm quite in the dark about it!"

"I'm nearly as bad," she confessed. "But at least I can tell you where we went. We went to Solomon Ishak. You know—the funny old jeweller?"

"Solomon Ishak is one of the greatest mysteries of Ispahan. But I understand he gets hold of some very rare antique pieces. Probably the chief is negotiating a deal."

"I don't think so. I had to take along the negatives of about forty photographs, and uncle left me wandering about that indescribable, stuffy shop for more than an hour while he remained locked in an inner room with old Solomon."

"And what became of the photographs?"

"He had them with him but brought them out at the end of the interview. They are back here now."

"That may explain the mystery," I said reflectively. "The photographs were of the relics of the Prophet, I take it?"

Rima nodded.

"The workmanship on the hilt of the sword has defied even the chief's knowledge," I added. "He probably wanted Solomon Ishak's opinion but didn't care to risk taking the sword itself."

Rima slipped a slender bare arm about my neck and snuggled her head down against my shoulder.

"Oh, Shan!" she whispered. "I have never felt so homesick in my life."

I stooped and kissed her curly hair, squeezing her very tightly; then:

"Rima, darling," I whispered, my lips very close to one half-hidden ear, "when we get to some place a little nearer civilisation, will you come and see the consul with me?"

She made no reply but hid her face more closely against me.

"If the chief still insists on a spectacular wedding, that can come later. But…"

Rima suddenly raised her face, looking up at me.

"Next time you ask me, I'm going to say, Yes, Shan. But please don't ask me again until we're out of Ispahan."

"Why?" I asked blankly. "Is there any special reason for this?"

"No," she replied, kissed me on the chin, and nestled down against me again. "But I've promised. And if you are good you'll be satisfied."

I stooped and nearly smothered her with kisses. I suppose my early training was to blame, and I didn't know, or even seek to find out, Rima's views upon the subject. As for the chief, I had known for a long time past that he was thoroughly enjoying the situation.

Had Rima and I openly become lovers, I am convinced he wouldn't have turned a hair. He was a wonderful old pagan, and his profound disrespect for ritual in any form had led to some awkward moments—awkward, that is, for me, but apparently enjoyed by Sir Lionel.

And at the moment that these thoughts were crossing my mind his great voice came from the window above:

"Break away. there!" he roared. "There's more serious work afoot than making love to my staff photographer!"

I jumped up—my blood was tingling—and turned angrily. But in the very act I met Rima's upcast glance. My mood changed. She was convulsed with laughter; and:

"The old ruffian!" she whispered.

"Come hither, my puritan friend," Sir Lionel continued. "Two cavaliers would have speech with thee!"

CHAPTER EIGHT

"EL MOKANNA!"

A conference took place in the chief's room at the end of the long corridor on the first floor of that queer old house.

The place was untidy as only Sir Lionel could make it. There were riding boots on the bed, and strewn about on the floor were such diverse objects as a battered sun helmet, a camera case, odd items of underwear, a pair of very ancient red leather slippers, a number of books—many of them valuable; the whole rising in a sort of mound towards an old cabin trunk, from which one would assume as by an eruption they had been cast forth.

There was a long, high window on the right through which I could see sunshine on the yellow wall of the Ghost Mosque. A low, shallow cupboard occupied the space below this window. Set left of this cupboard was a big table on which lay piled an indescribable litter. There were manuscripts, firearms, pipes, a hat box, a pair of shoes, a large case containing flasks of wine of Shiraz, a big scale map, a beautifully embroidered silk robe, and a fossilised skull.

On a low stool at the foot of the bed stood the grim green iron box.

Sir Denis Nayland Smith was standing staring at the box. The chief had thrown himself into an armchair.

"Greville," said Nayland Smith, "have you ever explored the mosque over the way?"

"Yes," I replied, to his evident surprise. "But I didn't find that it possessed any features of interest. Does it, Sir Lionel?"

"According to Smith," was the reply, "it does!"

"Had you any special reason for exploring the place?" Sir Denis asked.

"I had," I admitted. "I made my way in this morning through a window on the north side. You see, I imagined—it was probably no more than imagination—that I saw someone watching us from there on one occasion—"

"What occasion?"

"The inquiry into Van Berg's death—when Mr. Jean and Captain Woodville were here—"

"Never mentioned this to me!" the chief began, when:

"All I wanted to know," said Nayland Smith rapidly. "Be quiet, Barton." And now he turned. His face had grown very stern. "I want to make it perfectly clear to you both, that we three, and Rima, and Ali Mahmoud, stand in greater peril of our lives, at this present moment, than any of us has ever been before."

"That's putting it pretty strongly, Sir Denis," I said, for I recalled other experiences which I had shared with him.

"Not too strongly," he replied. "I rarely say what I don't mean, Greville. But apart from Rima—I sincerely wish she were a thousand miles from Ispahan—there's a further and a graver consideration. Sir Lionel here—inadvertently, I admit—has stirred up a thing which at this particular stage of world politics is calculated to sway the balance in the wrong direction.

"I know all the facts, Greville"—he threw a quick glance in my direction—"and I assure you that what I say is true. The blowing up of the tomb of El Mokanna revived the tradition of that minor prophet and brought into unexpected prominence certain living believers of his doctrine, of which accident they were not slow to take advantage. I have the names of several men in Afghanistan, Khorassan, and Persia whom I know to be associated with this movement, whether as legitimate fanatics or seekers after power remains to be seen. But the spread of the thing is phenomenal."

The chief had begun to walk up and down the room in that caged-bear fashion of his; and since Nayland Smith was also addicted to promenading in moments of intense thought, the latter checked his own restless movements at the first stride and dropped into an armchair which Sir Lionel had vacated, tugging reflectively at the lobe of his left ear.

His words had chilled me. All my fears, which throughout had centred around Rima, came to a head now. I had known for more than a week past that our little party was the focus of malignant forces. Now, chance, or divine Providence, had sent us the man best equipped to deal with such a situation. But his words held no comfort.

"The way in which this cry of 'El Mokanna' has swept through the East," he continued, speaking in his rapid staccato fashion, "points to organisation. Someone has seized this mighty opportunity. Don't glare at me, Barton. You, and you alone, are responsible for the position in which we find ourselves. Captain Woodville has already told you so, I believe."

I don't think the chief would have remained silent under such treatment from any but Sir Denis. He was certainly glaring, and he continued to glare. But the steely gray eyes met his unfalteringly; and Sir Lionel merely grunted and continued his promenade.

"Our chief enemy," Nayland Smith went on, "recognises the importance of possessing the New Creed, the Sword of God, and the gold mask. This was why poor Van Berg died."

I heard Sir Lionel groan. He halted, and stood with his back to us for some moments.

"The first attempt failed," that cool, even voice went on. "It was attended by very peculiar features; they were not insignificant. But—" he paused for a moment, impressively—"the attempt will be repeated. Our enemy knows that the method by which be obtained access to Van Berg's room has so far defied all investigation. He knows that the green box is no longer in that room—but is here."

"How can you be sure of that?"

"Because Barton has advertised the fact," Nayland Smith returned savagely. "Two Persian officials were present at the inquiry, here, in this house. And they know that the box now rests in Sir Lionel's room. Don't answer, Barton—just listen. And you, too, Greville."

It was hard going for Sir Lionel to swallow his words, but he succeeded in doing so. And with the brief clarity which was one of his peculiar gifts Nayland Smith outlined his plan of defence.

That he seemed to take it for granted that there would be an attack positively terrified me, since Rima was in the house. But what I did not understand at the time was an underlying anger which appeared to be directed against the chief...

"I hope that my presence may be unknown to the enemy," he concluded. "But, frankly, in spite of all the precautions I have taken, I doubt this. I am almost certain that I was covered. The man Amir Khan, originally your guide, has deserted to the other side. This, to me, is particularly, in fact dreadfully, significant. My object, Greville—" evidently he detected bewilderment in my expression— "is this: I mean to bring things to a head."

"What d'you mean?" Sir Lionel demanded, with a sudden angry outburst—"Bring things to a head! Haven't they come to a head already?"

"Listen, Barton," Nayland Smith spoke unusually slowly. "You have taken some risks in your time. But this time you have stirred up something too big for you. Forget that I'm here, but go to work without delay and instruct Ali Mahmoud accordingly, to prepare for departure in the morning. Do everything that occurs to you to make it known that tonight is the last night you will spend under this roof. Upon your success. Barton—I include you, Greville—my plan for discovering the murderer of poor Van Berg will depend…"

CHAPTER NINE

THE FLYING DEATH

The extraordinary events of that night brought me nearer to a belief in supernatural agencies than I could have believed myself capable of approaching.

Nayland Smith's programme was perfectly definite. Clearly enough he had formed a theory covering the singular facts of the death of Dr. Van Berg. This theory he bluntly declined to reveal to the chief.

"I'm going to handle this thing, Barton, in my own way," he said firmly. "For once in your life you'll take orders, or stand aside, whichever you please."

In consequence we were disposed in what seemed to me a very strange manner. My own post was in the chief's room, in which our long conference had taken place. I was seated upon a pile of pillows and other odds and ends, screened from the observation of anyone in the room by a large upstanding trunk, the property of Rima.

Through an opening between the wall and the side of this trunk I could see practically the whole of the room, which, as I have already said, was a large one. The shutters of the window above and to my right were closed; only a glimmer of moonlight showed through the slats. In consequence, the place was in semi-darkness, to which, however, after a time, my eyes grew accustomed.

I could see all the objects there very clearly. The window at the further end, that overlooking the street and the side of the mosque, had the shutters closed but not latched. Through the slit between them I could see reflected light on the ancient wall beyond.

The bed, which jutted out along to my left, showed the outline of a heavy body under its sheet. A gray army blanket was rolled across the foot in accordance with Sir Lionel's custom—a provision against the chill of early morning; and the sheet was pulled up right over the pillow so as entirely to conceal the head of the sleeper—another characteristic trick of the chief's in insect-infested countries.

That mound of odds and ends still remained upon the big table, and garments were littered about the floor. On a low stool at the foot of the bed, an object now associated in my mind with murder, stood the long green box. A pistol lay beside me, and I had an electric torch in my pocket.

I anticipated a dreary vigil, nor was I by any means satisfied that the enemy would fall into the trap laid for him by Nayland Smith. Our preparations for departure in the early morning had been almost too ostentatious, in my opinion.

The room was silent as a tomb.

Ali Mahmoud, in the lobby below, would be watching the street intently through the iron-barred grill of the house door. Rima was in one of the rooms above, from which she also commanded a view of the street. Of Sir Denis's position I remained in ignorance, except that definitely he was not in the house…

Time wore on. I grew very restless and cramped. Smoking was prohibited, as well as the making of the slightest sound.

I watched the shutters of the window above the cupboard so long and so intently that my sight became blurred. This, I felt assured, would be the point of attack. I formed dreadful mental pictures of the creature heard many nights ago by poor Van Berg—the thing which had alighted with a sound resembling that caused by the alighting of a heavy bird—in his own words.

What could it be—this flying thing? I conceived horrors transcending the imagination of the most morbid story-tellers.

For the keen weapon which had pierced through Van Berg's back and reached his heart, I substituted a dreadful kind of beak—the beak of a thing not of this world; a flying horror, such as the Arab romancers have conjured up—a ghoulish creature haunting the ancient cemetery just beyond the city walls…

It was the cry of this creature, I told myself, that moaning, wailing cry, which had given rise to the legend of the Ghost Mosque, which had led to this little street becoming deserted, and had made the house in which we lived uninhabitable for so many years.

At which point in my grisly reflections a sound caused me to draw a sharp breath. I crouched, listening intently.

Footsteps!

Someone was walking along the street below. The regular, measured steps paused at a point which I estimated to be somewhere just in front of the door of the house. I anticipated a challenge from Ali Mahmoud, but recalled that Sir Denis's instructions on this point had been implicit.

There was no challenge. The footsteps sounded again, echoing hollowly now, so that I knew the walker to be passing that out-jutting wall of the mosque and approaching the dark, tunnel-like archway and the three steps leading to the narrow lane which skirted the base of the minaret.

I heard him mount the three steps; then again he paused…

What would I not have given for a glimpse of him! A passer-by was a phenomenon in that street at night. I dared not move, however. The footsteps continued—and presently died away altogether.

Silence descended again upon this uncanny quarter.

How long elapsed I had no means of judging; probably only a few minutes. But I had begun to induce a sort of hypnosis by my concentrated staring at the slit between the shutters, when—from high up and a long way off, I heard *the sound*…

It brought my mind back in a flash to those horrible imaginings which had absorbed me at the moment that footsteps had broken the stillness. It was coming!… The flying death!

A sort of horrible expectancy claimed me, as, pistol in hand, I watched the opening between the shutters.

Silence fell again. I could detect no sound either within the house or outside.

Whereupon it happened—the thing I had been waiting for; a thing seemingly beyond human explanation.

There came a faint pattering sound on the narrow ledge outside and below the shutters. A dull impact and a faint creaking of woodwork told of a weight imposed upon the projecting window. Something began to move upward—a dim shadow behind the slats—upward and inward—towards the opening…

The tension of watching and waiting grew almost too keen to tolerate. But my orders were definite, and wait I must.

Beyond that faint straining of woodwork, no sound whatever was occasioned by the intruder. No sign came from below to indicate that Ali Mahmoud had seen anything of this apparition, which indeed, since it had apparently flown through the air, was not remarkable.

Then—the shutters began very silently to open…

CHAPTER TEN

I SEE THE SLAYER

The shutter opened so silently and so slowly that only by the closest watching could I detect the movement. There was absolutely no creaking.

A window of the Ghost Mosque on the opposite side of the street, looking like a black smudge on a dirty yellow canvas, came just in line with the edge of the left-hand shutter. And only by the ever increasing gap of yellow between the woodwork and the smudge of shadow, could I tell what was happening.

The effect was slowly to add to the light in the room. So accustomed had I become to the dimness that I felt myself shrinking back farther into my hiding place; although in actual fact the access of light was less, I suppose, than would have been gained by the introduction of a solitary candle.

My ghoulish imaginings came to a head.

Some vampire creature from the ancient cemetery was about to spring in. More than once since the relics of El Mokanna had come into our possession I had laughed at Rima's superstitious terrors, but at this moment I admit frankly that I shared them.

Ispahan lay around me, silent as a city of the past. I might have been alone in Persia. And always the fear was with me that Nayland Smith, for all his peculiar genius, had misjudged the circumstances which had led to the death of Van Berg; that I was about to be subjected to a test greater perhaps than my spiritual strength could cope with.

What I should have done at this moment had I been a free agent, I cannot even guess. But I doubt it I could have remained there silent and watching.

Fortunately, I was under orders. I meant to carry those orders out to the letter. But in honesty I must record that during the interminable moments which elapsed from the time that some incredible creature had alighted outside the window, to the moment that the shutters became fully opened, I doubted the wisdom of Nayland Smith…

A vague mass rose inch by inch over the window ledge; grew higher—denser, as it seemed to me; and, with a wriggling movement indescribably horrible, reached the top of that low cupboard which extended below the window—and crouched or lay there.

I had formed absolutely no conception of outline. The entrance of the nocturnal creature had been effected in such a manner that definition was impossible. This was the point, I think, at which my courage almost touched vanishing point.

What was the thing on top of the cupboard? Something which could fly—something which had no determinate shape…

I knew that the visitor was inspecting the room keenly. To me, as I have said, it seemed to have become brightly illuminated. Colt in hand, I shrank farther and farther away from the narrow opening through which I was peering, until my back was flat against the wall.

That vague outline which disturbed the square of the open window disappeared. A very soft thud which must have been inaudible to ears less keenly attuned than mine told me that the visitant, almost certainly the slayer of Van Berg, had dropped onto the floor and was now in the room with me!

I peered into the darkness left of the big, littered table. Something was approaching the bed… going, I thought, on *all fours*.

Definitely, the approaching was oblique—that is, not in my direction. I was conscious of a shock of relief. I had not been seen.

Something glittered dully in the reflected light, and I heard a faint swishing sound, almost the first, expecting the thud, which had betrayed the presence of this nocturnal assassin.

At first it puzzled me, and then, suddenly, to my mind an explanation sprang.

The creature was spraying the bed…

Ideas quickly associated themselves; for at this same moment there was swept to my nostrils an almost overpowering perfume of mimosa—the same that had haunted poor Van Berg's room.

It was some unfamiliar but tremendously potent anaesthetic.

In the instant that realisation came to me, I knew also that the horrible visitor was not a supernatural creature but human. True, his agility was far above the ordinary, and his powers of silent movement were uncanny.

He was evidently armed with some kind of spray; and during the time that its curiously soothing sound continued, I found, so oddly does the mind react to indefinable fear, that my thoughts had wandered. I was thinking about an account I had once read of a mysterious creature known as Spring-heeled Jack, who terrorised outlying parts of London many years ago.

For the fact remained that this man, now endeavouring to reduce the occupant of the bed to unconsciousness, could apparently spring to high windows, quite beyond the reach of any human jumper, and indeed, beyond the reach of any member of the animal kingdom!

The swishing sound ceased. Absolute silence followed…

Peer intensely as I would, I could detect no trace of another presence in the room. But I knew exactly what was happening. The unimaginable man who had come through the window was crouching somewhere and listening. Probably he was counting, silently, knowing how many seconds must elapse before the unknown drug which smelled like mimosa could reduce the sleeper to unconsciousness—or, perhaps, bring about death…

Distant though I was from the bed, that sickly sweet odour was making me dizzy.

Fully a minute elapsed. No sound could I hear; nor could I detect a movement. But during that age-long minute I observed a vague white patch in the darkness, and presently I identified it. It was made by the initials painted on the green iron box.

And as I watched, this white patch became obscured.

A sound disturbed that all-but-insufferable silence—a sound of heavy breathing. Then, silhouetted against the window… I saw the intruder.

I saw a small, lithe body, muscular arms uplifted, the green box born upon the right shoulder.

My hand trembled upon the trigger, but Nayland Smith's instructions had been definite. The man bore the box to the end of the room. Here, shadow from the cupboard swallowed him up. Preceded by very little noise the square outline of the box now appeared upon the top of the cupboard.

He had raised it above his head and placed it there, by which circumstances, since he appeared to be a small man, I was able to judge of his extraordinary strength.

My heart was beating very fast and I realised that I was holding my breath. I inhaled deeply, watching, now, the square of the opened window. A silhouetted arm appeared above the box, then a shoulder, and finally the whole of a lean body.

The midnight visitor was a Negro, or a member of some very dark race, wearing only a black loincloth: his features I could not see.

His movements interested me intensely. Stooping, he bent over the box. Certain metallic sounds told me that the iron handles at either end were being moved.

Then, as I watched... the box disappeared!

The black man alone, a crouching silhouette, remained outlined in the open window. The box had gone; incredible fact—but the box had gone! Silently, save for a distant thud that heavy iron chest had been "vanished" from the room as a conjurer vanishes a coin!

An interval followed, my reactions during which I cannot hope to describe, until presently I saw that the crouching figure was performing a sort of hauling movement. This movement ceased.

He stood suddenly upright... and disappeared.

CHAPTER ELEVEN

THE MAN ON THE MINARET

That vague supernatural dread which latterly I had shaken off swept back again like a cloud, touching me coldly. The window space was perfectly blank, now. The iron box had gone; the black man had gone. This miracle had been achieved with scarcely any sound!

The legend of Spring-heeled Jack crossed my mind again. Then I was up. My period of enforced inactivity was ended.

I pressed the button of my torch and, springing out from behind the big trunk, directed a ray along the narrow room. The air was still heavy with a vague sickly perfume of mimosa; but I gave no glance at the pillow which had been sprayed with this strange anaesthetic. The bed had been carefully prepared by Nayland Smith to produce the appearance of a sleeper.

"An old dodge of mine, Greville," he had said, "which will certainly fail if the enemy suspects that I am here."

Either the enemy did not suspect, or, like the ancient confidence trick, it was a device which age did not wither nor custom stale…

As though it had been a prearranged cue, that flash of light in the empty room heralded a sound—*the sound*... an indescribable humming which rose and rose, developed into a sort of wail, then died away like muted roaring...

I must explain at this point that from the moment of the figure's disappearance from the window to that when, switching on the light, I ran forward, only a very few seconds had elapsed.

Leaping upon the low cupboard, and staring down into the street, I witnessed a singular spectacle.

That extraordinary sound, the origin of which had defied all speculation, was still audible, and since it seemed to come from somewhere high above my head, my first instinct was to look up.

I did not do so, however.

At the moment that I sprang into the open window, my glance was instantly drawn *downward*. I saw a figure—that of the black creature who had just quitted the room—apparently suspended in space, midway across the street!

His arms raised above his head, he was *soaring* upward towards a window of the Ghost Mosque!

"Good God!" I said aloud—"it isn't human..."

There came a wild scream. The flying figure faltered—the upraised arms dropped—and he was dashed with a dull thud against the wall of the mosque, some eight feet below the window. From there he fell sheerly to the street below. A second, sickening, thud reached my ears...

The crack of a pistol, a sharp spurt of flame from the gallery of the minaret far above my head, drew my glance upward now. I saw a black-robed black-faced figure there, bathed in brilliant moonlight, bending over the rail and firing down upon the roof of the mosque below!

Once he fired, and moved further around the gallery. A second time. And then, as he disappeared from view, I heard the sound of a third shot...

Pandemonium awakened in the house about me. Ali Mahmoud was unfastening the heavy bolt which closed the front door. Rima's voice came from the landing above.

"Shan! Shan! Are you all right?"

"All right, dear!" I shouted.

Turning, I ran along the room and out into the corridor. I heard Barton's great voice growling impatiently in the lobby below. But before I could reach him he had raced out into the street. Ali, rifle in hand, followed him, and I brought up the rear.

Far above, Rima leaned from an open window, and:

"For God's sake, be careful!" she cried. "I can see something moving along the roof of the mosque!"

"Don't worry!" I called reassuringly. "We're all armed."

I was bending over a figure lying in the dust, a figure at which Sir Lionel was already staring down with an indescribable expression. It was that, as I saw now quite clearly, of a small but powerfully built Negro.

He presented an unpleasant spectacle by reason of the fact that he had evidently dashed his skull against the wall of the mosque at the end of that incredible flight from side to side of the street. He wore, as I had thought, nothing but a dark loincloth.

Thrust into this, where it was visible as he lay huddled up and half upon his face, was a dull metal object which gleamed in the light of our torches. For, although moonlight illuminated the minaret and upper part of the mosque, the street itself was a black gully. Stooping, I examined this object more closely.

It was a metal spray, such as dentists use. Its purpose I had already seen demonstrated; then:

"Look at his hands!" the chief said huskily. "What is he holding?"

At first I found it difficult to reply; then I realised that the Negro was clutching two large iron hooks to which had been attached a seemingly endless thread of what looked like catgut, no thicker than the D string of a violin. The truth was still far from my mind; when:

"A West African," Sir Lionel continued—"probably from the Slave Coast. What in hell's name brought such a bird to Persia?"

"Perhaps," I suggested, "he was sold. Slavery is still practised in these parts."

Further speculation on the point was ended by a sudden loud cry from the minaret.

"Stand by, there!"

Sir Lionel, Ali Mahmoud, and I raised our heads. A tall figure draped in a black native robe stood on the gallery. Upright, now, moonlight silvering his hair, I knew him. It was Nayland Smith!

"Ali Mahmoud!" he shouted, "round to the side door of the mosque and shoot anything you see moving. Barton! Stand by the main door, where you can cover three windows. Let nothing come out. Quick, Greville! You know the way into the minaret. Up to me!"

CHAPTER TWELVE

IN THE GHOST MOSQUE

An open stone stairway built around the interior wall, afforded a means of reaching the platform of the minaret from that point of entrance to which Nayland Smith had directed me. There was an inner gallery high above my head, to which formerly the mueddin had gained access from a chamber of the mosque.

My footsteps as I clambered upward, breathing hard, echoed around the shell of that ancient tower in a weird, uncanny tattoo. It may seem to have been a bad time for thought, but my brain was racing faster than my feet could carry me.

Some dawning perception of the means by which poor Van Berg had been assassinated was creeping into my mind. In some way the acrobatic murderer had *swung* into the room, probably from one of the windows of the mosque. The hooks which he still clasped in his hands had afforded him a grip, no doubt, and earlier had been hitched to the handles of the iron box which had been swung to its destination in the same way.

But remembering the slender line—resembling a violin string— which we had found attached to those hooks, I met with doubt again. The thing was plainly impossible.

I reached the opening into the gallery and paused for awhile. This gallery extended, right, into darkness which the ray of my torch failed to penetrate. Before me was a low, narrow door, giving access to a winding wooden stair which would lead me to the platform above.

The idea of that passage penetrating into the darkness of the haunted mosque was definitely unpleasant. And casting one final glance along it, I resumed my journey. I stumbled several times on those stairs, which were narrow and dilapidated, but presently found the disk of the moon blazing in my face and knew that I had reached the platform.

"Greville!" came in Nayland Smith's inimitable snappy voice.

"Yes, Sir Denis."

I came out and stood beside him. It was a dizzying prospect as one emerged from darkness. The narrow street upon which our house faced looked like a bottomless ravine. I could see right across the roof of the mosque on one hand, to where Ispahan, looking like a city of mushrooms from which tulip-like minarets shot up, slumbered under a velvet sky, and, left, to the silver river. Then, my attention was diverted.

A dark shape lay almost at my feet, half hidden in shadow. I drew back sharply, looking down; and:

"Damned unfortunate, Greville," said Nayland Smith rapidly.

He was standing near the door out of which I had come, a tall, angular figure, flooded by moonlight on the right, but a mere silhouette on the left. He wore a loose black *gibbeh* which I thought I recognized as the property of Ali Mahmoud. The angularity of his features was accentuated, and the one eye which was visible shone like polished steel. He glanced down.

"I used an extemporised sandbag from behind," he explained, "and I'm afraid I hit too hard. I'm not masquerading, Greville—" indicating his black robe. "I borrowed this to help me to hide in the shadows. Is the other Negro dead?"

"Yes, he dashed his brains out against the wall of the mosque."

"Damnably unfortunate!" Nayland Smith jerked. "I have no personal regrets, but either would have been an invaluable witness. There was a third on the roof of the mosque. His job was to keep a lookout. I missed him twice, but hit him the third time. He managed to get away, nevertheless. But I'm hoping he can't escape from the building."

Dimly, from far below, rose a murmuring of approaching steps and voices. Nayland Smith's shots had awakened the neighbourhood.

"Damn it!" he rapped. "If a crowd gathers, it may ruin everything."

He stooped and removed a loop of that strange tenuous line from a projection of the ornamental stonework decorating the railing of the balcony.

"Look!" he said, and held it up in the moonlight. "It doesn't seem strong enough to support a kitten. Yet the black murderer and the iron box were swung from window to window upon a carefully judged length of it." He thrust the line into his pocket. "I came prepared for wire," he added grimly, and exhibited an implement which I recognized as part of Sir Lionel's kit: a steel wire cutter.

"For heaven's sake, what is it?" I asked.

Even now, I found difficulty in believing that a line no stouter than sewing thread could carry a man's weight.

"I haven't the slightest idea, Greville. But it's tremendously tough. It took a mighty grip to cut through it. Suspended from this balcony, you see, its length carefully estimated, it enabled one of these acrobatic devils to swing from a window of the mosque right onto a corresponding window of the house opposite. It also enabled him to swing the iron box across. But there's work for us!"

He pushed me before him in his impetuous fashion; and:

"There was a *fourth* in the game, Greville," he added…"perhaps a fifth. He, or they, were stationed behind the window of the mosque. The controlling influence—the man we're looking for—was there!"

I started down at the wooden stair, Nayland Smith following hard behind me; until:

"One moment!" he called.

I paused and turned, directing the ray of my torch upward. He was fumbling in a sort of little cupboard at the head of the steps, and from it he presently extracted his shoes, and proceeded to put them on, talking rapidly the while.

"It was touch and go when that black devil came up, Greville. I also was black from head to feet; black robe, black socks, and a black head cover, made roughly from a piece of this old *gibbeh*, with holes cut for eyes and mouth! He didn't see me, and he couldn't hear me. I dodged him all round the gallery like a boy dodging around the trunk of a tree! When he made fast the line, on the end of which I could see two large iron hooks, and lowered it, I recognized the method."

He had both his shoes on now and was busily engaged in lacing them.

"It confirmed my worst suspicions—but this can be discussed later. Having lowered it to its approved length, he swung it like a pendulum; and presently it was caught and held by someone hidden behind a window of the mosque. You will find, I think, that there is a still lighter line attached to the hooks. This enabled the Negro, having swung across from the mosque to the house, to haul the pendulum back until the box was safely disposed of. It was as he swung across in turn, that I got busy with the wire cutter."

He came clattering down, and:

"Left!" he said urgently—"into the mosque."

I found myself proceeding along that narrow, mysterious passage.

"Light out!"

As I switched the torch off, he opened a door. I was looking along a flat roof, silvered by moonlight—the roof of the mosque.

"I hit him just before he reached this door. There's a bare chance he may have left a clue."

"A clue to what?"

A considerable group of people had collected in the street, far below, including, I thought, Armenians from across the river, as many excited voices told me. But I was intent upon the strange business in hand; and:

"*The sound!*" said Nayland Smith; "that damnable, howling sound which was their signal."

No torch was necessary now. The roof was whitely illuminated by the moon. And, stooping swiftly:

"My one bit of luck tonight," he exclaimed. "Look!"

Triumphantly, for I could see his eyes gleaming, he held up an object which at first I was unable to identify, I suppose because it was something utterly unexpected. But presently recognition came. It was a bone... a human frontal bone!

"I'm afraid," I said stupidly, "that I don't understand."

"A *bull-roarer!*" cried Nayland Smith. "Barton can probably throw light upon its particular history."

He laughed. A length of stout twine was attached to the bone, and twisting this about his fingers he swung the thing rapidly round and round at ever increasing speed.

The result was uncanny.

I heard again that awesome whining which had heralded the death of Van Berg, which I had thought to be the note of some supernatural nocturnal creature. It rose to a wail—to a sort of muted roar—and died away as the swing diminished…

"One of the most ancient signaling devices in the world, Greville—probably prehistoric in origin. Listen!"

I heard running footsteps, many running footsteps, in the street below—all receding into the distance…

Sir Denis laughed again, shortly.

"Our bull-roarer has successfully dispersed the curious natives!" he said.

CHAPTER THIRTEEN

THE BLACK SHADOW

Dawn was very near when that odd party assembled in the room which we used as an office, the room in which Van Berg had died. Nayland Smith presided, looking haggardly tired after his exertions of the night. He paced up and down continuously. The chief stood near the door, shifting from foot to foot in his equally restless fashion. Rima sat in the one comfortable chair and I upon the arm of it.

A Persian police officer who spoke perfect English completed the party.

"Dr. Van Berg, as you know," said Sir Denis, "died in this room. I have tried to explain how the murderer gained access. The room being higher than Sir Lionel's, the line used was shorter, but the method was the same. I found fingerprints and footmarks on the roof of the mosque and also on the ledge below these shutters. A man stabbed as Van Berg was stabbed bleeds from the mouth; therefore I found no bloodstains. The Negro was swung across, not from the window, but from the roof of the mosque. He employed the same device, having quietly entered, of spraying the head of the sleeper with some drug which so far we haven't been able to identify. It smells like mimosa. Fortunately, a portion remains in the spray upon the dead African, and analysis may enlighten us."

"But Dr. Van Berg was stabbed, as I remember?" said the Persian official.

"Certainly!" Nayland Smith snapped. "He had a pair of Caspian kittens sleeping at the foot of his bed. The bed used to stand there, just where you are sitting. They awakened immediately and in turn awakened him. He must have realised what was afoot, and he sprang straight for the box. It was his first and only thought—for already he was under the influence of the drug. The Negro knifed him from behind."

He pointed to a narrow-bladed knife which lay upon a small table.

"He came provided for a similar emergency tonight… That unhappy mystery, I think, is solved."

"I cannot doubt it," the Persian admitted. "But the strength of this material," touching a piece of the slender yellow-gray line, "is amazing. What is it?"

"It's silkworm gut," Sir Lionel shouted. "I recognized it at once. It's the strongest animal substance known. It's strong enough to land a shark, if he's played properly."

"I don't agree with you, Barton," Nayland Smith said quietly. "It certainly *resembles* silkworm gut, but it is infinitely stronger."

Before the chief could reply:

"A very singular business. Sir Lionel," the suave official murmured. "But I am happy to leam that no Persian subject is concerned in this murderous affair."

There was a pause, and then:

"A fourth man was concerned," said Nayland Smith, speaking

unusually slowly. "He, as well as the Negro whom I wounded, has managed to get away. Probably there are exits from the mosque with which I am unacquainted?"

"You suggest that the fourth man concerned was one of our subjects?"

"I suggest nothing. I merely state that there *was* a fourth man. He was concealed in a window of the mosque."

"Probably another of these Negroes—who are of a type quite unfamiliar to me…"

"They are Ogboni!" shouted the chief. "They come from a district of the Slave Coast I know well! They're members of a secret Voodoo society. You should read my book *The Sorcerers of Dahomey*. I spent a year in their territory. When I saw that bull roarer there—" he pointed to the frontal bone with the twine attached, which also lay upon the small table—"it gave me the clue. I knew that these West African negroes were Ogboni. They're active as cats and every bit as murderous. But I agree with Smith, that they were working under somebody else's direction."

The Persian official, a dignified and handsome man of forty-odd, wearing well tailored European clothes, raised his heavy brows and smiled slightly.

"Are you suggesting. Sir Lionel," he asked, "that the religious trouble, which I fear *you* have brought about, is at the bottom of this?"

"I am," the chief replied, glaring at him truculently.

"It's beyond doubt," said Nayland Smith. "The aim of the whole conspiracy was to gain possession of the green box."

The Persian continued to smile.

"And in this aim it would seem that the conspirators have been successful."

"They certainly managed to smuggle the box out of the mosque,"

Nayland Smith admitted grimly, "although one of the pair was wounded, as I know for a fact."

Our visitor stood up.

"Some sort of rough justice has been done," he said. "The actual assassin of your poor friend Dr. Van Berg has met his deserts, as has his most active accomplice. The green box, I believe, contained valuable records of your recent inquiries in Khorassan…"

His very intonation told me unmistakably that he believed nothing of the kind…

"I feel, Sir Lionel, that this may represent a serious loss to Oriental students—nor can I imagine of what use these—records can be to those who have resorted to such dreadful measures to secure them."

The chief clapped his hands, and Ali Mahmoud came in. The Persian official stooped and kissed Rima's fingers, shook hands with the rest of us, and went out. There was silence for a few moments, and then:

"You know, Barton," said Nayland Smith, pacing up and down rapidly, "Ispahan, though quite civilised, is rather off the map; and frankly—local feeling is against you. I mean this Mokanna movement is going to play hell in Persia if it goes on. As you started it—you're not popular."

"Never have been," growled the chief; "never expect to be."

"Not the point," rapped Smith. "There's going to be worse to come—when they know."

A silence followed which I can remember more vividly than many conversations. Rima squeezed my arm and looked up at me in a troubled way. Sir Denis was not a man to panic. But he had made it perfectly clear that he took a grave view of the situation.

Sir Lionel had fenced with the local authorities throughout, knowing that they could have no official information regarding the relics—since, outside our own party (and now Captain Woodville and Stratton Jean), nobody but Amir Khan knew we had found them.

At the cost of one life in our camp and two in their own the enemy had secured the green box... but the green box was empty! I knew now why the chief had been so conscience-stricken by the death of Van Berg; I knew that the relics had never been where we all supposed them to be from the time that we came to Ispahan.

Van Berg had died defending an empty box...

Sir Lionel began to laugh in his boisterous fashion.

"We've scored over them. Smith!" he shouted, and shook his clenched fist. They had Van Berg—but we got a pair of the swine tonight! Topping it all—they've drawn a blank!"

His laughter ceased, and that wonderful, lined old face settled down again into the truculent mask which was the front Sir Lionel Barton showed to the world.

"It's a poor triumph," he added, "to pay for the loss of Van Berg."

Nayland Smith ceased his promenade at the window and stood with his back to all of us, staring out.

"I don't know where you've hidden the relics, Barton," he said slowly, "but I may have to ask you to tell me. One thing I do know. This part of the East is no longer healthy for any of us. The second attempt has failed—but the third…"

"What are you suggesting?" Sir Lionel growled; "that I give 'em up? Suppose it came to that. Who am I dealing with?"

Nayland Smith did not turn. But:

"I believe I can tell you," he answered quietly.

"Then tell me! Don't throw out hints. Speak up, man!"

At that, Nayland Smith turned and stared at the speaker, remaining silent for some moments. At last:

"I flew here in a two-seater from Basra," he replied. "There was no other aircraft available in the neighbourhood. I have already made arrangements, however. Imperial Airways have lent us a taxi. You must realise. Barton, the position is serious."

Something in his manner temporarily silenced the chief; until:

"I do realise it," he admitted grudgingly. "Some organiser has got hold of this wave of fanaticism which my blowing up of El Mokanna's tomb started, and he realises—I suppose that's what you're driving at?—that production of the actual relics would clinch the matter. Am I right?"

"You are!" said Nayland Smith. "And I must ask you to consider one or two facts. The drug which was used in the case of Van Berg, and again last night, is, I admit, unfamiliar. But the method of employment is not. You see what I mean?"

Rima's grip on my arm tightened; and:

"Shan," she said, looking up at me, "it was what happened two years ago in England!"

The chief's face was a study. Under tufted eyebrows he was positively glaring at Nayland Smith. The latter continued:

"Rima begins to realise what I mean. The device for passing from house to house without employing the usual method of descending to the street is also familiar to me. It was *experience*, and nothing else, that enabled me to deal with the affair of last night."

He paused, and I found my mind working feverishly. Then, bringing that odd conversation to a dramatic head, came a husky query from Sir Lionel.

"Good God! Smith!" he said. "He can't be behind this?"

The emphasis on "he" resolved my final doubt.

"You're not suggesting, Sir Denis," I asked, "that we are up against *Dr. Fu-Manchu*?"

Rima clutched me now convulsively. Once only had she met the stupendous genius, Dr. Fu-Manchu, but the memory of that one interview would remain with her to the end of her days, as it would remain with me.

"If I had had any doubts, Barton," said Nayland Smith, "your identification of the murderer and his accomplice would have settled them. They belong, you tell me, to a secret society on the Slave Coast."

He paused, staring hard at Sir Lionel.

"I believe that there is no secret society of this character, however small or remote, which is not affiliated to the organisation known as the Si-Fan. That natives of the Pacific Islands are indirectly controlled by this group, I know for a fact; why not Negroes of West Africa? Consider the matter from another angle. What are natives of the Slave Coast doing in Persia? Who has brought them here?

"They are instruments, Barton, in the hands of a master schemer. For what object they were originally imported, we shall probably never know, but their usefulness in the present case has been proved. There can be no association between this West African society and the survivors of the followers of El Mokanna. These Negroes are in the train of some directing personality."

It was morning, and the East is early afoot. From a neighbouring market street came sounds of movement and discords human and animal. Suddenly Sir Denis spoke again.

"If any doubt had remained in my mind. Barton, it would have been removed last night. You may recall that just before the first signal came, someone passed slowly along the street below?"

"Yes! I heard him—but I couldn't see him."

"I heard him, too!" I cried…

"I both heard him and *saw* him," Nayland Smith continued— "from my post on the minaret. Action was impossible—

unfortunately—in the circumstances. But the man who walked along the street last night just before the second attempt on the green box… was Dr. Fu-Manchu!"

CHAPTER FOURTEEN

ROAD TO CAIRO

Weary though I was of all the East, nevertheless, Cairo represented civilisation. I think I have never felt a greater wave of satisfaction than at the moment when, completing the third and longest stage of our flight from Ispahan, we climbed down upon the sands of Egypt.

Dr. Petrie was there to meet us; and the greeting between himself and Sir Denis, while it had all the restraint which characterises our peculiar race, was nevertheless so intimate and affectionate that I turned away and helped Rima down the ladder.

When the chief, last to alight, joined his old friend, I felt that Rima and I had no further part in the affair.

It should have been a happy reunion, but a cloud lay over it—a cloud which I, personally, was helpless to dispel.

Dr. Petrie, no whit changed since last I had seen him, broke away from Sir Denis and the chief and hugged Rima and myself in both arms. The best of men are not wholly unselfish; and part of Petrie's present happiness was explainable by something which I had overheard as he had grasped Nayland Smith's hand:

"Thank God, old man! Kara is home in England…"

Mrs. Petrie, the most beautiful woman I have ever met (Rima is not jealous of my opinion), was staying with Petrie's people in Surrey, where the doctor shortly anticipated joining her.

I was sincerely glad. For the gaunt shadow of Fu-Manchu again had crept over us, and the lovely wife whom Petrie had snatched from that evil genius was in safe keeping beyond the reach of the menace which stretched over us even here.

Nevertheless, this was a momentary hiatus, if no more than momentary. Rima extended her arms, raised her adorable little head, and breathed in the desert air as one inhaling a heavenly perfume.

"Shan," she said, "I don't feel a bit safe, yet. But at least we are in Egypt, *our* Egypt!"

Those words "our Egypt" quickened my pulse. It was in Egypt that I had met her, and in Egypt that I had learned to love her. But above and beyond even this they held a deeper significance. There is something about Egypt which seems to enter the blood of some of us, and to make that old, secret land a sort of super-motherland. I lack the power properly to express what I mean, but over and over again I have found this odd sort of cycle operating—suggesting some mystic affinity with the "gift of the Nile," which, once recognized, can never be shaken off.

"Our Egypt!" Yes, I appreciated what she meant…

Dr. Petrie had his car waiting, and presently we set out for Cairo. Our pilot, Humphreys, had official routine duties to perform, but arrangements were made for his joining us later.

The chief, with Nayland Smith and Rima, packed themselves in behind, and I sat beside Dr. Petrie in front. Having cleared the outskirts of Heliopolis and got out onto the road to Cairo:

"This last job of yours, Greville," said Petrie, "in Khorassan, has had its echoes even here."

"Good heavens! You don't tell me!"

"I assure you it is so. I hadn't the faintest idea, until Smith's first message reached me, that this extraordinary outburst of fanaticism which is stirring up the Moslem population (and has its particular centre at El Azhar) had anything to do with old Barton. Now I know."

He paused, steering a careful course through those immemorable thoroughfares where East and West mingle. Our pilot had just tricked sunset, and we drove on amid the swift, violet, ever changing dusk; dodging familiar native groups; a donkey-rider now and then—with villas shrinking right and left into the shadows, and dusty palms beginning to assume an appearance of silhouettes against the sky which is the roof of Egypt.

"It may have reached me earlier than it reached the authorities," Dr. Petrie went on; "I have many native patients. But that the Veiled Prophet is reborn is common news throughout the native quarter!"

"This is damned serious!" said I.

Petrie swept left to avoid a party of three aged Egyptians trudging along the road to Cairo as though automobiles had not been invented.

"When I realised what lay behind it," Petrie added, "I could only find one redeeming feature—that my wife, thank God! was in England. The centre of the trouble is farther east, but there's a big reaction here."

"The centre of the trouble," rapped Nayland Smith, evidently having overheard some part of our conversation, "is here, in your car, Petrie!"

"What!"

The doctor's sudden grip on the wheel jerked us from the right to the centre of the road, until he steadied himself; then:

"I don't know what you mean. Smith," he added.

"He means the big suitcase which I have with me!" the chief shouted. "It's under my feet now!"

We were traversing a dark patch at the moment with a crossways ahead of us and a native café on the left. Petrie, a careful driver, had been trying for some time to pass a cart laden with fodder which jogged along obstinately in the middle of the road. Suddenly it was pulled in, and the doctor shot past.

Even as Sir Lionel spoke, and before Petrie could hope to avert the catastrophe, out from the nearer side of this café, supported by two companions, a man (apparently drunk or full of hashish) came lurching. I had a hazy impression that the two supporters had sprung back; then, although Petrie swerved violently and applied brakes, a sickening thud told me that the bumpers had struck him...

A crowd twenty or thirty strong gathered in a twinkling. They were, I noted, exclusively native. Petrie was out first—I behind him—Nayland Smith came next, and then Rima.

Voices were raised in high excitement. Men were gesticulating and shaking clenched fists at us.

"Carry him in," said Petrie quietly. "I want to look at him. But I think this man is dead..."

On a wooden seat in the café we laid the victim, an elderly Egyptian, very raggedly dressed, who might have been a mendicant. A shouting mob blocked the doorway and swarmed about us. Their attitude was unpleasant.

Nayland Smith grabbed my arm.

"Give 'em hell in their own language!" he directed. "You're a past master of the lingo."

I turned, hands upraised, and practically exhausted my knowledge of Arab invective. I was so far successful as to produce a lull of stupefaction during which the doctor made a brief examination.

Rima throughout had kept close beside me; Nayland Smith stood near the feet of the victim—his face an unreadable mask, but his piercing gray eyes questioning Petrie. And at last:

"Where's Barton?" said Petrie astonishingly, standing upright and looking about him—from Rima to myself and from me to Nayland Smith.

"Never mind Barton," said the latter. "Is the man dead?"

"Dead?" Petrie echoed. "He's been dead for at least three hours! He's rigid... Where's Barton?"

CHAPTER FIFTEEN

ROAD TO CAIRO (CONTINUED)

Sir Denis forming the head of the wedge, the four of us fought our way out of the café to the street, Petrie and I acting as Rima's bodyguard.

The hostility of the crowd was now becoming nasty. The mystery of the thing had literally turned me cold. Then, to crown it all, as we gained the open, I was just in time to see the chief, standing beside Petrie's car, deliver a formidable drive to the jaw of a big Nubian and to see the Negro sprawl upon his back.

"A *frame-up*, Smith!" came his great voice, as he sighted us. "To me, Cavaliers! We're in the hands of the Roundheads!"

So strange a plot I could never have imagined, but its significance was all to obvious. The chief's cry was characteristic of the man's entire outlook on life. He was a throwback to days when personal combat was a gentleman's recreation. His book *History and Art of the Rapier* might have been written by a musketeer, so wholly was the spirit of the author steeped in his bloodthirsty subject. This boyish diablerie it was which made him lovable, but perhaps as dangerous a companion as any man ever had.

One thing, however, I could not find it in my heart to forgive him: that he should expose Rima to peril consequent upon his crazy enthusiasms. I had come to want her near me in every waking moment. Yet now, with that threatening crowd about us and with every evidence that a secret enemy had engineered this hold-up, I found myself wishing that she, as well as Mrs. Petrie, had been safe in England.

How we should have fared, and how that singular episode would have ended, I cannot say. It was solved by the appearance of a member of one of the most efficient organisations in the world: a British-Egyptian policeman, his tarbush worn at a jaunty angle, his blue tunic uncreased as though it had left the tailor's only that morning. His khaki breeches were first class, and his very boots apparently unsoiled by the dust. He elbowed his way into the crowd—aloof, alone, self-contained, all powerful.

I had seen the same calm official intrusion on the part of a New York policeman, and I had witnessed it with admiration in London. But never before had I welcomed it so as at the appearance of this semi-military figure that night on the outskirts of Cairo.

Gesticulating Egyptians sought to enlist his sympathy and hearing. He was deaf. It dawned upon me that the casual onlookers had been deceived as completely as ourselves. We were regarded as the slayers of the poor old mendicant. But the appearance of that stocky figure changed everything.

As we reached Barton:

"Is the case safe?" snapped Nayland Smith, glancing down at the Negro, now rapidly getting to his feet.

"It is," the chief replied grimly. "That's what they were after." Sir Denis nodded shortly and turned to the police officer.

"*Your* car, sir?" asked the latter. "What's the trouble?"

"Remains to be investigated! You turned up at the right moment. My name is Nayland Smith. Have you been advised?"

The man started—stared hard, and then:

"Yes, sir." He saluted. "Two days ago. Carry on, sir. I'll deal with all this."

"Good. You're a smart officer. What's your name?"

"John Banks, sir, on special duty here tonight." "I'll mention you at headquarters…"

CHAPTER SIXTEEN

A MASKED WOMAN

"I am not prepared to believe," said Sir Lionel, walking up and down the big room reserved for him at Shepheard's, "that even Dr. Fu-Manchu could have had a stock of dead men waiting on the road from Heliopolis."

"Neither am I," said Nayland Smith. "We may have avoided earlier traps. Those three old fellows, Petrie—" turning to the Doctor— "who seemed so reluctant to get out of your way, you remember, and the cart laden with fodder. I don't suggest for a moment, Barton, that that poor old beggar was killed to serve the purpose; but Petrie here is of opinion that he died either from enteritis or poisoning, and the employment of a body in that way was probably a local inspiration on the part of the agents planted at that particular stage of our journey. He was pushed out, to the best of my recollection, from a shadowy patch of waste ground close beside the café. Where he actually died, I don't suppose we shall ever know, but—" tugging at the lobe of his left ear—"it's the most extraordinary trick I have ever met with, even in my dealings with…"

He paused, and Rima finished the sentence:

"Dr. Fu-Manchu."

There came an interval. The shutters of the window which overlooked the garden were closed. Muted voices, laughter, and a sound of many footsteps upon sanded paths rose to us dimly. But that group in the room was silent, until:

"Only *he* could devise such a thing," said the chief slowly, "and only you and I, Smith, could go one better."

He pointed to a battered leather suitcase lying on a chair and began to laugh in his own boisterous fashion.

"I travel light, Smith!" he cried, "but my baggage is valuable!"

None of us responded to his mood, and Sir Denis stared at him very coldly.

"When is Ali Mahmoud due in Cairo?" he asked.

That queer question was so unexpected that I turned and stared at the speaker. The chief appeared to be quite taken aback; and:

"He'll do well if he's here with the heavy kit in four days," he replied. "But why do you ask, Smith?"

Nayland Smith snapped his fingers irritably and began to walk up and down again.

"I should have thought, Barton," he snapped, "that we knew one another well enough to have shared confidences."

"What do you mean?"

"Simply what I say. If it conveys nothing—forget it!"

"I shan't forget it," said the chief gloweringly, his tufted brows drawn together. "But I shall continue to conduct my own affairs in my own way."

"Good enough. I'm not going to quarrel with you. But I should like to make a perfectly amiable suggestion."

"One moment," Petrie interrupted. "We're all old friends here. We've gone through queer times together, and after all—there's

85

a common enemy. It's useless to pretend we don't know who that common enemy is. You agree with me, Smith? For God's sake, let's stand four square. I don't know all the facts. But I strongly suspect—" turning to Sir Denis—"that *you* do. You're the stumbling block, Barton. You're keeping something up your sleeve. Lay all the cards on the table."

The chief gnawed his moustache, locked his hands behind him, and stood very upright, looking from face to face. He was in his most truculent mood. But at last, glancing aside from Petrie:

"I await your amiable suggestion, Smith," he growled.

"I'll put it forward," said the latter. "It is this: A Bibby liner is leaving Port Said for Southampton tomorrow. I suggest that Rima secures a berth."

Rima jumped up at his words, but I saw Petrie grasp her hand as if to emphasise his agreement with them.

"Why should I be sent home, Sir Denis?" she demanded. "What have I done? If you're thinking of my safety, I've been living for months in remote camps in Khorassan and Persia, and you see—" she laughed and glanced aside at me—"I'm still alive."

"You have done nothing, my dear," Sir Denis returned, and smiled in that delightful way which, for all his seniority, sometimes made me wonder why any woman could spare me a thought while he was present. "Nor," he added, "do I doubt your courage. But while your uncle maintains his present attitude, I don't merely fear—I know— that all of us, yourself included, stand in peril of our lives."

There was an unpleasant sense of tension in the atmosphere. The chief was in one of his most awkward moods—which I knew well. He had some dramatic trick up his sleeve. Of this I was fully aware. And he was afraid that Sir Denis was going to spoil his big effect.

Sir Lionel, for all his genius, and despite his really profound learning, at times was actuated by the motives which prompt a mischievous schoolboy to release a mouse at a girl's party.

Incongruously, at this moment, at least from our point of view, a military band struck up somewhere beneath; for this was a special occasion of some kind, and the famous garden was en fête. None of us, however, were in gala humour; but:

"Let's go down and see what's going on, Shan," said Rima. She glanced at Sir Lionel. "Can you spare him?"

"Glad to get rid of him," growled the chief. "He's hand and hoof with Smith, here, and one of 'em's enough…"

And so presently Rima and I found ourselves crossing the lobby below and watching a throng entering the ballroom from which strains of a dance band came floating out.

"What a swindle, Shan!" she said, pouting in a childish fashion I loved. "I'm simply dying for a dance. And I haven't even the ghost of a frock with me."

We were indeed out of place in that well dressed gathering, in our tired-looking travelling kit. For practically the whole of our worldly possessions had been left behind with the heavy gear in charge of Ali Mahmoud.

After several months more or less in the wilderness, all these excited voices and the throb and drone of jazz music provided an overdose of modern civilisation.

"I feel like Robinson Crusoe," Rima declared, "on his first day home. Do you feel like Man Friday?"

"Not a bit!"

"I'm glad, because you look more like a Red Indian."

Exposure to sun and wind, as a matter of fact, had beyond doubt reduced my complexion to the tinge of a very new brick, and I was wearing an old tweed suit which for shabbiness could only be compared with that of gray flannel worn by Sir Denis.

Nevertheless, I thought, as I looked at Rima, from her trim glossy head to the tips of her small gray shoes, that she was the daintiest figure I had seen that night.

"As we're totally unfit for the ballroom," I said, "do you think we might venture in the garden?"

We walked through the lounge with its little Oriental alcoves and out into the garden. It was a perfect night, but unusually hot for the season. Humphreys, our pilot, joined us there, and:

"You know, Greville," he said grinning, "I don't know what you've been up to in Khorassan, or wherever it is. But somebody in those parts is kicking up no end of a shindy."

He glanced at me shrewdly. Of the real facts he could know nothing—unless the chief had been characteristically indiscreet. But I realised that he must suspect our flight from Persia to have had some relation to the disturbances in that country.

"I should say you bolted just in time," he went on. "They claim a sort of new Mahdi up there. When I got to Cairo this evening I found the news everywhere. Honestly, it's all over the town, particularly the native town. There's a most curious feeling abroad, and in some way they have got the story of this Veiled bloke mixed up with the peculiar weather. I mean, it's turned phenomenally hot. There's evidently a storm brewing."

"Which they put down to the influence of El Mokanna?"

"Oh, what nonsense!" Rima laughed.

But Humphreys nodded grimly, and:

"Exactly," he returned. "I'm told that a religious revival is overdue among the Moslems, and this business may fill the bill. You ought to know as well as I do, Greville, that superstition is never very far below the surface in even the most cultured Oriental. And these waves of fanaticism are really incalculable. It's a kind of mass hypnotism, and we know the creative power of thought."

I stared at the speaker with a new curiosity. He was revealing a side of his nature which I had not supposed to exist. Rima, too, had grown thoughtful.

"Someone would have to lead this movement," she suggested. "How could there be followers of a Veiled Prophet if there were no Veiled Prophet?"

"I'm told that up at El Azhar," Humphreys replied seriously, "they are proclaiming that there is a Veiled Prophet—or, rather, a Masked Prophet. He's supposed to be moving down through Persia."

"But it's simply preposterous!" Rima declared.

"It's likely to be infernally dangerous," he returned dryly. "However," brightening up, "I notice you're devoid of evening kit, Miss Barton, same as Greville. But as I'm attired with proper respectability, I know of no reason why we shouldn't dance out here. The band's just starting again."

Rima consented with a complete return of gaiety. And as her petite figure moved off beside that of the burly airman, I lighted a cigarette and looked around me. I was glad she had found a partner to distract her thoughts from the depression which lay upon all of us. And, anyway, I'm not much of a dancing man myself at the best of times.

Up under the leaves of the tall palms little coloured electric lamps were set, resembling fiery fruit. Japanese lanterns formed lighted festoons from trunk to trunk. In the moonlight, the water of the central fountain looked like an endless cascade of diamonds. The sky above was blue-black, and the stars larger and brighter than I remembered ever to have seen them.

Crunching of numberless feet I heard on the sanded paths; a

constant murmur of voices; peals of laughter rising sometimes above it all—and now the music of a military band.

There were few fancy costumes, and those chiefly of the stock order. But there was a profusion of confetti—which seems to be regarded as indispensable on such occasions, but which I personally look upon as a definite irritant. To shed little disks of coloured paper from one's clothing, cigarette case, and tobacco pouch wherever one goes for a week after visiting a fête of this kind is a test of good-humour which the Southern races possibly survive better than I do.

I strolled round towards the left of the garden—that part farthest from the band and the dancers—intending to slip into the hotel for a drink before rejoining Rima and Humphreys.

Two or three confetti fiends had pot shots at me, but I did not find their attentions stimulating. In fact, I may as well confess that this more or less artificial gaiety, far from assisting me to banish those evil thoughts which claimed my mind, seemed to focus them more sharply.

Sir Denis and the chief, when I had left them, were still pacing up and down in the latter's room, arguing hotly; and poor Dr. Petrie was trying to keep the peace. That Sir Lionel had smuggled the Mokanna relics out of Persian territory he did not deny, nor was this by any means the first time he had indulged in similar acts of piracy. Nayland Smith was for lodging them in the vault of the Museum: Sir Lionel declined to allow them out of his possession.

He had a queer look in his deep-set eyes which I knew betokened mischief. Sir Denis knew too, and the knowledge taxed him almost to the limit of endurance, that the chief was keeping something back.

A sudden barrage of confetti made me change my mind about going in. Try how I would, I could not force myself into gala humour, and I walked all around the border of the garden, along a path which seemed to be deserted and only imperfectly lighted.

Practically everybody was on the other side, where the band was playing—either dancing or watching the dancing. The greater number of the guests were in the ballroom, however, preferring jazz and a polished floor to military brass and al fresco discomfort. I had lost my last cigarette under the confetti bombardment, and now, taking out my pipe, I stood still and began to fill it.

Dr. Fu-Manchu!

Nayland Smith believed that agents of Dr. Fu-Manchu had been responsible for the death of Van Berg and for the theft of the green box. This, I reflected, could mean only one thing.

Dr. Fu-Manchu was responsible for the wave of fanaticism sweeping throughout the East, for that singular rumour that a prophet was reborn, which, if Humphreys and Petrie were to be believed, El Azhar already proclaimed.

My pipe filled, I put my hand in my pocket in search of matches, when—a tall, slender figure crossed the path a few yards ahead of me.

My hand came out of my pocket, I took the unlighted pipe from between my teeth, and stared… stared!

The woman, who wore a green, sheath-like dress and gold shoes, had a delicate indolence of carriage, wholly Oriental. About one bare ivory arm, extending from just below the elbow to the wrist, she wore a massive jade bangle in six or seven loops. A golden girdle not unlike a sword belt was about her waist, and a tight green turban on her head.

Her appearance, then, was sufficiently remarkable. But that which crowned the queerness of this slender, graceful figure, was the fact that she wore a small half-mask; and this half-mask was apparently of gold!

That the costume was designed to represent El Mokanna there

could be no doubt. This in itself was extraordinary, but might have been explained by that queer wave of native opinion which was being talked about everywhere. It was such an ill-considered jest as would commend itself to a crazy member of the younger set. But there was something else…

Either I had become the victim of an optical delusion, traceable to events of the past few days, or the woman in the gold mask was Fu-Manchu's daughter!

CHAPTER SEVENTEEN

THE MOSQUE OF MUAYYAD

Normally the air would have been growing chilly by now, but on the contrary a sort of oppressive heat seemed to be increasing. As the alluring figure crossed diagonally and disappeared into a side path, I glanced upward.

The change was startling.

Whereas but a few minutes before the stars had been notably bright, now not a star was visible. A dense black cloud hung overhead, and, as the band stopped, I noted a quality of stillness in the atmosphere such as often precedes a storm.

These things, however, I observed almost subconsciously. I was determined to overtake the wearer of the gold mask; I was determined to establish her identity. All those doubts and fears which I had with difficulty kept at bay seemed to swoop down upon me as if from the brooding sky.

An imperfect glimpse only I had had of long, tapering ivory fingers. But I believed there was only one woman in the world who possessed such hands—the woman known as Fah Lo Suee, the fascinating but witch-like daughter of the Chinese doctor.

Slipping my pipe back into my pocket, I stepped forward quickly, turning right, into a narrow path. Owing, I suppose, to the threatening skies, a general exodus from the garden had commenced, and since I was walking away from the hotel and not towards it, I met with no other guests.

I had hesitated only a few seconds before starting in pursuit. Nevertheless, there was no sign of my quarry. I pulled up, peering ahead. A sudden doubt crossed my mind.

Had Fah Lo Suee seen me? And did she hope to slip away unmasked? If so, she had made a false move.

For a glance had shown that, now, she could not possibly avoid me. She had turned left, from the narrow path, and was approaching the railings of the garden at a point where there was a gate.

I chanced to know that this gate was invariably locked...

She had nearly reached it when I began to walk forward again, slowly and confidently. Her movements convinced me even in the semi-darkness that my conjecture had been correct. This was Fu-Manchu's daughter, beyond any shadow of doubt.

I was not twelve paces behind her when she came to the gate. She stooped, and, although I heard no sound—the gate swung open! I saw her for a moment, a tall, slim silhouette against lights from the other side of the street; then the gate clanged to behind her.

Without even glancing over her shoulder, although I knew she must have heard my approach, she turned left in the direction of Sharia Kamel, still at that leisurely, languid pace.

I ran to the gate—it was locked!

This discovery astounded me.

By what means obtained, I could not even guess, but clearly this strange woman possessed a key of the disused entrance. I contemplated scaling the railings, but realised the difficulty of the operation. There was only one thing for it.

I turned and ran back to the hotel, hoping I might meet no one to whom I should feel called upon to give an explanation of my eccentric conduct.

There came an ominous rumbling, and I saw with annoyance that crowds were pouring in at the entrance. However, I made a rush for it; earned some stinging comments on the part of guests into whom I bumped—dashed across the lobby and out onto the terrace.

A line of cars and taxicabs was drawn up outside. This I had time to note as I went flying down the steps. I turned sharply right. I was only just in time. A wonderfully slender ankle, an arched instep, and a high-heeled golden shoe provided the only clue.

The woman had just entered a car stationed, not outside the terrace of the hotel, but over by the arcade opposite. At the very moment that I heard the clang of its closing door, the car moved off, going in the direction of Esbekiyeh Gardens.

I ran to the end of the rank of waiting cabs and cars, and, grabbing an Egyptian driver who brought up the tail of the procession:

"Look!" I said rapidly in Arabic, and pulled him about, "where I am pointing!"

The hour being no later than ten o'clock, there was still a fair amount of traffic about. But I could see the car, a long, low two-seater, proceeding at no great speed, in the direction of the Continental.

"You see that yellow car? The one that has just reached the corner!"

The man stared as I pointed; and then:

"Yes, I see it."

"Then follow it! Double fare if you keep it in sight!"

That settled the matter. He sprang to the wheel in a flash. And whilst I half knelt on the seat, looking back, he turned his cab with reckless disregard of oncoming traffic and started off at racing speed…

Other cars were in the way, now, but I could still discern that in which the woman had driven off. I saw it turn left. I bent forward, shouting to the driver.

"They have turned left—did you see?"

"Yes."

An English policeman shouted angrily as my driver swerved to avoid a pedestrian and drove madly on. But the magic of a double fare infected him like a virus. He took the corner by the Gardens, when we reached it, at breakneck speed, and foreseeing disaster if this continued:

"Take it easy!" I shouted, leaning forward. "I can see them ahead. I don't want to catch them—only to keep them in sight."

The man nodded, and our progress became less furious. The atmosphere remained oppressive, but a few stars began to creep out overhead, and I saw ragged borders of the black cloud moving away over the Mokattam Hills. Rumbling of thunder grew more distant.

I could see the car ahead very clearly, now, for indeed we were quite near to it. And I found time to wonder where it could possibly be going.

We were leaving the European city behind and heading for the Oriental. In fact, it began to dawn upon me that Fah Lo Suee was making for the Muski—that artery of the bazaar streets, hives of industry during the day, but desolate as a city of the dead at night.

I was right.

The last trace of native night life left behind us, I saw the yellow car, proceeding in leisurely fashion, head straight into that deserted thoroughfare. My driver followed. We passed a crossways but still carried on, presently to turn right. I saw a mosque ahead, but my brain was so excited that at the moment I failed to identify it. My knowledge of native Cairo is not extensive at the best.

We left the mosque behind, the narrow street being far from straight and I in a constant fever lest we should lose sight of the yellow car. Then, I saw it—just passing another, larger mosque.

"Where are we?" I asked.

"Sukkariya," he replied, slowing down still more and negotiating a right-angle turn.

Empty shops and unlighted houses were all about us. For some time now we had met not a single pedestrian. It was utterly mystifying. Where could the woman possibly be heading for?

"Where does this lead to?"

"Mosque of Muayyad-Bab ez-Zuwela..."

Fah Lo Suee, of course, must have known now that she was pursued, but this I considered to be unavoidable, since in that maze of narrow streets that only a native driver could have negotiated, to lose sight of her for a moment would have meant failure.

Right again went the long, low French car.

"Don't know the name," my driver announced nonchalantly.

We turned into the narrowest street we had yet endeavoured to negotiate.

"Pull up!" I ordered sharply.

The place was laden with those indescribable smells which belong to the markets of the East, but nowhere could I see a light, or any evidence of human occupation. Narrow alleys intersected the street—mere black caverns.

Ahead, I saw the yellow car moving away again. But, for the second time that night, I had a glimpse of an arched instep, of a golden shoe.

Fah Lo Suee had alighted from the car, which evidently someone else was driving, and had walked into a narrow alley not twenty yards along.

I jumped out.

"Stay here," I ordered. "Don't move, whatever happens, until I come back."

I set out at the double, pulling up when I gained the entrance to the alley, and peering into its utter blackness. I heard the distant rumbling of thunder. It died away into oppressive silence.

No sound of footsteps reached me, and there was no glimmer of light ahead.

CHAPTER EIGHTEEN

DR. FU-MANCHU

I began to grope my way along a dark, unevenly paved passage, but I had taken no more than two steps forward when the folly of my behaviour crashed upon me like a revelation. If the woman who had disappeared somewhere ahead were indeed she whom we had known as Madame Ingomar, what a fool I was to thrust myself into this rat trap!

For a man to experience such terrors in regard to a woman may seem feeble; but from bitter experience I knew something of the weapons at command of Fah Lo Suee. That I might be mistaken about the identity of the gold mask was remotely possible, but no more than remotely so.

In a few fleeting seconds I reviewed the queer episode from the moment when I had seen that green-robed figure in Shepheard's garden—and I realised with bleak certainty that her behaviour had been directly to one end and to one end only. A trap had been baited… and I had fallen into it like the veriest fool.

I pulled up sharply, stretching out my hands to learn if any obstruction lay ahead. In the heat of the chase I had thrown precaution aside. I realised now, too late, that I was unarmed, alone; no one but the driver of the taxicab had the slightest idea where I had gone.

This same counsel came in the same moment that panic threatened. What else I could have done if the woman were not to escape unmasked was not clear. But to have sent a message to Smith, to Petrie, to the chief, before setting out, seemed, now, a more reasonable course.

And as the things which I had not done presented themselves starkly before me, a wave of that abominable perfume of mimosa which to the end of my days I must associate with the death of poor Van Berg was swept into my face...

It stifled me, engulfed me, struck me dumb. I remember that I tried to cry out, recognising in this awful moment that my only chance was to attract the attention of the Egyptian driver.

But never a sound came, only an increase of darkness, a deadly sickness, and a maddening knowledge that among fools in the land of Egypt I might claim high rank...

My next impression was of acute pain in the left ankle. My head was swimming as though I had recently indulged in a wild debauch, and my eyelids were so heavy that I seemed to experience physical difficulty in raising them.

I did raise them, however, and (a curious circumstance, later to be explained) my brain immediately began to function from the very moment that I had smelled that ghastly perfume.

My first thought, now, overlapped my last before unconsciousness had claimed me. I thought that I lay in that nameless alley somewhere behind the Mosque of Muayyad and that in falling I had twisted my ankle. I expected darkness, but I saw light.

Raising my hands, I rubbed my aching eyes, staring about me

dazedly. I was furiously thirsty, but in absolute possession of my senses. I looked down at my ankle, which pained me intensely, and made a discovery so remarkable that it engaged my attention even in the surroundings amid which I found myself.

I was lying on a divan; and about each of my ankles was fastened a single loop of dull, gray-yellow line resembling catgut and no thicker than a violin string. Amazing to relate—there were apparently *no knots*!

One of these loops was drawn so tightly as to be painful, and a single strand, some twelve inches long, connected the left ankle with the right. I struggled to my feet—and was surprised, since I knew I had been drugged, to find that my muscular reactions were perfectly normal.

Evidently my common sense was subnormal (or I am slow to profit by experience); for, resting one foot firmly on the floor, I kicked forward with the other, fully anticipating that this fragile link would snap.

The result must have been comic; but I had no audience. I kicked myself backward with astonishing velocity, falling among the cushions of the divan, from which I had not moved away!

Fortunately, the tendon escaped serious injury; but this first experiment was also the last. I had, tardily, recognized my bonds to be of that mysterious substance which had figured in our Ispahan adventure. I should not have been more helpless, save that I could shuffle about the room, if iron fetters had confined me.

I lay where I had fallen, gazing about. And I knew, as I had known in the very moment of opening my heavy-lidded eyes, that this was an amazing room in which I found myself.

It was a long, low salon, obviously that of an old Egyptian house, as the woodwork, a large *mushrabiyeh* window, and the tiling upon part of the wall clearly indicated. There were a few good rugs upon the floor, and light was furnished by several lamps, shaded incongruously in unmistakable Chinese fashion, which swung from the wooden ceiling.

The furniture was scanty, some of it Arab in character but some of it of Chinese lacquer. Right and left of the recessed window (which, wrongly, as after events showed, I assumed to overlook a street adjoining that alleyway behind the mosque) were deep bookcases laden with volumes. These, to judge from their unfamiliar binding, might have been rare works.

There were a number of glass cases in the room, containing most singular objects. In one was what looked like a living human head, that of a woman. But, as I focused my horrified gaze upon it, I saw that it was an unusually perfect mummy head. In another, which was obviously heated, I saw growing foliage and, watching it more closely, realised that a number of small, vividly green snakes moved among the leaves. A human skeleton, perfect, I thought, even to the small bones, stood in a rack in a gap between the bookcases. The window recess was glazed to form a sort of small conservatory, and through the glass, dimly, I could see that bloated flesh-coloured orchids were growing.

I stood up again, testing my injured ankle. It pained intensely, but the tendon had survived the jerk. I began to shuffle forward in the direction of a large, plain wooden table, resembling a monkish refectory table, before which was set one of those polished, inlaid chairs which are produced in the bazaars of Damascus.

There were some of those strange-looking volumes upon this table, as well as a number of scientific instruments, test tubes, and chemical paraphernalia. As I stood up, I saw that the table was covered with a sheet of glass.

Changing my position, other glass cases came into view; they contained rows of chemical bottles and apparatus. The place was more than half a laboratory. And I noticed, looking behind me, that there was a working bench in one corner fitted with electrical devices, although of a character quite unfamiliar.

The truth came subconsciously ahead of its positive confirmation. There were three doors to the salon, perfectly plain white teak doors. And in the very moment that I recognized a peculiar fact—viz: that they possessed neither bolts, handles, nor keyholes—one of these doors opened and slid noiselessly to the left.

I found myself alone with Dr. Fu-Manchu.

CHAPTER NINETEEN

FORMULA ELIXIR VITAE

He wore a green robe upon which was embroidered a white peacock, and on the dome of his wonderful skull a little cap was perched—a black cap surmounted by a coral ball. The door slid silently to behind him, and he stood watching me.

Once and once only, hitherto, had I seen the mandarin Fu-Manchu. He had impressed me, then, as one of the most gigantic forces ever embodied in a human form: but amazing—and amazingly horrible—he seemed, now, as he stood looking at me, to have shaken off part of the burden of years under which he had stooped on that unforgettable night in London.

He carried no stick; his long, bony hands were folded upon his breast. He was drawn up to his full, gaunt height, which I judged to be over six feet. His eyes, which were green as the eyes of a leopard, fixed me with a glance so piercing that it extended my powers to the full to sustain it.

There are few really first-class brains in the world today, but no man with any experience of humanity, looking into those long brilliant eyes, could have doubted that he stood in the presence of a super-mind.

I cannot better describe my feelings than by saying I felt myself to be absorbed; mentally and spiritually sucked empty by that awful gaze.

Even as this ghastly sensation, which I find myself unable properly to convey in words, overwhelmed me, a queer sort of film obscured the emerald eyes of Dr. Fu-Manchu, and I experienced immediate relief.

I remembered in that fleeting moment a discussion between Nayland Smith and Dr. Petrie touching this phenomenal quality of Fu-Manchu's eyes, which the doctor frankly admitted he had never met with before, and for which he could not account.

Walking slowly, but with a cat-like dignity, Fu-Manchu crossed to the long table, seating himself in the chair. His slippered feet made no sound. The room was silent as a tomb. The scene had that quality which belongs to dreams. No plan presented itself, and I found myself tongue-tied.

Fu-Manchu pressed the button of a shaded lamp upon a silver pedestal, and raising a small, pear-shaped vessel from a rack, examined its contents against the light. It contained some colourless fluid.

His hands were singular: long, bony, flexible fingers, in which, caricatured, as it were, I saw the unforgettable ivory fingers of Fah Lo Suee.

He replaced the vessel in the rack and turned to a page of one of those large volumes which lay open beside him. Seemingly considering it, he began to speak absent-mindedly.

His voice was as I remembered it, except that I thought it had acquired greater power: guttural but perfectly clear. He gave to every syllable its true value. Indeed, he spoke the purest English of any man I have ever heard.

"Mr Greville," he said, "I trust that any slight headache which you may have experienced on awakening has now disappeared."

I stood watching him where he sat, but attempted no reply.

"Formerly," he continued, "I employed sometimes a preparation of Indian hemp and at other times various derivatives of opium with greater or less success. An anaesthetic prepared from the common puffball for many years engaged my attention also; but I have now improved upon these."

He extended one long, green-draped arm, picking up and dropping with a faint rattling sound a number of brownish objects which looked like dried peas and which lay in a little tray upon the table.

"Seeds of a species of *Mimosa pudica*, found in Brazil and in parts of Asia," he continued, never once glancing in my direction. "I should like you to inform our mutual friend Dr. Petrie, whom I esteem, that Western science is on the wrong track, and that the perfect anaesthetic is found in *Mimosa pudica*. You succumbed to it tonight, Mr. Greville, and you have been unconscious for nearly half an hour. But if you were a medical man you would admit that the effects are negligible. The mental hiatus, also, is bridged immediately. Your first conscious thought was liked with your last. Am I right?"

"You are right," I replied, looking down at my feet and wondering if a sudden spring would enable me to get my hands around that lean throat.

"Your reflexes are normal," the slow, guttural voice continued. "The visceral muscles are unimpaired; there is no cardiac reaction. You are even now contemplating an assault upon me." He turned to another page of the large volume. "But consider the facts, Mr. Greville. You are still young enough to be impetuous: permit me to warn you. That slender thread which confines your ankles, and which I understand Sir Lionel Barton mistook for silkworm gut, is actually prepared from the flocculent secretion of *Theridion*—a well known but interesting spider…

"You seem to be surprised. The secret of that preparation would make the fortune of any man of commerce into whose hands it might fall. I may add that it will not fall into the hands of any man of commerce. But I am wasting time."

He stood up.

"I have studied you closely, Mr. Greville, in an endeavour to discern those qualities which have attracted my daughter."

I started violently and clenched my fists.

"I find them to be typically British," the calm voice continued, "and rather passive than active. You will never be a Nayland Smith, and you lack that odd detachment which might have made our mutual friend. Dr. Petrie, the most prominent physician of the Western world had he not preferred domesticity with an ex-servant of mine."

Inch by inch I was edging nearer to him as he spoke.

"You cannot have failed to note an improvement in my physical condition since last we met, Mr. Greville. This is due to the success of an inquiry which has engaged me for no less a period than twenty-five years."

He moved slowly in the direction of the *mushrabiyeh* window, and, frustrated, I pulled up.

"These orchids," he continued, extending one bony hand to the glass case which occupied the recess, "I discovered nearly thirty years ago in certain forests of Burma. They occur at extremely rare intervals—traditionally only once in a century, but actually with rather greater frequency. From these orchids I have at last obtained, after twenty-five years of study, an essential oil which completes a particular formula—" he suddenly turned and faced me—"the formula *elixir vitae* for which the old philosophers sought in vain."

Transfixed by the glare of those green eyes, I seemed to become rigid: their power was awful. I judged Fu-Manchu to be little short of seventy, but as he stood before me now I appreciated in the light of his explanation, more vividly than I had understood at the moment of his entrance, how strangely he had cheated time.

I was fascinated but appalled—fascinated by the genius of the Chinese doctor; appalled by the fact that he employed that genius, not for good, but for evil.

"You are a very small cog, Mr. Greville," he continued, "in that wheel which is turning against me. If I could use you, I would do so. But you have nothing to offer me. I bear you no ill-will, however, and I have given my word to my daughter—whom you know, I believe, as Fah Lo Suee—that no harm shall come to you at my hands. She is a woman of light loves, but you have pleased her—and I have given my word."

He spoke the last sentence as one who says, "I have set my royal seal to this." And indeed he spoke so with justice. For even Sir Denis, his most implacable enemy, had admitted that the word of Dr. Fu-Manchu was inviolable. Volition left me. Facing this superhuman enemy of all that my traditions stood for, I found my mental attitude to be that of a pupil at the feet of a master!

"My daughter's aid was purchased tonight at the price of this promise," Dr. Fu-Manchu added, his voice displaying no emotion whatever. "I had thought that I could use you to achieve a certain end. But consideration of the character of Sir Lionel Barton has persuaded me that I cannot."

"What do you mean?" I asked, my voice sounding unfamiliar.

"I mean, Mr. Greville, that you love him. But you love a shell, an accomplishment, a genius if you like; but a phantom, a hollow thing, having no real existence. Sir Lionel Barton would sacrifice you tomorrow—tonight—to his own ambitions. Do you doubt this?"

It was a wicked thought, and I clenched my teeth. But God knows I recognized its truth! I knew well enough, and Rima knew too, that the chief would have sacrificed nearly everything and almost everybody to that mania for research, for achievements greater than his contemporaries' which were his gods. That we loved him in spite of this was, perhaps, evidence of our folly or of something fine in Sir Lionel's character, something which outweighed the juggernaut of his egoism.

"For this reason"—Dr. Fu-Manchu's voice rose to a soft, sibilant note—"I have been compelled slightly to modify my original plans." Returning to his chair, he seated himself. I was very near to him now, but:

"Sit down!" he said.

And I sat down, on an Arab stool which stood at one end of the table and which he indicated with a bony extended forefinger. Since that all but incredible interview I have tried to analyse my behaviour; I have tried to blame myself, arguing that there must have been some course other than the passive one which I adopted. Many have thought the same, but to them all I have replied: "You have never met Dr. Fu-Manchu."

He rested his long hands before him upon the glass covering of the table. And, no longer looking in my direction:

"Sir Lionel Barton has served me for the first time in his life," he said, his voice still touching that high, sibilant note. "By discovering and then destroying the tomb of El Mokanna he awakened a fanaticism long dormant which, properly guided, should sweep farther than that once controlled by the Mahdi. And the Mahdi, Mr.

Greville, came nearer to achieving his ends than British historians care to admit. Your Lord Kitchener—whom I knew and esteemed—had no easy task."

He suddenly turned to me, and I lost personality again, swamped in the lake of two green eyes.

"The Mokanna may be greater than the Mahdi," he added. "But his pretensions must survive severe tests. He must satisfy the learned Moslems of the Great Mosque at Damascus, and later pass the ordeal of Mecca. This he can do who possesses the authentic relics…"

Vaguely, I groped for the purpose behind all this…

"I would not trust Sir Lionel Barton to respond even to that demand about to be made upon him, if Dr. Petrie and Sir Denis Nayland Smith were not there. Since they are—I am satisfied."

He struck a little gong suspended on a frame beside his chair. One of the three doors—that almost immediately behind him, opened; and two of those dwarfish and muscular Negroes entered, instantly carrying my mind back to the horrors of Ispahan.

They wore native Egyptian costume, but that they were West Africans was a fact quite unmistakable.

"New allies of mine, Mr. Greville," said the awful Chinaman, "although old in sympathy. They have useful qualities which attract me."

He made a slight signal with his left hand, and in an instant I found myself pinioned. He spoke gutturally in an unfamiliar tongue—no doubt that of the Negroes. And I was led forward until I stood almost at his elbow.

"This document is precious," he explained, "and I feared that you might attempt some violent action. Can you read from where you stand?"

Yes, I could read—and reading, I was astounded…

I saw a note in my own handwriting, addressed to Rima; phrased as I would have phrased it, and directing her to slip away and to join me in a car which would be waiting outside Shepheard's! Particularly, the note impressed upon her that she must not confide in anyone, but must come *alone*...

I swallowed audibly; and then:

"It's a marvellous forgery," I said.

"Forgery!" Dr. Fu-Manchu echoed the word. "My dear Mr. Greville, you wrote it with your own hand during that period of thirty minutes' oblivion to which I have drawn your attention. My new anaesthetic"—he drooped some of the dried seeds through his long fingers—"has properties approaching perfection."

My arms held in a muscular grip:

"She will never be fool enough to come," I exclaimed.

"Not to join *you*?"

"She will run back when she finds I am not there."

"But you will be there."

"What?"

"When one small obstacle has been removed—that which the obstinacy of Sir Lionel Barton has set before me—your behaviour, Mr. Greville, will excite Dr. Petrie's professional interest. I wish it were in my power to give him some small demonstration of the potentialities, which I have not yet fully explored, of another excellent formula."

A sudden dread clutched me, and I found cold perspiration breaking out all over my body.

"What are you going to do with me?" I asked—"and what are you going to do with Rima?"

"For yourself, you have my word..." the green eyes which had been averted turned to me again; "and I have never warred with women. I am going to recover the relics of the Masked Prophet and return them to those to whom they properly belong. You are going to assist me."

I clenched my teeth very tightly.

Dr. Fu-Manchu stood up and moved with his lithe, dignified gait, to one of the glass cases. He opened it. Speaking over his shoulder:

"If you care to swallow a cachet," he said, "this would suffice. The liquid preparation"—he held up a small flask containing a colourless fluid—"is not so rapid. Failing your compliance, however, an injection is indicated."

He stood with his back to me. The grip of the two dwarfish Negroes held me as in iron bands. And I found myself studying the design of the white peacock which was carried from the breast of the doctor's robe, over the shoulders and round to the back. I watched his lean yellow neck, and the scanty, neutral-coloured hair beneath his skullcap; the square, angular shoulders, the gaunt, cat-like poise of the tall figure. He seemed to be awaiting a reply.

"I have no choice," I said in a dry voice.

Dr. Fu-Manchu replaced the flask which he held in one bony hand and selected a small wooden box. He turned, moving back towards the table.

"The subcutaneous is best," he murmured, "being most rapid in its effect. But the average patient prefers the tablets…"

He opened a leather case which lay upon the table and extracted a hypodermic syringe. Unemotionally he dipped the point into a small vessel and wiped it with a piece of lint. Then, charging it from a tiny tube which he took from the box, he stepped towards me.

CHAPTER TWENTY

THE MASTER MIND

I remember saying, as that master physician and devil incarnate thrust back the sleeve of my tweed jacket and unfastened my cuff link:

"Since I have your word, Dr. Fu-Manchu, you are loosing a dangerous witness on the world!"

The needle point pierced my flesh.

"On the contrary," the guttural voice replied without emotion, "one of your own English travellers, Dr. McGovem, has testified to the fact that words and actions under the influence of this drug—which he mentions in its primitive form as *kaapi*—leave no memory behind. I have gone further than the natives who originally discovered it. I can so prescribe as to induce fourteen variations of amnesia, graded from apparently full consciousness to complete anaesthesis. The patient remains under my control in all these phases. Anamnesis, or recovery of the forgotten acts, may be brought about by means of a simple antidote…"

He extracted the needle point.

"This preparation"—he laid the syringe on the glass-topped table and indicated the working bench—"might interest Sir Denis."

I experienced a sudden unfamiliar glow throughout my entire body. A burning thirst was miraculously assuaged. Whereas, a moment before, my skin had been damp with perspiration, now it seemed to be supernormally dry. I was exhilarated. I saw everything with an added clarity of vision...

Some black, indefinable doubt which had been astride me like an Old Man of the Sea dropped away. I wondered what I had been worrying about. I could perceive nothing wrong with the world nor with my own condition and place in it.

Dr. Fu-Manchu took up a dull white flask, removed the stopper, and dipped a slender rod into the contents.

"This, Mr. Greville"—holding up a bar of metal—"is Sheffield steel."

He dropped upon the bar some of the liquid adhering to the rod. "Now—observe..."

In obedience to a slight signal, the Negroes released my arms; one with surgical scissors, cut the fastenings from my ankles...

But I was conscious of no desire to attack the speaker. On the contrary, I recognized with a sudden overwhelming conviction the fact that my own happiness and the happiness of everyone I knew rested in his hands! He was all-powerful, beneficent, a superman to be respected and obeyed.

I watched him, entranced. Holding the steel bar in his bony fingers, he snapped it as though it had been a stick of chocolate!

"Had I been a burglar, Mr. Greville, this small invention would have been of value to me. You see, even I have my toys..."

He turned and walked slowly from the room with that dignified, yet cat-like gait which I knew. As lightning flickers in a summer sky, the idea crossed my mind that once I had feared, had loathed this

Chinese physician. It disappeared, leaving me in a state of mental rapture such as I had never known.

I rejoiced that I was to serve Fu-Manchu. Of the details of my mission I knew nothing, but that it aimed at the ultimate good of us all, I did not doubt. We were in charge of an omnipotent being; it was not for us to question his wisdom.

Led by one of the Slave Coast Negroes whose broad shoulders and slightly bandy legs lent him a distinct resemblance to an ape dressed in human clothing, I found myself passing rapidly along a dimly lighted passage. I was delighted at my discovery that these active little men resembled apes. It seemed to me, in that strange mood, one worthy of reporting to the chief—an addition to scientific knowledge which should not be lost.

I understood, and it was a deep-seated faith, why Dr. Fu-Manchu had willing servants all over the world. Hitherto I had merely existed: this was *life*. I laughed aloud, and snapped my fingers in time to my swift footsteps.

Down a flight of stairs I was led. A silk-shaded lamp on the landing afforded the only light, but I was aware of a surety of foot which would have enabled me to negotiate the most perilous mountain path with all the certainty of a wild goat. An iron-barred and studded door was opened, and I looked out into a square courtyard.

No cloud obscured the sky, now, which seemed to be filled with a million diamonds.

A landaulet stood before the steps. Respecting its driver, I could be sure only of one thing in that semi-darkness: he wore a *tarbush* and was therefore presumably an Egyptian.

The Negro opened the door for me, and I stepped in. One of the headlights was switched on momentarily, and I saw a heavy gate being opened. Then, the driver had swung out into a narrow street. It was not that behind the Mosque of Muayyad…

Through a number of such narrow streets, with never a light anywhere, we went at fair speed. I found myself constantly chuckling at the surprise which I had in store for Rima and the chief. Its exact character was not apparent to me, but I was perfectly satisfied that when the time came all would be well.

A shock of doubt, which passed quickly, came, when leaving the last of these streets we bumped up an ill-made road, turned sharply, and at greatly accelerated speed set off along a straight tree-bordered avenue. Beyond question this was the road from Gizeh to Cairo!

Mental confusion resembling physical pain claimed me in that moment. My drugged brain, of course, was trying to force realities upon me. The spasm passed. There was some good reason for this circuitous route…

And now we were nearing Cairo. The moment of the great revelation was fast approaching.

I took very little heed of passing automobiles or pedestrians, nor did I note by what route the driver made his way through to the Sharia Kamel. But almost exactly at the spot where Fah Lo Suee had entered the yellow car, that is, nearly opposite Shepheard's, we pulled up.

"Stand here, please, in the light," said the driver, springing out and opening the door for me, "where she can see you when I find her."

"I know," I replied eagerly; "I understand perfectly."

The man nodded and ran across to the terrace steps. The number of waiting cars was not so great as at the time of my departure, but it was obvious that revelry still proceeded.

So unusually warm was the night that fully half a dozen tables on the terrace were occupied by dancers who had evidently come there to seek comparative quiet. Dimly I could hear strains of music. One thing I knew urgently I must avoid above all others—I must not be seen by anyone who knew me.

It was vitally important that Rima alone should know what was afoot.

I saw the driver go up the steps. He looked about him swiftly and then went into the hotel. He was carrying my letter. I became the victim of a devouring impatience.

Rima was not well known at Shepheard's and perhaps it might prove difficult to find her, unless she chanced to be in her room. All would be lost if Sir Lionel got to know, or even if Sir Denis or Dr. Petrie should suspect what was afoot.

My impatience grew by leaps and bounds.

A group of four people came out onto the terrace, walking down the strip of carpet towards the steps. I shrank back apprehensively. One was a big, heavily built man, and for a moment I mistook him for the chief, until I saw that he wore evening kit. A car drew up, and the party drove away.

Suspense became all but intolerable. Evidently some difficulty was being experienced in finding Rima, and the moments were precious—each one adding to the chances of detection. I found myself regarding failure of the plot with absolute horror!

Such was the genius of Dr. Fu-Manchu…

The doors revolved again. The Egyptian driver came out, walked to the head of the steps, and signaled to me.

I stepped forward into the roadway where I must be clearly visible from the terrace. Rima came out, dressed as I had seen her last, hatless and flushed with excitement. She held an open letter in her hand—mine. And she was staring eagerly across the street in quest of me.

None of the people seated on the terrace took any notice of these manoeuvres; indeed, as I realised joyfully, there was nothing extraordinary in a man calling to pick up a girl from a dance.

Rima saw me, raced down the steps, and ran across.

I noticed, with a quick pang of sorrow—which, however, instantly gave place to that thrilling exaltation which was the keynote of my mood—that she was, or recently had been, very frightened. She threw her arms around me with a little gasping cry and looked into my eyes.

"Shan, Shan darling! You have terrified us all! Wherever have you been? Whose car is this?"

"It is *his* car, dearest," I replied. "Quick! get in. It's important that nobody should see us."

"*His* car?"

As I half lifted her in onto the cushions she grasped my arm and looked up with startled eyes at me. The chauffeur already was back at the wheel.

"Shan dear, whatever do you mean? Sir Denis got in touch with police headquarters half an hour ago. And Uncle is simply raving. Dr. Petrie has asked everybody he knows in the hotel if you were seen to leave."

I held her close as the car moved off, but she began to tremble violently.

"Shan!—my dear, my dear!" she cried, and pulled my head down, trying to search my eyes in that semidarkness. "For God's sake, where are we going?"

"We are going to *him*," I replied.

"My God! He's mad!"

The words were barely audible—a mere whisper. Thrusting both hands against my breast, Rima tried to push me away—to free herself. Already we had passed the Continental.

"You don't understand, darling…"

"God help me, Shan, I *do*! Make him stop! Make him stop, I tell you!"

An English policeman was on duty at the corner, and as we raced past him, I saw him raise his arm. Rima, wrenching free, leaned from the window, and:

"Help!" she screamed.

But I drew her forcibly back, putting my hand over her mouth before she could utter another word.

"My darling!" I said, holding her very close. "You will spoil everything! You will spoil everything!"

She relaxed and lay very still in my arms…

The way was practically deserted, now, and we passed few lighted patches, but I could see her big, upcast eyes fixed upon me with an intensity of expression which puzzled me. I could see, too, that she had grown very pale. She did not speak again, but continued to watch me in that strange manner.

She seemed to be communicating some silent message and to be changing my mood, cooling that feverish exaltation.

What had she asked? Where we were going? Yes, that was it… And where *were* we going? Mental turmoil like a physical pain claimed me again as I tried to grapple with that question…

CHAPTER TWENTY-ONE

"HE WILL BE CROWNED IN DAMASCUS"

I have related what really happened on that night in Cairo in the proper order of those events—but in their order as I knew it later. As a matter of fact, quite a long interval elapsed, as will presently appear, before I was able to recall anything whatever from the time when I set out in pursuit of Madame Ingomar to that when I acted as a decoy in the abduction of Rima.

A master player had used me as a pawn. The very seat of reason had been shaken by a drug not to be discovered in any pharmacopoeia. These events and those which immediately followed I was to recover later. I must return now to the conclusion of a phase in my life which I still consider the most remarkable any man has known…

"Shan dear, I know you are very sleepy, but it's getting cold, and very late…"

I stirred dreamily, opening my eyes. I was pillowed on a warm ivory shoulder, a bare arm encircled my neck, and the silvery voice which had awakened me was tenderly caressing. I hugged my fragrant pillow and felt no desire to move.

A long jade earring touched me coldly. Soothing fingers stroked my hair, and the silvery voice whispered:

"Truly, Shan, you must wake up! I'm sorry, dear, but you must."

Reluctantly I raised my head, looking into brilliant green eyes regarding me under half lowered lashes. Their glance was a caress as soothing as that of the slender fingers.

Fah Lo Suee, I mused languidly, conscious of nothing but a dreamy contentment, and thinking what perfect lips she had, when, smiling, she bent and whispered in my ear:

"Love dreams are so bitter-sweet because we know we are dreaming."

But yet I was reluctant to move. I could see a long reach of the Nile, touched to magic by the moon. *Dahabeahs* were moored against the left bank, their slender, graceful masts forming harmonious lines against a background of grouped palms and straggling white buildings. Of course! I was in Fah Lo Suee's car; her arms were about me. I turned my head, looking over a silken shoulder to where a bridge spanned the Nile. It must be very late, I mused, later than I had supposed; the Kasr el-Nil bridge was deserted.

Memory began to return—or what I thought then to be memory— from the moment when I determined to follow Fah Lo Suee from the garden of Shepheard's… I had been uncertain of her identity until she had removed the gold mask…

"I think someone has been watching, Shan, and I am positively shivering. I am going to drive you back now."

I sat bolt upright, one hand raised to my head, as Fah Lo Suee bent slightly and started the car. With never another glance aside, she drove on, presently to turn, right, into the maze of Cairo's empty streets.

Furtively I watched the clear profile of the driver. It was beautiful, and strangely like that of the mystery queen, Nefertiti, whose cold loveliness has caused so much controversy. The small chin was delicately but firmly modelled, the straight nose from a strictly classical standpoint was perhaps too large, but very characteristic. I exulted in the knowledge that this brilliant and alluring woman had selected me—Shan Greville—from the rest of mankind.

Cairo's streets were depopulated as the streets of sleeping Thebes; and at the corner of Sharia el-Maghriabi, which I recognized with a start of awakening, Fah Lo Suee pulled up.

I did not know then, but I knew later, the real character of a kind of wave of remorse which swept over me. It was, of course, my true self fighting against this strange abandonment, partly drug-induced and partly hypnotic, which held me voluptuously…

Rima! How could I ever face Rima? What explanation could I offer which she would accept? And Sir Denis! Oddly enough, it was his grim brown face which appeared most vividly before me in that odd moment of clarity: the chief and Dr. Petrie were mere shadows in a mist background…

I had held a link of a deathly conspiracy in my hand. I could have snapped it; my duty was plain. Instead, I had passed the hours in dalliance with Fah Lo Suee! I clutched my head, trying to recall where we had gone. I could not believe that I had spent the night like some callow undergraduate on a petting party; but:

"You must walk from here, Shan," said Fah Lo Suee. "I dare not drive you any farther."

She linked her arms about me and crushed her lips against mine, her long, narrow eyes closed. And in the complete surrender of that parting embrace I experienced a mad triumph which no other conquest could have given me. Rima, Nayland Smith, the chief—all were forgotten!

"Goodnight, dear! And remember me until we meet again…"

I stood on the pavement struggling with the most conflicting emotions, as the car swept around in the empty Sharia el-Maghrabi and disappeared in the direction of Ismailia. The perfume of that parting kiss still lingered on my lips. As a man marooned, condemned, forgotten, I stood there—I cannot say for how long. But at last I turned and stared about me.

Cairo was asleep. What did it matter? I laughed aloud—and began to walk back to Shepheard's.

I met never a soul in the Sharia Kamel, until just before reaching the terrace. At this point, where there are a number of shops lying back from the street, a hideous object, a belated beggar man, suddenly emerged from the shadows.

Ragged, bearded, indescribably filthy, he hobbled upon a crude crutch. As he ranged up beside me, muttering unintelligibly, I thrust my hand into my trouser pocket, found some small coins, and dropped them in his extended palm.

"He will be crowned in Damascus," said the mendicant, and hobbled away…

I despair of making my meaning clear; but those words formed the termination of what I can only term the *second phase* of my dream-like experience. Oddly enough, they remained with me: I mean, when all else was forgotten, I remembered the words, "He will be crowned in Damascus."

For, as they were spoken, and as I listened to the *tap-tap-tap* of the mendicant's crutch receding in the distance, a complete mental blackout came for a third time in that one night!

All that I have related of my experience with Fah Lo Suee, as well as that which went before, I was to recall later, as I shall presently explain; but, so far as I knew at the time, in effect what occurred was this:

I found myself standing, swaying rather dizzily, and with a splitting headache, looking towards the steps of Shepheard's with the words buzzing in my ears: "He will be crowned in Damascus."

The sound of the crutch had died away, and I had no idea who had spoken those words! I know now, of course, that they formed part of an amazing sequence of hypnotic suggestions; that they were my cue for *final forgetfulness*. At the time, I merely knew that, wondering when and where I had heard that sentence spoken, I staggered forward, trying to remember why I was there—and what business had brought me to Cairo.

Then came *true* memory—I mean memory without interference.

I had reached the foot of the steps when the facts returned to me... That narrow alley behind the Mosque of Muayyad! From the moment I had entered it until the present, I was conscious of nothing but darkness!

How had I reached the Sharia Kamel? I asked myself. Could I have walked? And where had I heard those words: "He will be crowned in Damascus"?

Shepheard's was in darkness, and it suddenly occurred to me to look at my wrist watch.

Three A.M.

Heavy-footed, I mounted the steps. The door was barred, but I pressed the bell. In the interval of waiting for the night porter to open, I cudgeled my brains for an explanation of what had happened.

I had followed Fu-Manchu's daughter (of her identity I was all but certain) in a taxicab. I should remember the man. Leaving him at a corner near the Bab ez-Zuwela, I had unwisely run on into a narrow alleyway; and then?

Then... I had found myself a few steps away from the point at which I now stood at three in the morning!

The night porter unbarred the door.

CHAPTER TWENTY-TWO

THE HAND OF FU-MANCHU

The night porter, who knew me well, stared like a man who sees a ghost.

"Good heavens, Mr. Greville!"

I saw that the lobby was in the hands of an army of cleaners, removing traces of the night's festivities. A man standing over by the hall porter's desk turned and then came forward quickly.

"Where is Sir Lionel Barton?" I had begun when:

"Are you Mr. Shan Greville?" the stranger asked.

He was an alert-looking man wearing dinner kit and carrying a soft felt hat. There was something about him which was vaguely familiar.

"I am," I replied.

The hall porter had stepped back as the newcomer arrived upon the scene, but he continued to stare at me, in a half-frightened way.

"My name is Hewlett. I'm in charge of police headquarters in the absence of Superintendent Weymouth. I was never more pleased to see a man in my life than I am to see you, Mr. Greville."

I shook his hand mechanically, noting that he was looking at me in a a queer fashion; and then:

"Where is Sir Denis?" I asked rapidly, "and Miss Barton?"

Hewlett continued to look at me, and I have since learned that I presented a wild-eyed and strange appearance.

"All your friends, Mr. Greville," he replied, "are out with the search party, operating from Bab el-Khalk. I came back here ten minutes ago for news. I'm glad I did."

"Where are they searching?" I asked dazedly.

"All around the neighbourhood of the Bab ez-Zuwela—acting on information supplied by the taxi-man who drove you there."

"Of course," I muttered; "he returned here and reported my absence, I suppose?"

Hewlett nodded. His expression had changed somewhat, had become very grave.

"You look completely whacked," he said. "But, nevertheless, I'm afraid I must ask you to come along and join Sir Denis. My car is just round the corner."

My confusion of mind was such that I thought the search (which presumably had been for me) would now be continued in the hope of discovering the hiding place of Fah Lo Suee.

"Very well," I replied wearily. "I should like a long drink before we start, and then I shall be entirely at your service."

"Very well, Mr. Greville."

I gave the necessary orders to the night porter, whose manner still remained strange, and dropped upon a lounge. Hewlett sat down beside me.

"In order that we don't waste one precious moment," he went on, "suppose you tell me exactly what happened tonight?"

"I'll do my best," I said, "but I fear it's not going to help very much."

"What? How can that be?"

"Because the most important period is a complete blank."

Whereupon I related my movements in the garden that night: how I had seen a woman, whom I was convinced was none other than the daughter of Fu-Manchu, going out by that gate of the garden which I had supposed always to be locked. How I had run through to the front of the hotel just in time to see her entering a car which waited upon the other side of the street.

"Describe this car," said Hewlett eagerly.

I did so to the best of my ability, stressing its conspicuous yellow colour.

"I have no doubt that my driver's account is more accurate than mine," I continued. "He knew the names of all the streets into which we turned, with the exception of the last."

"He led us there," said Hewlett with a certain impatience, "but we drew a complete blank. What I want you to tell me, Mr. Greville, is into which house you went in that street."

I smiled wryly, as the night porter appeared, bearing refreshments on a tray.

"I warned you that my evidence would be a disappointment," I reminded him. "From that point up to the moment when I found myself standing outside Shepheard's, here, my memory is a complete blank."

Hewlett's expression became almost incredulous. "But what happened?" he demanded. "The man tells us that he saw you run into a narrow turning on the left, as the yellow car—your description of which tallies with his—was driven off. He followed you a moment later and found no trace whatever. For heaven's sake, tell me, Mr. Greville, what happened?"

"I had fallen into a trap," I replied wearily. "I was drenched with some kind of anaesthetic. I don't know how it was applied. Perhaps a cloth saturated in it was thrown over my head. Unconsciousness was almost instantaneous. Beyond telling you that this drug, which was used in the murder of Dr. Van Berg in Persia, has a smell resembling that of mimosa, I can tell you nothing more—absolutely nothing!"

"Good heavens!" groaned Hewlett, "this is awful. Our last hope's gone!"

My brain seemed to be spinning. I was conscious of most conflicting ideas; and suddenly:

"Wait a moment!" I cried. "There is one other thing. At some time—I haven't the faintest idea when, but at some time during the night I heard the words, 'He will be crowned in Damascus'!"

"By whom were they spoken?"

I shook my head impatiently.

"I have no recollection that they were spoken by anybody. I merely remembered them, just before I came up the steps a little while ago. When and where I heard them I haven't the slightest idea. But I'm ready, Mr Hewlett. I'm afraid I can't be of the least assistance, but all the same I'm at your service."

He stood up, and I detected again that queer expression upon his face.

"I suppose," I added, "Miss Barton is in her room?"

Hewlett bit his lip and glanced swiftly aside. He was a man suddenly and deeply embarrassed. In a grave voice which he tried to make sympathetic:

"It's hard to have to tell you, Mr. Greville," he replied, "but it's for Miss Barton we are searching."

"*What!*"

I had turned, already heading for the door, when those words fell upon my ears. I grasped the speaker by both shoulders and, staring into his eyes like a madman, I suppose:

"Miss Barton! What do you mean? What do you mean?" I demanded.

"Go steady, Mr. Greville," said Hewlett, and gripped my forearms tightly, reassuringly. "Above all things, keep your nerve."

"But—" my voice shook almost hysterically—"she was with Reggie Humphreys, the Airways pilot... I left her dancing with him!"

"That was a long time ago, Mr. Greville," was the reply, spoken gently. "Half an hour after the time you mention, there was a perfect hue and cry because you had disappeared. The hotel was searched, and finally Sir Denis got through to my office. Then the cabman turned up reporting your disappearance and where it had taken place. He reported to the central police station, first, and then came on here."

"But," I began, "but when—"

"I know what you're going to ask, but I can't answer you, because nobody seems to know. There's only one scrap of evidence. An Egyptian chauffeur brought a note to one of the servants here and requested him to give it to Miss Barton. He telephoned to her room, found her there, and she immediately came down. From that moment the man (I have examined him closely) lost sight of her. But his impression, unconfirmed, is that she ran out onto the terrace. From which moment, Mr. Greville, I regret to say, nothing has been seen or heard of her."

CHAPTER TWENTY-THREE

AMNESIA

My frame of mind when the new day broke, is better left to the imagination. I was convinced that my brain could not long sustain such stress. Maltreated already by an administration of some damnable drug, this further imposition was too great. I sat in the chief's room in the light of early morning. Birds were flying from tree to tree outside in the garden; and I could hear the sound of a broom as a man below swept the sanded path.

Sir Lionel had gone to his room to rest, and Dr. Petrie had been recalled to his house by professional duties. Nayland Smith walked up and down in front of the open window. He looked haggard—a sick man; and his eyes were burning feverishly. Suddenly he stopped, turned, and stared at me very hard.

"Look at me, Greville," he said, "and listen closely."

His words were spoken with such a note of authority that I was startled out of my misery. I met that steady glance, as:

"He will be crowned in Damascus," said Nayland Smith distinctly.

I felt my eyes opening more widely as if under the influence of that compelling stare. Even as I realised that this was a shot at random, and grasped the purpose of the experiment, it succeeded—in a measure.

For one incalculable instant I saw with my mind's eye an incredibly dirty old beggarman, hobbling along on a crutch. My expression must have given the clue, for:

"Quick!" rapped Nayland Smith; "what are you thinking about?"

"I am thinking," I replied in a flat, toneless voice, which during these last agonising hours I had come to recognise as my own, "that those words were spoken by a very old man, having one leg and carrying a crutch."

"Keep your mind on that figure, Greville," Nayland Smith ordered; "don't lose it, but don't get excited. You are sure it was a crutch—not a stick?"

I shook my head sadly. I thought I knew what he was driving at. Dr. Fu-Manchu, on the one occasion (so far as I remembered) that I had ever set eyes on him, had supported his weight upon a heavy stick.

"It was a crutch," I replied. "I can hear the tap of it, now."

"Did it *crunch*? Was the man walking on gravel—or sand?"

"No, a clear tap. It must have been on stone."

"Did he speak in English?"

"Yes. I am almost sure the words were spoken in English."

"Did he say 'Damas' or 'Damascus'?"

"Damascus."

"Anything else?"

"No—it's all gone again."

I dropped my head into my hands as Nayland Smith began to walk up and down before the window.

"Do you know, Greville," he said, speaking slowly and deliberately, "that your memory of those words—for I am perfectly convinced that you really heard them—relieves my mind of a certain anxiety in regard to Rima."

I looked up.

"What ever do you mean?"

"It confirms my first opinion that her disappearance was arranged, and arranged with fiendish ingenuity, by the Fu-Manchu group. This can only mean one thing, Greville. She has been abducted for a definite purpose. Had it been otherwise, in these rather disturbed times, I should have feared that her abduction had been undertaken for personal reasons. You understand what I mean?"

I nodded miserably.

Nayland Smith stepped across and laid his hand upon my shoulder.

"Buck up, old chap. I think I know how you feel. But there's nothing to despair about. Take my word for it: we shall have news of her before noon."

Hoping, doubting, I looked up at the speaker.

"You don't say that just to try to ease my mind?"

"To do so would be false kindness. I say it because I believe it.

"You mean… ?"

"I mean that Rima is to be used as an instrument to bring Sir Lionel to reason."

"By heavens!" I sprang up, hope reborn in my heart. "Of course! Of course! It will be a case of ransom!"

"Rima's life against the relics of the Prophet," Nayland Smith returned dryly. He begun to walk up and down again. "And this time, Greville, the enemy will score. Not even Barton could hesitate."

"Hesitate!" I cried. "Why, if he has to be forced to give them up at the point of a gun—give them up he shall!"

"I don't think such persuasion will be necessary, Greville. Barton is a monument of selfishness where his professional enthusiasms are concerned, but he has a heart, and a big one at that."

I dropped back into my seat again. A flood of relief had swept over me, for I believed Nayland Smith's solution of the mystery to be the correct one. Truth to tell, I was physically tired to the point of exhaustion; yet sleep, I knew, was utterly impossible. And I sat there, watching that apparently tireless man; haggard, but alert, bright-eyed, pacing up and down—up and down—his brain as clear and his nerves as cool as if he were fresh from his morning bath. Even the chief, who had the constitution of a healthy ox, had collapsed some time before and was now sleeping like a log.

I was conscious of an acute pain in the tendon behind my left ankle, and stooping, I began to rub it. As I did so:

"What's the matter?" Nayland Smith asked sharply.

"I don't know," I replied, and lifting my foot I rolled my sock down and examined the painful spot.

"By Jove! something has cut in there. And my other ankle is painful, too, but in front."

"Let me see," he said rapidly. "Rest both feet on this chair here."

Whereupon he stooped and examined my ankles with the utmost care, and finally:

"You have been tied," he said, "and from the appearance of your ankles, brutally tied, with some very thin but presumably very strong material." He glanced up, smiling sourly. "I think, Greville, I have a length of that same mysterious material carefully preserved among my belongings!"

He watched me steadily, and I knew what he hoped for.

"No!" I shook my head sadly. "I have undoubtedly been tied, as you surmise, but I have no recollection whatever of the matter."

"Damn!" he rapped, and stood upright. "I can't help you in this case. There's no cue word, you see, to arouse that drugged memory. By heaven, Greville—" he suddenly shook his clenched fist in the air—"if I and those behind me can defeat the genius of this one old man, we shall have accomplished a feat which Homer might have sung. He is stupendous!"

He ceased suddenly and began to stare at me again.

"H'm!" he added. "I am forgetting how to keep my head in difficult moments. I have allowed elementary routine to go to the winds. Have you by any chance examined the contents of your pockets since you returned?"

"No!" I replied in surprise; "it never occurred to me."

"Be good enough to turn out all your pockets and place their contents upon this table."

Mechanically I obeyed. A wallet, a pipe, a pouch, a cigarette case, I extracted from various pockets and laid down upon the table. A box of matches, a pocketknife, a bunch of keys, some loose money, a handkerchief, a trouser button, two toothpicks, and an automatic lighter which never functioned but which I carried as a habit.

"That's the lot," I announced dully.

"Anything missing?"

"Not that I can remember."

Nayland Smith took up my cigarette case, opened it, and glanced inside.

"How many cigarettes were in your case when you left?"

I paused for a moment, and then:

"None," I replied confidently. "I remember dropping my last in the garden, here, just before I sighted Fah Lo Suee."

He took up my pipe: it was filled but had not been lighted.

"Odd! Isn't it?" he asked. "Remember anything about this?"

I dropped my weary head into my hands again, thinking hard, and at last:

"Yes," I replied. "I remember that I never lighted it."

Nayland Smith sniffed at the tobacco, opened my pouch and sniffed at the contents, also; then:

"Is your small change all right?"

"To the best of my recollection."

"Examine the wallet. You probably know exactly what you had there."

I obeyed; and at the first glance, I made a singular discovery.

A small envelope of thick gray paper containing a bulky enclosure protruded from one of the pockets of the wallet!

"Sir Denis!" I said excitedly, "this wasn't here. This doesn't belong to me!"

"It does now," he replied grimly, and, stooping, he pulled out the envelope from the wallet which I held in my hand.

"'Shan Greville, Private,'" he read aloud. "Do you know the writing?"

I stared at the envelope which he had placed on the table before me. Yes, that handwriting was familiar—hauntingly familiar, but difficult to place. Where had I seen it before?

"Well?"

It was queer, square writing, the horizontal strokes written very thickly, and the ink used was of a peculiar shade of green. I looked up.

"Yes, I have seen it—somewhere."

"Good. As it is addressed to you and marked 'private,' perhaps you had better open it."

I tore open the small square envelope. It contained a single sheet of the same thick, gray paper folded in which was a little piece of muslin, a tiny extemporised bag, tied with green silk. It contained some small, hard object, and I placed it on the table glancing at Nayland Smith, and then began to read the note written in green ink upon the gray paper. This is what I read:

I do not want you to suffer because of what I have been compelled to do. You love Rima. If she does not come back—trust me. I am not jealous. I send you a tablet which must be dissolved in a half litre of matured white wine, and which you must drink as quickly as possible. I trust you also—TO BURN THIS LETTER. To help you I say: He will be crowned in Damascus.

This I read aloud, then dropped the letter on the table and glanced at Nayland Smith. He was watching me fixedly.

"'He will be crowned in Damascus,'" he echoed. "Quick! Do those words, now, take you back any further?"

I shook my head.

"Do you know the writing? Think."

"I am thinking. Yes, I have it! I have only seen it once before in my life."

"Well?"

"It's the writing of Fu-Manchu's daughter—Fah Lo Suee!"

Sir Denis snapped his fingers and began to walk up and down again.

"I knew it!" he snapped. "Greville! Greville! It's the old days over again! But this time we're dealing with a she-devil. And dare we trust her? Dare we trust her?"

I was untying the little packet, and from it I dropped an ordinary-looking tablet, small, round, and white, which might have been aspirin, upon the table.

"Personally," I said, with a ghastly attempt at a smile, "I would as soon think of following the instructions in her letter as of jumping out of that window."

Nayland Smith continued to walk up and down.

"For the moment I express no opinion," he replied. "I may have a better knowledge of the mentality of Eastern women than you have, Greville. And I may have paid a high price for my knowledge. But don't misunderstand me."

I picked up the tablet and was in the act of throwing it out into the garden, when:

"Don't do that!" He sprang forward and grasped my wrist. "You leap to conclusions too hastily. Think! Thought is man's prerogative. You definitely recognise this as the writing of Fu-Manchu's daughter? Granting it even to be a forgery—what then?" He stared at me coldly. "Can you conceive of any object which would be served by bringing your death about in so complicated a manner?"

It was a new point of view—but a startling one.

"Frankly, no." I admitted. "But we have had experience in the past, Sir Denis, of remarkable behaviour on the part of persons subjected to the poisons of Dr. Fu-Manchu."

"You are thinking of an attempt once made unconsciously by Rima to murder *me*?" he suggested. I had thought of this. Don't imagine I haven't taken it into account. But no agent of Dr. Fu-Manchu, with such an object in mind, could be so clumsy as this."

He pointed to the tablet upon the table.

"I suppose you're right," I said dully. "But all the same, you are not suggesting that I should follow out these instructions?"

Nayland Smith shook his head.

"I am merely suggesting," he answered, "that you should keep this remarkable clue. It may have its uses later."

Already he was sniffing at the paper and envelope, scrutinising the writing—holding the sheet up to the light—examining its texture.

"Very remarkable," he "murmured, and, turning, stared at me fixedly.

Personally, I was on the verge of collapse and knew it. My brain was a veritable circus; my body was deadly weary. Desperately though anxiety rode me, I would have given all I had for one hour of sleep, of forgetfulness, of relief from this fever which was burning me up. Nayland Smith came forward and, seating himself beside me, put his arm around my shoulders.

"Listen, Greville," he said. "Petrie is due back in a few minutes, now. He won't have long to spare. But I'm going to make him put you to sleep. You understand?"

I had never in my life stood so near to the borders of hysteria.

"Thanks," I replied; "of course I do. And I'll submit to it; but there's a proviso…"

"What is it?"

"Not for more than an hour. I can't bear the thought of lying like a log while I might be of use to her."

He gripped my tightly for a moment, and then stood up.

"You are off duty," he snapped dryly. "I'm in charge, and you'll take my orders. When Petrie comes, you'll do exactly as Petrie directs. In the meantime, have I your permission to examine and photograph this letter? You will then, quite properly, wish to destroy it, as your correspondent directs."

I agreed. At which very moment the door was thrown open and Petrie came in. One glance he cast at Sir Denis, and then directed that searching professional gaze upon me; the analytical look of a diagnostician. I saw that he was not favourably impressed.

"Smith," he said, with another glance at Sir Denis, "our friend here must sleep."

Nayland Smith nodded.

"It's not going to be easy," Petrie continued; "you're most terribly overwrought, Greville. But if you share my opinion that sleep is necessary, I think I can manage you."

"I do," I replied.

"In that event, the matter is simple enough. We will go up to your room, now."

CHAPTER TWENTY-FOUR

THE MESSENGER

"**W**ake up, old chap, there's good news!"

I opened my eyes to find myself staring up into the face of Nayland Smith. My brain was confused; I could not coordinate circumstances, and:

"What is it?" I asked drowsily; "what's the time?"

"Never mind the time, Greville. Wake up! There's work for you."

Then full consciousness came. But before I had time to clear the borderland:

"He will be crowned in Damascus," said Nayland Smith staring intently into my eyes.

His gaze held me; but in the moment that he spoke I had seen that Dr. Petrie stood behind him, that I was lying in my room. Even as I realised what he was endeavouring to do, I realised also that he had partially succeeded.

For my memory was thrown back as he willed it to be, to the pavement of the Sharia Kamel. Dawn, as I recalled the scene, was not far off. And I was walking in the direction of Shepheard's. Out of the shadows of the recess where the shops lie back, a ragged figure approached me, whining for *bakshish*. I saw him clearly; every line and lineament of his dirty face, his straggly gray beard, his ragged garments, his crutch. I could hear it tapping on the pavement...

I saw myself give him alms and turn away; I heard his words: "He will be crowned in Damascus." I knew again the mystification which had descended upon me in that moment; and felt the depth of wonder about where I had been and of how I came to find myself in that place, at that time.

Starting up in bed:

"It was an old *beggarman*," I cried hoarsely, "in the Sharia Kamel, who spoke those words!"

And while Nayland Smith and Petrie listened eagerly I told them all that I had remembered. And, concluding:

"What's the news?" I demanded, now fully awake, and conscious that my hours of sleep had given me new life.

"It's as I predicted, Greville," Nayland Smith replied. "She is being held to ransom."

I sprang out onto the floor. Queerly enough, that news came like balm to my troubled mind. Rima was in the hands of Dr. Fu-Manchu! A dreadful thought, one would suppose—but better, far, far better than doubt. One thing at least I knew definitely: that if terms had been demanded by the Chinaman, it remained only strictly to carry them out.

The most evil man I had ever known, he was also, according to his own peculiar code, the most honourable. I met Nayland Smith's glance and knew that he understood me.

"I have burned your letter, Greville," he said quietly.

"Thank you," I replied. "And now, tell me: Who brought the news?"

"The messenger is in Barton's room," Dr. Petrie answered,

watching me with keen professional interest. "How do you feel? Fairly fit?"

"Thanks to you, I feel a new man."

Nayland Smith smiled and glanced aside at Petrie.

"You may recall," he said, "that no less an authority than Dr. Fu-Manchu always regarded your great talents as wasted, Petrie!"

CHAPTER TWENTY-FIVE

MR. ADEN'S PROPOSAL

"Leave this to me, Barton," Nayland Smith said sharply. "If you interfere in any way I won't be answerable for the consequences."

Sir Lionel clenched his fists and glared at our visitor; then, crossing, he stood with his back to us, looking out of the window. He was dishevelled, unshaven, wrapped in his dilapidated old dressing gown, and in a mood as dangerous as any I had ever known.

Professional duties had compelled Dr. Petrie to leave, and so there were four of us in the long pleasant room, with its two windows overlooking the garden. I was little better groomed than the chief, for I had been fast asleep five minutes before, thanks to Petrie's ministrations. But Sir Denis, although his gray suit had seen much wear, looked normally spruce.

I stared with murderous disfavour at a man seated in an armchair over by the writing table.

Heavily built, he wore the ordinary morning dress of a business man, and indeed was of a type which one may meet with in any of the capitals of the world. His face, inclined to be fat, was of a dead white colour. Thick iron-gray hair was cut close to his skull, and he had a jet-black moustache. I hated his dark, restless eyes.

"This is Mr.—er—Aden," Nayland Smith continued; "and as the business upon which he has come interests you personally, Greville, I thought you should be present."

Mr. Aden bowed and smiled. My detestation grew by leaps and bounds.

"Mr. Aden is a solicitor practising in Cairo. By the way—" suddenly turning to our visitor—"I believe I met your brother some years ago."

"That is not possible," said the Greek; and his oily voice did nothing to redeem his character in my eyes.

"No?" Sir Denis queried rapidly. "Not a Mr. Samarkan, one-time manager of the New Louvre Hotel in London? But surely?"

Mr. Aden visibly started, but endeavoured to conceal the fact with an artificial cough and a swiftly upraised hand.

"You are mistaken. Sir Denis," he declared suavely, "not possibly in the resemblance, but certainly in the relationship. I never *heard* of Mr. Samarkan."

"Indeed!" snapped Nayland Smith, and turned aside. "Let it pass, then. Briefly, Greville the position is this: Mr.—er—Aden, here in the ordinary way of his professional duties—"

"Damned nonsense!" shouted the chief, stamping one slippered foot upon the floor, but not turning around. "He's one of the gang and an impudent liar!"

"Barton!" Nayland Smith interrupted angrily, "I have requested you to leave this matter to me. If you insist upon interrupting, I shall order you to do so."

"Order be damned!"

"I have the necessary authority."

Some few moments of ominous silence followed, during which Nayland Smith stood staring at the broad back of Sir Lionel. The latter remained silent, and:

"Very well," Sir Denis went on. "As I was explaining, Greville, Mr.—er—the name persistently escapes me…"

"Adrian Aden," our visitor prompted smoothly.

"Yes. Mr. Aden has been instructed by one of his clients to approach Barton professionally."

"The situation is difficult," Mr. Aden explained, extending a fat white hand. "But what could I do? I act for the great interests in Egypt. I cannot afford to offend."

"Ah!" shouted the chief, "truth at last! I admit you're not the man to offend Dr. Fu-Manchu."

"Dr. Fu-Manchu?" Mr. Aden murmured. "That name also is unfamiliar to me."

Nayland Smith glanced in Barton's direction, snapped his fingers irritably, and:

"The name of your client it is unnecessary to discuss at the moment," he said. "But I gather your instructions to be these: A body of religious fanatics has abducted Miss Rima Barton. Your client has learned that she will be returned unharmed if the demands of these religious fanatics are complied with?"

"Ah!" beamed Mr. Aden, "but this is common sense, Sir Denis. How perfectly you understand my position."

"If *you* understood it," growled the chief, "you would know that you might be kicked through the window at any moment."

"This is the lowest and foulest kind of blackmail," I broke in savagely. "If you are what you claim to be, a solicitor, you deserve to be struck off the rolls."

"Really, Greville," said Nayland Smith, "you are unduly hard upon Mr. Aden. I have no doubt that he has undertaken infinitely more delicate cases."

Mr. Aden shot a quick glance at the speaker, but either missed the point or professed to do so.

"You speak hastily, Mr. Greville," he replied. "I act for those who would help you."

"His clients, you see, Greville," Nayland Smith continued dryly, "seem to know all that goes on in the Near East. They deeply deplore the outrage which has been committed—I understood you to say so, Mr. Aden."

"Oh, but completely!"

"And they suggest a means by which Miss Barton's release may be secured. In fact, the exact terms are mentioned, I believe?"

"But certainly!" But certainly!" the Greek assured him. "They claim, these religious people, that Sir Lionel Barton has stolen property which belongs to them."

To my intense surprise the chief did not speak, did not move.

"They say also, my clients inform me, that, if this property is returned, the missing lady will also be returned."

"Quite reasonable," Sir Denis murmured. "Have you details of the property which they claim has been stolen?"

"I have it here."

Mr. Aden opened a portfolio lying beside him on the floor and extracted a sheet of paper.

"A sword or scimitar of Damascus steel inlaid with gold, having a curved, double-edged blade and the hilt encrusted with emeralds, rubies, and pearls…"

He slipped on a pair of horn-rimmed spectacles, the better to read, and continued:

"A mask of thin gold finely engraved; and fifteen thin gold plates sixteen inches long by twelve inches wide, bearing the text of the New Koran of El Mokanna."

He ceased speaking, took off his spectacles, and looked up.

As he did so, Sir Lionel turned. And before Nayland Smith could check him:

"Suppose I admitted that I had these things in my possession," he said, glaring down upon the white-faced Greek, "what would you do?"

"I should believe you."

"Thanks. But how much better off would Rima be?"

"Barton," said Nayland Smith, "absolutely for the last time—will you either shut up or get out!"

The chief plunged his hands into the pockets of his dressing gown, glared down at the Greek again, and glared at Sir Denis. Then, walking across to a settee, he threw himself upon it, stamping his feet on the floor.

"We will assume," Nayland Smith continued, "that the objects you enumerate are actually in Sir Lionel's possession. What next?"

"I understand that those who have her in charge will give up Miss Barton in exchange for these relics."

"Under what conditions?"

I was positively boiling over, and hot words leapt to my tongue; but Sir Denis stared me down.

"You will bring those things which I have specified to an appointed place," Mr. Aden replied, "and there you will meet Miss Rima Barton."

"Sounds like an ambush," Nayland Smith snapped.

The Greek shrugged his fat shoulders.

"I should be glad to communicate any other suggestion you might care to make. But first—my instructions on this point are explicit—"

he turned with unconcealed nervousness to Sir Lionel: "I must see these items, please," he held up the sheet of paper, "and notify my clients that all is correct."

"Don't speak, Barton," said Nayland Smith. "The suitcase is under the settee, just by your feet. Haul it out, unstrap it, unlock it, and comply with Mr. Aden's request."

The chief's face grew positively purple as he angrily sustained the fixed stare of Sir Denis.

"Neither Greville nor I can understand your hesitation," the latter added. "Nothing else counts while Rima is in the hands of—Mr. Aden's client."

At those words Sir Lionel's furious glare was transferred to Mr. Aden, upon whose white forehead I could see beads of perspiration. Then he stooped, hauled forth the heavy suitcase, and unfastened it.

Out from the interior he lifted and laid upon a small table those priceless relics of the Masked Prophet, the possession of which had brought about such disaster and in its consequences driven me to the verge of madness.

CHAPTER TWENTY-SIX

A STRANGE RENDEZVOUS

We sat on the terrace in a corner near the entrance to the American Bar. It was getting on towards lunch time, and this was a fairly busy season in Cairo. I had seen several people I knew, but had deliberately avoided them. Now I faced Sir Lionel across the cane-topped table, and:

"There's one thing I can't stand, Greville," he said, "and that's being ordered about! Latterly, I've had too much of it—altogether too much of it." He brought his fist down on the table with a bang. "But we shall see who scores in the end. As for that slimy swine Aden, he's no more a solicitor than I'm a barber."

"Wrong again, Barton," came quietly, and glancing up I saw that Nayland Smith had just come through the doors behind us.

"I'm apparently always wrong," growled the chief.

"Not always," said Sir Denis, drawing up a chair. "But it happens that the Mr. Samarkan whom I mentioned an hour ago—you remember him, of course?"

"My memory isn't failing me. Smith! He died in England, in those damned caves—near my own place. Of course I remember him!

Thanks to you, the sticky business was hushed up!"

"Ah!" murmured Nayland Smith, and his stern face suddenly broke into a smile.

That smile rather cleared the air.

"You know, Barton," he went on, "although you're the last man to admit it, you've been behaving like a sick cow ever since Rima disappeared. I understand your feelings, but I don't understand why you should vent them on your friends. However (it was Petrie who gave me the clue), the record of M. Samarkan—one-time manager of a hotel no great distance from this, and, later, of the New Louvre in London—is filed at Scotland Yard. Therefore I happen to know that he had a brother. I know also that his brother changed his name by deed poll and took out naturalisation papers."

He paused, staring hard at Sir Lionel.

"I saw the resemblance, of course," the chief admitted, "but…"

"So did I," Nayland Smith went on. "But it was Petrie who placed him. I have just been checking up on the gentleman. He has a legal practice in Cairo, as he stated. But it's of a very shady character."

"So I imagine," I interjected.

"In short, there's no doubt whatever that his main source of revenue is the affairs of the Si-Fan. He's one of their spies, and an agent of Dr. Fu-Manchu, as his brother was before him."

Simply eaten up with impatience and anxiety, I could scarcely contain myself during this conversation. And, as Sir Denis paused again:

"This doesn't help me in the least to understand," I said, "why you let the brute slip!"

"Same here," growled the chief. "Personally, I should have thrown him out of the window."

Sir Denis lay back in his chair, giving an order to a waiter who had just come up; and, as the man went away:

"Your primitive tactics, Barton," he remarked coldly, "would probably result in the total disappearance of Rima. If that's what you are after—take charge."

"But—" the chief began.

"There's no 'but'!" snapped Nayland Smith impatiently. "We have absolutely no clue to Rima's whereabouts. Greville, here, has been doped—his brain on that point is useless. The man you wanted to throw out of the window probably knows no more than we know. But he's a link—a link which *you* would have snapped!"

He paused so suddenly, staring obliquely across the street at a high window, that automatically I turned and looked in the same direction. And as I looked, I saw what he had seen.

From the window of a native house—for Shepheard's borders closely upon the Oriental city—a woman was leaning out, apparently watching us where we sat on the step. She withdrew from the window immediately, but as she did so I turned and met a piercing glance from Sir Denis.

"Was I right, Greville?"

I nodded.

"I *think* so."

Even without his confirmation I should have been certain that Fah Lo Suee had been watching us from across the street!

I jumped up.

"Let's search the house!" I cried. "I know you have powers, Sir Denis!"

My excitement had attracted attention, and I suddenly realised with embarrassment that a number of people were looking at me.

"Sit down, Greville," was the quiet reply. "Your tactics are as bad as Barton's."

I dropped back in my chair and met his steady gaze—not, I believe, with too great an amiability.

"What the devil's all this about?" growled the chief. "I can't see anything."

"Outside your particular province," Nayland Smith returned, "you rarely *do* see anything. Petrie, with his stolid mentality, is worth both of you put together when it comes to grasping facts. If I hadn't been here last night, Barton, all Cairo would know now that Rima was missing."

"Why shouldn't all Cairo know?"

"Because it would result in her being smuggled away. If you can't see that, you can see nothing."

Nevertheless, I could not refrain from glancing up at that high window at which, I was assured, Fu-Manchu's daughter had been stationed—watching us. And Nayland Smith suddenly detected this.

"For heaven's sake!" he snapped irritably, "pretend you didn't see her." He pulled out pouch and pipe and threw them down on the table. "I must smoke!"

As he began to load the cracked old briar:

"What I want to know—" Sir Lionel began.

"What you want to know," Sir Denis took him up, "is why I selected so strange a meeting place. If you'll be good enough not to interrupt me, I'll explain. Ah! here's Petrie."

I saw the doctor, who had just come up the steps, looking about in search of us, and standing up I waved my hand. He nodded, and threading his way among the tables, joined us.

"Sit down, Petrie," said Nayland Smith; "here's a chair. You will notice that, anticipating your arrival, I thoughtfully ordered a drink for you."

"Tell me, Smith," Petrie began eagerly, "have you come to terms?

For God's sake, say that you have."

"I have, old man," Nayland Smith replied, laying his hand upon the speaker's arm, and squeezing it reassuringly. "But neither Barton nor Greville seems to appreciate my purpose."

"Fah Lo Suee—" I began, glancing towards that window across the street.

"Greville!" snapped Sir Denis, "there will be plenty of time later; at the moment I wish to explain the position to Petrie."

His manner was overbearing to the point of rudeness. I felt like a recruit in the hands of a company sergeant major. But I suffered it and took out my cigarette case.

"I have arranged," he continued, "with Mr. Aden—who is, as you suspected, Petrie, a brother of the lamented Samarkan—"

"I knew it!" Petrie cried.

"You were right," Nayland Smith admitted, "and I am indebted to you for the clue. But, as I was saying, I have arranged that the relics of the Masked Prophet—which God knows have caused sufficient misery already—shall be handed over to those who demanded them, and Rima returned to us tonight at twelve o'clock in the King's Chamber of the Great Pyramid."

Probably no more perfect registration of astonishment could have been achieved by any Hollywood star than that now displayed by Dr. Petrie. He stared from face to face in positive bewilderment, and:

"You think what I think, Petrie," the chief shouted; "that it's stark raving lunacy!"

Sir Denis began to light his pipe.

"Frankly, I don't know what to think," Petrie confessed. "It sounds fantastic to a degree. Really, Smith, in the circumstances…"

Sir Denis, having failed to light up with the first match, turned irritably to the speaker.

"Have you ever had occasion to observe, Petrie," he inquired acidly, "that my average behaviour tends to the absurd?"

"Not at all."

"Very well." He struck a second match. "I will quote, from memory, the terms of the agreement to which Barton and I have set our hands, witnessed by Greville, here."

The second match failed also. Laying his pipe upon the table:

"The phrasing doesn't matter," he went on, "but the hub of the thing is this:

"Dr. Fu-Manchu's agent was authorised to propose that at a meeting place to be mutually agreed on, but one not less than half a mile from any inhabited dwelling, no more than two persons should present themselves with the relics of the Prophet. Of the other part it was agreed that no more than two persons should be with Rima. Rima having been accepted on our side, and the relics on the other, all should be permitted to depart unmolested."

"Well?" said the chief, leaning across the table; "it was playing into our hands!"

"Listen," Nayland Smith's even voice continued: "Knowing with whom I was dealing, I made a further condition. It was this: that after the interchange of valuables (pardon me, Greville, but I don't quite know how otherwise to express myself) there should be a ten minutes' truce. Note the time—*ten minutes*."

"I still remain in the dark," I confessed.

"So do I," said Petrie.

"Wait!" the chief growled, watching Nayland Smith intently. "I begin to see—I think I begin to see."

"Good for you, Barton," was the reply. "I naturally anticipated an ambush. If Fu-Manchu can secure what he wants and at the same time dispose of two people in the world who know much of himself and his methods, this would be a master stroke. I looked for loopholes in the agreement. While the doctor would not hesitate to murder any of us, he is incapable of dishonouring his bond. I played for safety."

"Hopeless!" I exclaimed. "It appears to me that tonight we are walking with our eyes open right into a trap."

"Wait!" With a third match the speaker got his pipe going. "By the courtesy of Mr. Aden it was left to me to suggest this meeting place. And I selected the King's Chamber of the Great Pyramid. It was a momentary inspiration, and I may have been wrong. But consider its advantages."

He paused, and now we were all watching him intently.

"Apart from the condition that we shall be represented by no more than two persons at the meeting place, there is no clause in the agreement prohibiting our being *covered* by as many persons as we care to assemble!

"Police headquarters are advised. Tonight at twelve o'clock Gizeh will be deserted; there's no moon. A cordon will be drawn around the Pyramid. Nothing in my agreement with Mr. Aden prohibits this. When Rima is brought there from whatever place they have her in hiding, the fact will be reported to me."

"By heaven!" cried the chief, and banged the table so violently that Petrie's glass was upset; but, as if not noticing the fact. "By heaven! This is sheer genius. Smith. Your pickets will get her on the way?"

"It's possible."

Sir Lionel laughed boisterously and clapped his hands for a waiter.

"They won't even get—" he began—and then paused.

I saw Sir Denis watching him, and I realised that he, as well as I, had noticed that schoolboy furtiveness creeping over Sir Lionel's face. The arrival of the waiter interrupted us temporarily, but then:

"You see, Greville," said Sir Denis, turning to me eagerly, "even if they slip past the pickets, and we have to enter the Pyramid, those inside will be at our mercy. Because the police will close around the entrance behind us, and—"

"And there's only *one* entrance!" I concluded. "I see it all! We can't fail to regain the relics!"

"This would be playing into our hands," cried the chief, "if Fu-Manchu agreed to it. We began cheering too soon! I admit the brilliancy of the scheme, Smith; I can see your point, now. But when a meeting place half a mile from any inhabited dwelling was suggested, Fu-Manchu hadn't thought about the Great Pyramid! He's a devil incarnate and could probably work conjuring tricks almost anywhere else within the terms of the agreement. But the Pyramid! He'll veto the whole thing when the slimy Aden reports."

"I had fully anticipated it," Nayland Smith admitted, "but only ten minutes ago, just before I joined you, the arrangement was confirmed on the telephone."

"By whom?" I asked.

"By the only voice of its kind in the world—by the voice of Dr. Fu-Manchu."

"Good God!" I exclaimed—"then he's *here*, in Cairo!"

CHAPTER TWENTY-SEVEN

THE GREAT PYRAMID

We set out at eleven-thirty in Petrie's car.

I suppose, of all the dark hours I have known, this was as black as any. I rested upon Sir Denis Nayland Smith as upon a rock... If he should fail me—all was lost.

That his singular plan was a good one I had accepted as a fact; failing this acceptance, I should have been in despair. Perhaps it was the aftermath of drugs to the influence of which I had been subjected; but I was in an oddly *muted* frame of mind. Frenzy had given place to a sort of Moslem-like resignation; a fatalistic, deadening recognition of the fact that if Rima, who was really all that mattered to me in the world, should have come to harm, life was ended.

At the village, where few lights were burning when we passed, a British policeman was on duty. Nayland Smith checked Petrie, and leaning out of the car:

"Anything passed?" he asked rapidly.

"Nothing much, sir. Two or three hotel parties. I've noticed a lot of funny-looking Bedouins about here tonight, but I suppose that's nothing to do with the matter."

"Making for Gizeh?"

"No, sir. They all went that way—into the village."

"Go ahead, Petrie."

As we swung around onto that long, straight tree-lined avenue which leads to the Plateau of Gizeh, I counted three cars which passed us, bound towards Cairo. There was nothing ahead, and nobody seemed to be following. As the hotel came into view:

"We have time in hand," said Petrie, "shall I drive right ahead?"

"Pull up," Nayland Smith directed sharply.

An Egyptian, who might have been a dragoman, had sprung from the shadow of the wall bordering the gardens of Mena House, where during the day a line of cars and camels may be seen. Nayland Smith craned out.

"Who is it?" he asked impatiently.

"Enderby, Sir Denis. You met me at headquarters today."

"Right! What have you to report?"

"Not a thing! I have four smart gyppies watching with me, and we have checked everybody. There's absolutely nothing to report."

"Leave the car here, Petrie," said Nayland Smith, "we have time to walk. It may be better."

Petrie backed the car in against the wall, and we all got out. The "Arab" whose name was Enderby, and whom I took to be a secret service agent, conversed aside with Sir Denis for some time. Then, saluting in the native manner, he withdrew and disappeared into the shadows again.

"Queer business," said Nayland Smith, pulling the lobe of his ear. "A gathering of the heads of the many orders of dervishes is taking place in the Village tonight. As a rule they don't mix… And why at Gizeh?"

"Don't like the sound of it myself," the chief growled; but:

"D'you mind grabbing the case, Greville?" said Nayland Smith tersely.

With ill-concealed reluctance, Sir Lionel passed his leather suitcase into my possession; and we started up the sandy slope.

I had abandoned speculation—almost abandoned hope; having, in fact, achieved acceptance of the worst. Diamond stars gleamed in an ebony sky. The Great Pyramid, most wonderful, perhaps, of the structures of man, blotted out a triangle of the heavens. Our feet crunched on the sandy way. We were sombrely silent.

At one point, as we turned the bend at the top of the road, I remember that I wondered, momentarily, what the others were thinking about; and particularly if Sir Denis's confidence remained unimpaired. My own, alas, had long since deserted me…

And dervishes were assembling at Gizeh. That certainly was odd. Why, as Nayland Smith had asked, at Gizeh?

Just as we were topping the slope a man appeared, apparently from nowhere, and so suddenly that I was startled out of my confused reverie. Petrie, who was beside me, grabbed my arm; and then:

"You're early, Sir Denis," said a voice.

I knew it at once: it was that of Hewlett, Acting Superintendent of Police.

"Not so loud," snapped Nayland Smith. "What's the news?"

"None, I regret to say, sir."

"You mean no one has entered The Pyramid?"

"Not a soul—if I can rely on my men!"

My heart sank—went down to zero. The scheme, the fantastic scheme, had failed. He was dealing with a super-mind, and Fu-Manchu was laughing at him. It was unthinkable that the Chinese doctor should have exposed any of his agents to a danger so obvious.

"How many men have you here?"

"Sixty. The place is entirely surrounded."

"What does this mean, Smith?" Petrie asked urgently. He turned to Hewlett, whom he evidently knew well, and: "How long have you been covering the Pyramid?" he added.

"Since the guides knocked off," was the reply. "If anybody's smuggled through in the interval, he must have been invisible."

"It's a booby trap," said the chief shortly. "You've ruled me out, Smith, and perhaps it doesn't matter. But, by heaven—"

"Disappear, Hewlett," Nayland Smith directed tersely; and as Hewlett obediently merged into the shadows: "I don't know what this means, Petrie," he went on, "any more than you do. From the evidence, and I count it pretty sound, nobody has gone into the place tonight since sunset. But three of us have signed an agreement with an enemy I would strangle with my own hands if I had the opportunity, but with an enemy who has one redeeming virtue: he always keeps his word. We must keep ours."

"He's spotted the cordon," Sir Lionel growled, "and he's called his men off."

"We have stuck strictly to the terms of the understanding. He must have anticipated that we should do our utmost to arrest his agents immediately the ten-minute truce ended."

"Then he finds he can't cope with the situation. He's backed out—"

"My God!" I groaned, "where's Rima? She can't possibly be here!"

"Wait and see!" snapped Nayland Smith.

His words were spoken so savagely that I recognized the tension under which he was labouring and regretted my emotional outburst.

"I'm sorry, Sir Denis," I said. "It's vital to me, and—"

"It's equally vital to *me*! I'm not risking Rima's life for any pet theory, Greville. I'm doing my damnest to make sure she's returned safely."

His words made me rather ashamed of myself.

"I know," I replied. "I'm terribly worked up."

"Barton," came a tense order, "get in touch with Hewlett, and stand by, here. You too, Petrie."

"I hate you for this," said the chief violently. "Hate on! You are too damned impetuous for the job before us…"

Together, he and I set out.

I glanced back once, and Sir Lionel and Dr. Petrie presented a spectacle which might have been funny had my sense of humour been properly alert. Dimly visible, for the night was velvety dark, they stood looking after us like schoolboys left outside a circus…

And presently I found myself alone with Nayland Smith at the foot of that vast, mysterious building which has defied the researches of Egyptologists and exercised the imaginations of millions who have never seen it. Personally, I had lived down that sense of mystery which claims any man of average intelligence when first he confronts this architectural miracle.

Sir Lionel had carried out an inquiry here in 1930, just prior to our excavations on the site of Nineveh. I knew the Great Pyramid inside out, remembering the job more vividly because Rima had been absent in England during the time, the chief having given her leave of absence which he refused to grant to me.

We had reached the steps which led to the opening; and:

"You're in charge now," said Nayland Smith. "Lead, and I'll follow. Give me the case."

CHAPTER TWENTY-EIGHT

INSIDE THE GREAT PYRAMID

In that little bay in the masonry which communicates with the entrance we stood and, turning, looked back.

Sixty men surrounded us; but not one of them was in sight. At some point there in the darkness, Sir Lionel and Dr. Petrie were probably watching. But in the absence of moonlight we must have been very shadowy figures, if visible at all. I looked down upon the mounds and hollows of the desert, and I could discern away to the left those streets of tombs whose excavation had added so little to our knowledge. There were two or three lighted windows in Mena House...

"Go ahead, Greville," said Nayland Smith. "From this point onward I am absolutely in your hands."

I turned, switching on the flash lamp which I carried, and began to walk down that narrow passage, blocked at its lower end, which leads to the only known entrance to the interior chambers. Familiar enough it was, because of the weeks I had spent there taking complicated measurements under Sir Lionel's direction— measurements which had led to no definite results.

We came to the end where the old and new passages meet. Our footsteps in the silence of that densely enclosed place aroused most eerie echoes; and in the flattened V where the ascent begins:

"Stand still, Greville," Sir Denis directed.

I obeyed. My light already was shining up the slope ahead. In silence we stood, for fully half a minute.

"What," I asked, are you listening for?"

"For anything," he replied in a low voice. "If I had not spoken to Dr. Fu-Manchu in person on the telephone today, Greville, I should be prepared to swear that you and I were alone in this place tonight."

"I have no reason to suppose otherwise," I replied. "The pickets have seen no one enter. What have we to hope for?"

"Nothing is impossible—particularly to Dr. Fu-Manchu. He accepted my terms and the meeting place. In short he declared himself. And, though contrary to normal evidence, I shall be greatly surprised if when we reach the King's Chamber, we do not find his representatives there with Rima."

I could not trust myself to reply, but led on, up the long, sloping, narrow way which communicates with the Great Hall, that inexplicable, mighty corridor leading to the cramped portals of the so-called King's Chamber. At the mouth of that opening beyond which the Queen's Chamber lies, Nayland Smith, following, grasped my arm and brought me to a halt.

"Wait," he said; "listen again."

I stood still. Some bats, disturbed by our lights, circled above us. My impatience was indescribable. I imagined Rima, a captive, being dragged along these gloomy corridors. I could not conceive it; I did not believe she was in the place.

But until I had reached that dead end which is the King's Chamber, my doubts could not be resolved; and this delay imposed by Nayland Smith was all but intolerable, the more so since I could not fathom its purpose.

I have never known a silence so complete as that which reigns inside the Great Pyramid. No cavern of nature has ever known it, for subterraneously there is always the trickle of water, some evidence of nature at work. Here, in this vast monument, no such sounds intrude.

And so, as we stood there listening, save for the whirl of bat wings, we stood in a silence so complete that I could hear myself breathing. When Nayland Smith spoke, although he spoke in a whisper, his voice broke that utter stillness like the blow of a hammer.

"Listen! Listen, Greville! Do you hear it?"

CHAPTER TWENTY-NINE

WE ENTER THE KING'S CHAMBER

Very dimly it came to my ears. From whence it proceeded I could not even imagine... In those surroundings, at that hour, it possessed a quality of weirdness which was chilling:

The dim note of a gong!

Its effect was indescribably uncanny; its purpose incomprehensible. In the harsh light of the flash lamps I saw Nayland Smith's features set grimly.

"For heaven's sake, what's that?" I whispered.

"A signal," he replied in a low voice, "to advise *someone* we are here. God knows how any of them got in, but you see, Greville, I was right. We are not alone!"

"There's something horrible about it," I said uneasily.

I glanced upward into the darkness we must explore.

"There is," Nayland Smith agreed quietly. "But it has a good as well as a bad aspect. The good that it seems to imply ignorance of our cordon; the bad, that it proves certain persons to have entered the Pyramid tonight unseen by the pickets."

Silence, that dead silence which is characteristic of the place, had fallen about us again like a cloak. Honestly, I believe it was only the thought of Rima which sustained me. It was at this moment that the foolhardiness of our project presented itself starkly to my mind.

"Aren't you walking into a trap, Sir Denis?" I said. "*I* don't count from the point of view of Dr. Fu-Manchu, but—?"

"But," he took me up, "as an expert, can you tell me how Dr. Fu-Manchu's agents, having disposed of me here—which admittedly might be convenient—could hope to profit? At the moment, six men are watching the entrance. A further sixty are available if anything in the nature of an Arab raid should be attempted."

"I agree. But the *gong*! If they got in unseen, surely they can get out?"

He stared at me; his eyes were steely in that cold light.

"I had hoped you might have overlooked this fact," he said, "because it reduces us to our only real safeguard: the word of Fu-Manchu! In all the years that I have fought for his destruction, Greville, I have never known him to break it. We shall go unmolested for ten minutes after Rima is restored to us! Then—unleash the dogs of war! Carry on."

"Ten minutes after Rima is returned to us!"... Did the light of his faith in the word of Fu-Manchu truly burn so bright?

I led on and upward—and presently we found ourselves in that awe-inspiring black corridor which communicates with the short passage leading to the room called the King's Chamber, but which (as Sir Lionel has always maintained) in its very form destroys at a blow the accepted theory, buttressed by famous names, that this majestic pile was raised as the tomb of Khufu.

Automatically, I directed the light of my lamp farther upward. The vast, mysterious causeway was empty, as far as the feeble rays could penetrate.

We mounted to the ramp on the left side and climbed onward. Ages of silence mantled us, and, strangely, I felt no desire to give voice to the many queries which danced in my brain. An image led me on; I seemed to hear my voice speaking a name:

Rima!

I climbed more swiftly.

This might be a trap; but according to available evidence, no one had entered the Pyramid that night; but plainly I had heard the gong... and dervishes were gathering at Gizeh...

We reached the horizontal passage to the King's Chamber; and instinctively both of us paused. I stared back down the slope as far as the light of my lamp would reach. Nothing moved.

"Will you be good enough to take over the duties of pack mule, Greville," said Nayland Smith crisply.

He handed me the case. The entrance to the place yawned in front of us. Sir Denis took a repeater from his pocket, examined it briefly, and slipped it back. Then, shining a light into the low opening:

"Follow closely," he directed.

For one instant he hesitated—any man living would have hesitated—then, ducking his head and throwing the light forward along the stone passage, he started forward. I followed; my disengaged hand gripped an automatic.

I saw the end of the passage as Nayland Smith reached it; I had a glimpse of the floor of that strange apartment which many thousands have visited but no man has ever properly comprehended; and then, following him in, I stood upright in turn. As I did so, I drew a sharp breath—indeed, only just succeeded in stifling a cry...

A bright light suddenly sprang up! So lighted, the place presented an unfamiliar aspect. No bats were visible. The chamber looked more lofty, but for that very reason more mysterious. The lamp which shed this brilliant illumination—a queer, globular lamp—was so powerful that I could not imagine from what source its energy was derived.

It stood upon a small table, set close beside the famous coffer; and behind it, so that the light of this lamp shone down fully upon him, a man—apparently the sole occupant of the King's Chamber—was seated in a rush chair of a type common in Egypt. He wore a little black cap surmounted with a coral ball, and a plain yellow robe. His eyes were fixed steadily upon Sir Denis.

It was Dr. Fu-Manchu!

CHAPTER THIRTY

DR. FU-MANCHU KEEPS HIS WORD

Nayland Smith stood quite still, the ray of his torch shining down on the floor at his feet. Those incredible green eyes beyond the globular lamp watched him unblinkingly.

As I supposed at the time—although, of course, I was wrong—I had seen Dr. Fu-Manchu once only in my life. And as I saw him now, an astounding change presented itself. That wonderful face, on which there rested an immutable dignity, seemed to be the face of a younger man. And the power which radiated from the person or this formidable being was of a character which I could never hope to portray. He seemed to exude force. The nervous energy of Sir Denis was of a kind which could almost literally be felt, but that which emanated from Dr. Fu-Manchu vibrated with an intensity which was uncanny.

How long a time elapsed in the utter silence of that strange meeting place before a word was spoken, I cannot say, but the dragging seconds seemed interminable.

The atmosphere was hot—stiflingly hot. My head seemed to be swimming. I glanced swiftly at Nayland Smith. His teeth were clenched tightly, and I knew that his right hand, which he held in his pocket, rested upon a Colt repeater. I could not guess what or whom he had expected to meet, but every lineament of his stern face told me that he had never anticipated meeting the Chinese doctor.

It was the latter who broke that unendurable silence.

"We meet again. Sir Denis—a meeting which I observe you had not anticipated. Yet you might have done so."

Fu-Manchu spoke coldly, unemotionally, and except for certain gutturals and at other times an odd sibilant, his English was perfect, deliberate to the point of the pedantic, but carrying no trace of accent. I remembered that, according to Petrie, the Chinese doctor spoke with facility in any of the civilised languages, as well as many savage tongues and dialects.

I had eagerly read all that my friend had written about him, during the years that he and Sir Denis had warred almost constantly with their great adversary, my reading embracing hundreds of Petrie's notes which had never been published. Memories returned to me now, as I found myself face to face with this great but evil man. I wish I possessed the doctor's facility of style. His pen, I think, could have done greater justice to a scene in attempting which I find my own more than halting.

"You saw me in Ispahan," the calm voice continued. Its effect in that enclosed chamber was indescribable. "Prior to which, you had recognized my methods. You had tricked those acting for me, and I arrived too late to rectify their errors of judgment, for which, however, two paid with their lives."

Nayland Smith continued to watch the speaker, but uttered never a word.

"Perhaps my personal appearance in that street on the night of my second attempt to secure the relics was an indiscretion. But I had lost faith in my agents. You foiled me, Sir Denis. You saw me; I did not see you. You seem to have overlooked the fact that I walked without the aid of a stick."

Nayland Smith visibly stared—but did not speak.

"Sir Lionel Barton's box-trick," Fu-Manchu went on—his peculiar utterance of the chief's name producing a horrifying effect upon my mind—"necessitated this hasty journey to Egypt, at great personal inconvenience. I arrived an hour after you. Therefore, Sir Denis, since you know with whom you are dealing, and since with my present inadequate resources I have none about me upon whose service I can rely, is there anything singular in my meeting you personally?"

"No." Sir Denis spoke at last, never taking his gaze from that lined, yellow face. "It is characteristic of your gigantic impudence."

No expression of any kind could be read upon Dr. Fu-Manchu's face, except that his eyes, long, narrow, and of a brilliant green colour which I can only term unnatural, seemed momentarily to become slightly filmed.

"You have played the only card which we couldn't defeat," Sir Denis went on; "and here—" he pointed to the case which I had set upon the floor—"is your price. But, before we proceed further…"

I knew what he was about to say, and I said it for him, shouted it, angrily:

"Where is Rima?"

For one instant the long green eyes flickered in my direction. I felt the force of that enormous intellect, and:

"She is here," said Dr. Fu-Manchu softly. "I said she would be here."

The last words were spoken as if nothing could be more conclusive. I was on the point of challenging them, but, somehow, there was that in their utterance which seemed unchallengeable. The crowning mystery of the thing presented itself nakedly before me.

How had Fu-Manchu gained access to this place, the entrance to which had been watched from sunset? How had Rima been smuggled in?

"Your motives," said Nayland Smith, speaking in the manner of one who holds himself tightly on the curb, "are not clear to me. This movement among certain Moslem sects—which, I take it, you hope to direct—must break down when the facts are published."

"To which facts do you more particularly refer?" the Chinese doctor inquired sibilantly.

"The fact that an extemporised bomb was exploded in the tomb of El Mokanna by Sir Lionel Barton, and that the light seen in the sky on that occasion was caused in this manner; the fact that the relics were brought by him to Egypt and returned to the conspirators under coercion. What becomes of the myth of a prophet reborn when this plain statement is made public?"

"It will not affect the situation in any way; it will be looked upon as ingenious propaganda of a kind often employed in the past. And since neither Sir Lionel Barton nor anyone else will be in a position to *prove* that the relics were ever in his possession, it will not be accepted."

"And your own association with the movement?"

"Is welcome, since the ideals of the Si-Fan are in harmony with the aims of those Moslem sects you have mentioned, Sir Denis. Subterfuge between us is useless. This time I fight in the open. One thing, and one thing only, can defeat the New Mokanna... his failure to produce those evidences of his mission which, I presume, you bring to me tonight..."

His strength and the cool vigour of his utterance had now, as I could see, arrested Sir Denis's attention as they had arrested mine; and:

"I congratulate you," he said dryly. "Your constitution would seem to be unimpaired by your great responsibilities."

Dr. Fu-Manchu slightly inclined his head.

"I am, I thank you, restored again to normal health. And I note with satisfaction that you, also, are your old vigorous self. You have drawn a cordon of Egyptian police around me—as you are entitled to do under the terms of our covenant. You hope to trap me, and have acted as I, in your place, should have acted. But I know that for ten minutes after our interview is concluded I am safe from molestation. I am not blind to the conditions. My safety lies in my knowledge that you will strictly adhere to them."

He clapped his hands sharply.

What I expected to happen, I don't know. But Nayland Smith and I both glanced instinctively back to the low opening. What actually happened transcended anything I could have imagined.

A low shuddering cry brought me swiftly about again.

"*Shan!*"

Rima, deathly pale in the strange light of that globular lamp, was standing upright behind the granite coffer!

My heart leapt, and then seemed to stop, as she fixed her wide-open eyes upon me appealingly. And Sir Denis, that man of steel nerve, exhibited such amazement as I had never known him to show in all the years of our friendship.

"Rima!" he cried. "Good God! Have you been lying there, hiding?"

"Yes!" she turned to him. I saw that her hands were clenched. "I promised." She glanced down at the motionless, high-shouldered figure seated before her. "It was *my* part of the bargain."

Describing a wide circle around the sinister Chinaman, she ran to me, and I had her in my arms. I could feel her heart beating wildly. I held her close, stroking her hair: she was overwrought, on the verge of collapse. She was whispering rapidly—incoherently—other fears for my safety, other happiness to be with me again, when those low even tones came:

"I have performed what I promised. Sir Denis. It is now your turn…"

CHAPTER THIRTY-ONE

THE TRAP IS LAID

My last recollection as I stopped and went out must always remain vivid in my mind.

Those golden records of the Masked Prophet, one of the unique finds in the history of archaeology, lay glittering upon the narrow table under the light of that strange globular lamp. Dr. Fu-Manchu, his long pointed chin resting upon his crossed hands, his elbows upon the table, watched us unfalteringly.

One grave anxiety was set at rest. In reply to a pointed question of Nayland Smith's, he had assured us that Rima had not been subjected to "damnable drugs or Lama tricks" (Sir Denis's own words). And, fearing and loathing Dr. Fu-Manchu as I did, yet, incredible though it may seem, I never thought of doubting his word. A hundred and one questions I was dying to ask Rima, but first and foremost I wanted to find the sky above my head again.

The Great Corridor was empty from end to end. And, I leading and Nayland Smith bringing up the rear, we stumbled down to the point where it communicates with the narrower passage. Here I turned, and looked back as far as the light of my lamp could reach.

Nothing was visible. I could only think that Dr. Fu-Manchu remained alone in the King's Chamber…

I glanced at Rima. She was clenching her teeth bravely, and even summoned up a pallid smile. But I could see that she was close to the edge of her resources.

"Hurry!" snapped Nayland Smith. "Remember—ten minutes!"

But even when, passing the lowest point, we began to mount towards open air, somehow, I could not credit the idea that Dr. Fu-Manchu had carried out this business unaided. I paused again.

"It was here that we heard," I began—

As though my words had been a cue, from somewhere utterly impossible in those circumstances to define, came the dim note of a gong!

Rima clutched me convulsively. In that age-old corridor, in the heart of the strangest building erected by the hands of man, it was as uncanny a sound as imagination could have conjured up.

"Don't be afraid, Rima," came Nayland Smith's voice. "It's only a signal that we are on the way up!"

"Oh!" she gasped, "but I can't bear much more. Please get me out, Shan!—get me out…"

I led on as swiftly as possible. Had Rima collapsed, it would have been no easy task to carry her along that cramped passage. But the purpose of those signals, apart from the mystery of the hiding place of whoever gave them, was a problem we were destined never satisfactorily to solve.

As we had arranged, five men with Dr. Petrie were immediately outside the entrance.

"Thank God, Petrie," said Nayland Smith hoarsely. "We've got her! Here she is! Take care of her, old man."

Whereupon, at sight of the Doctor, Rima's wonderful fortitude deserted her. She threw herself into his arms with a muffled scream and began to sob hysterically.

"Rima, dear," I exclaimed, "Rima!"

Petrie, supporting her with one arm, waved to me to go on, at the same time nodding reassuringly.

"Come on, Greville," said Nayland Smith. "She's in safe hands, and better without you at the moment."

We had arranged—I confess I had never dared to hope that our arrangements would be carried out—to take her to Mena House. Down on the sands at the foot of the slope Sir Lionel and Hewlett were stationed. And, as I jumped from the last step:

"Have you got her, Greville? Is she safe?" the chief asked hoarsely.

"Yes, she's with Petrie. She's broken down, poor little lady—and I don't wonder," Nayland Smith replied. "But she's come to no harm, Barton. Keep out of the way—leave her to Petrie."

"Where has she been? How did it happen?"

"It's impossible to ask until the nerve storm has worn itself out. Anything to report, Hewlett?"

"I'm staggered. Sir Denis! But thank God you have Miss Barton! There's only one thing. A few minutes after you went in, as we were closing up on the Pyramid, we heard a most awful wailing sound…"

"A *bull-roarer*, Smith!" the chief shouted. "But God knows where the nigger was hidden: we never had a glimpse of him."

Nayland Smith glanced aside at me.

"Possibly the opposite number of the gong signal," he whispered. "But what came first?—and how did one signaler hear the other?"

I saw Hewlett glancing at the dial of an illuminated wrist watch.

"Three minutes to go. Sir Denis," he announced. "How many are inside?"

"One only," Nayland Smith replied, in a curiously dull voice.

"Only one!" the chief cried incredulously.

"One, but the biggest *one* of all."

"What! You don't mean…"

"Exactly what I do mean. Barton. We left Dr. Fu-Manchu alone in the King's Chamber."

"Good God! Then for all his cunning—"

"He's trapped!" Hewlett concluded. "How he got in, and how he got Miss Barton in, is entirely beyond me. But that he can never get out, is certain."

He spoke truly; for other than the Grand Hall or Great Corridor along which we had recently come, there is no entrance to the King's Chamber—and the two exits from the Pyramid were guarded.

CHAPTER THIRTY-TWO

I SEE EL MOKANNA

D r. Petrie gave Rima a sleeping draught and saw her off to bed in the big hotel on the edge of the desert. In spite of all our precautions, news had leaked out that something was afoot.

Whereas, at the time of our arrival, the place had been quiet, with few lights showing, now an air of excitement prevailed. People who seemed to have hastily dressed were standing about in groups. We had smuggled Rima in by a side entrance. But in the lobby and on the terrace outside I met many curious glances.

And there was another, altogether more disturbing circumstance. In the roadway, and by the gate usually haunted by dragomans during the day, a group of some forty natives had assembled, of a type not usually met with there. They were men from the desert villages for the most part, and although all were oddly silent, I overheard several furtive asides which I construed as definitely hostile.

I recognized the black turbans of the *Rifaiyeh* and the red of the *Ahmadiyeh*. *Senussi* I saw among them too—and the white headdresses of many *Kadiriyeh*…

These were the dervishes who had gathered at Gizeh Village!

Wildly impatient as I was to join the party at the Pyramid, it was impossible for me to leave for some time. Petrie was with Rima, whom he had placed under the care of a resident nurse. She kept waking up and calling piteously for me. Twice I had been brought to her room to pacify her. Her frame of mind was most mysterious. She seemed to be obsessed with the idea that some harm had befallen me.

The second time, after she had gone to sleep contentedly, clasping my hand, I had managed to slip away without awakening her. And now, as I roamed restlessly about the lobby, Dr. Petrie suddenly appeared.

"She's right enough now, Greville," he reported, "and Mrs. Adams is with her. A most reliable woman."

"Dare we start?" I asked.

"Certainly! my car's outside. But we shall be too late for—"

I knew what he would have said; equally, I knew why he hesitated. The physical facts of the situation were beyond dispute; but the more I had considered the matter, the more clearly I had appreciated the fact that a man of Dr. Fu-Manchu's intellect would never voluntarily have walked into such a mouse trap.

No one knew how he had entered the Pyramid nor how Rima had been taken there. Furthermore, he had introduced that singular lamp into the place, the table and the Arab chair. Now, in addition, he had the relics of the Prophet.

As we walked down the sanded drive to the road, observed with great curiosity by several residents who obviously suspected that our business was a strange one, we came face to face with that ominous gathering of Arabs near the gate. I saw at a glance that reinforcements had joined them. The black turbans of the *Rifaiyeh* predominated now.

"This looks unwholesome, Greville," said Petrie in an undertone. "What are all these fellows doing here at this time of night?"

"They are the dervishes! Evidently they assembled at Gizeh Village and then marched here. I have been prowling about for some time, waiting for reports about Rima, and I watched them gathering."

We were among them now. Although they made way for us, I liked their attitude less and less.

"Tribesmen of some sort," said Petrie close to my ear. "Except in ones and twos, these birds are rarely seen."

As we reached his car, which stood a little to the left of the entrance, I looked back uneasily. The dervishes seemed to be watching us.

"What the devil's afoot?" Petrie asked, grasping the wheel. "I should think they meant mischief, if they were armed."

He started slowly up the slope; and as we passed that silent company I looked into many flashing eyes close beside the window. But no one attempted to obstruct us.

"A very queer business," Petrie muttered. "Smith should know at once. It can hardly be a coincidence."

We met several stragglers of the same type on that short winding road which leads up to the plateau, presumably going to join those already assembled outside Mena House. But the doctor's mind, as well as my own, now focused upon the major problem; and as we turned the final bend and the great black mass of the Pyramid loomed above us:

"You know, Greville," said Petrie, "a load has been lifted from my mind. Honestly, I don't think the possession of the relics of Mokanna will do much to help the movement. Rima's safety would be cheap at the price of every relic in the Cairo Museum."

"I feel much the same about it," I admitted. "Although, of course, those things are unique."

"Unique be damned!" said Petrie. "Hello! who's this?"

It was a police officer standing with upraised arm.

"You can't pass this way, sir," he shouted, and came forward as Petrie pulled up.

We both got out, but the night, as I have said, was very dark.

And as we did so, the policeman directed the ray of the lamp upon us.

"Oh!" he added. "It's Dr. Greville and Mr. Petrie, isn't it?"

Petrie laughed.

"The other way about, officer," he replied.

"You'll have to walk from here. Those are my orders, sir."

"It makes no difference. We couldn't have driven much further, anyway. Is there any news?"

"Not that I've heard, sir. I understand that they're still searching inside—"

"What!" I exclaimed. "There's nothing to search—only two rooms. That is, unless they're searching Davidson's shaft."

"Come on, Greville," said Petrie curtly. "Let's go and see for ourselves. You may be of use here. You ought to know every nook and cranny of the place."

"I do, but so does the chief—and he's on the spot."

We were challenged again as we reached the foot of the Pyramid, by a sergeant whom I took to be in charge of the cordon.

"O.K., sir," he said when he saw me.

"What's happened? Who's inside?"

"The acting superintendent, sir, Sir Denis Nayland Smith, and Sir Lionel Barton. Three men with them."

"And no one has come out?"

"Not a soul, sir."

Petrie turned to me in the darkness. "Shall we go up?" he said.

We found four men on duty when we had climbed up to the entrance. They passed us immediately, and I was about to lead the way in when a muffled voice reached me from the interior.

"I tell you it's a trick, Smith! He's slipped out in some way…"

The chief.

I stepped back again and felt, for I could not see their faces, an atmosphere of tension among the four police officers on duty.

"There's treachery. Somebody's been bought over."

That loud, irascible voice was drawing nearer; and:

"It's all but incredible, Greville," said Petrie, in a low voice; "but evidently Fu-Manchu has managed to get out as mysteriously as he got in!"

"I hope there's no question about us, sir," came sharply; and one of the four men, whom on close inspection I recognized for a sergeant, stepped forward. "I'm responsible to the acting superintendent, so I don't care what the other gentleman says. But you can take my word for it that nobody has come out of this place tonight, since you came out with the lady and Sir Denis."

"We don't doubt it, Sergeant," Petrie replied. "Sir Denis won't doubt it, either. You mustn't pay too much attention to Sir Lionel Barton. He's naturally very disturbed."

"That may be, sir—" the man began; when:

"Who's on duty, here?" bellowed the chief, suddenly appearing out of the opening.

"One moment, Sir Lionel," a quiet voice interrupted; and I saw Hewlett grasp his arm. "*I* am responsible for the men on duty. Sergeant!"

"Sir?"

"Have you anything to report?"

"Nothing, sir."

"It's some damned trick!" growled the chief.

Nayland Smith came out last, saw me in the darkness, and:

"Is everything all right, Greville?" he asked eagerly.

"We managed to get her to sleep," Petrie replied. "Everything is all right. But this business passes my comprehension, Smith."

"It does!" the latter rapped. "But, needless to say, I anticipated it."

"It's a trick!" the chief shouted. The man's a conjurer: always was. How did he get Rima in? Damn it! Can't we ask her?"

"You'll ask her nothing tonight, Barton," Petrie returned quietly. "And you'll ask her nothing in the morning until you have my permission."

"Thanks!" was the reply. "I'll remember you in my will." He was, in short, in a towering rage, and: "Where's Greville?" he finished up.

"Here I am."

"D'you think it feasible that Fu-Manchu could have slipped up into one of the construction chambers?"

"No, I don't."

"Neither do I. Even if he did, he's got to come down sometime."

"What are these construction chambers, Greville?" Nayland Smith asked in a low voice.

"Five low spaces above the King's Chamber," I replied, "terminating in a pointed roof, generally supposed to have been intended to relieve the stress on the room below."

"Any way into them?"

"Yes—by means of a long ladder."

"Is there anything in what Barton says?"

"Hardly. In any event, there is only one way out!" I turned to Sir Lionel. "Have you searched the shaft. Chief?"

"No!" he growled—"I haven't. And what's more I'm not going to. Have the damn place closed and watched; that's all that's necessary."

Nayland Smith turned to Hewlett.

"You must arrange for the Pyramid to be closed to visitors for the remainder of the week. And have men on duty at the entrance day and night."

"Very good," said Hewlett; "I'll see to it."

We had climbed down again to the base, and my feet were on the sand, when an idea occurred to me.

"By heavens! Sir Denis," I cried. "It isn't safe to leave just four men there tonight."

"Why?" he snapped.

"You remember the meeting of dervishes reported by Enderby? Well—they are here—fifty or sixty strong!"

"Where?"

"Just this side of Mena House."

"A rescue!" said the chief hoarsely. "They mean to rush the entrance! Fu-Manchu is hiding inside!"

I could see Nayland Smith pulling at the lobe of his ear.

"They began to gather about midnight," said Hewlett. "It's been reported."

"Who are they?"

"Mostly men from outlying villages, and as Mr Greville says, members of various dervish orders."

"I don't like this," rapped Nayland Smith. The Mahdi organised the dervishes, you know. What's your opinion, Hewlett?"

"I haven't one. I can't make it out—unless, as Sir Lionel suggests, they are going to attempt to rush us… But, by jove! here they come!"

We had set out down the slope and nearly reached that point where Petrie and I had left the car. Now, we pulled up like one man.

Dimly visible in the darkness of the night, their marching feet crunching upon the sand, we saw a considerable company of Arabs approaching from the opposite direction.

"It might be dangerous," Nayland Smith muttered, "if it weren't for the fact that sixty armed men are still on duty."

And as he spoke, that onward march ceased as if in response to some unspoken order. Vaguely, although at no great distance from where we stood, we could see that strangely silent company. The policeman who had stopped Petrie's car suddenly appeared.

"What do I do about this, sir?" he asked, addressing Hewlett. "They look nasty to me."

"Do nothing," was the reply. "We have the situation well in hand."

"Very good, sir."

We were near enough now to the crowd on the edge of the plateau to be able to distinguish the colours of robes and turbans—white, black, green and red; a confused blurred mass, but divisible into units. And as I looked doubtingly in their direction, suddenly I saw a hundred arms upraised, and in a muted roar their many voices reached me:

"*Mokanna!*"

Whereupon, unanimous as worshippers in a cathedral, they dropped to their knees and bowed their heads in the sand!

"Good God! What's this?"

Nayland Smith was the speaker.

We all turned together, looking back to the northern face of the Great Pyramid. And as we did so, I witnessed a spectacle as vivid in my mind tonight as it was on the occasion of its happening.

Perhaps two thirds of the way up the slope of the great building, but at a point which I knew to be inaccessible to any climber, a figure appeared… Even from where I stood, it was visible in great detail— for the reason that this figure was brilliantly lighted!

Many explanations occurred to us later of how this illumination might have been produced. We recalled the globular lamp in the King's Chamber; several such lamps, masked from the viewpoint of the onlookers and placed one step below the figure, backed by reflectors, would, I think, have accounted for the phenomenon. But at the time, no solution offered.

Personally, I was conscious of nothing but stark amazement, For there, enshrined in the darkness, *I saw El Mokanna!*

I saw a tall, majestic figure, wearing either a white or a very light green robe. The face was concealed by a golden mask and surmounted by a tall turban. Upraised in the right hand glittered a sword with a curved blade...

A weird chanting arose from the dervishes. I didn't even glance back. I was staring—staring at that apparition on the Pyramid. Distant shouting reached me—orders, as I realised. But I knew, had known it all along, that no climber could reach that point.

Then, as suddenly as it had appeared, the apparition vanished.

The lights had been extinguished or covered: such was the conclusion to which we came later. But at the time the effect was most uncanny. And as the figure vanished, again, from the dervishes, came a loud and now triumphant shout:

"*Mokanna!*"

In the dead silence which followed:

"Fu-Manchu has set us a problem," said Nayland Smith. "Either he or some selected disciple has been posing as the reborn prophet, from Afghanistan right down to the border of Arabia. You understand the dervish gathering, now, Hewlett?"

A murmuring of excited conversation reached us. The assembly of Arabs, palpably come there as to a tryst, was dispersing and already returning down the slope.

"It was urgent," Sir Denis went on; "hence the abduction of Rima.

This was an *appointment* with the leaders of the *Senussi* and other fanatical orders. He had tricked them hitherto, but if the real relics had once been placed beyond his reach detection sooner or later was inevitable. This spark, Greville—" he turned to me in the darkness—"is going to light a bonfire. The Mokanna promises to be a greater problem that the Mahdi."

Whereupon the chief began to laugh!

That laughter was so unexpected, and indeed so eerie in the circumstances, that I found in it some quality of horror.

"He's tricked us, Smith!" he shouted. "He's tricked us! But, by God, I've tricked *him*!"

CHAPTER THIRTY-THREE

FACTS AND RUMOURS

The story of the second Masked Prophet, although extreme precautions were taken by the British secret service and by Sir Denis Nayland Smith, nevertheless leaked out and into the newspapers of Europe and America. It is well known today to everybody, so far as externals go.

Journalistic espionage triumphed even before the prophet appeared in Egypt. That ominous disturbance moving from Afghanistan down through Persia was paragraphed in the London *Daily Telegraph*, in the *Times of New York* and in Le Temps of Paris. The Indian papers had fairly long accounts.

When that strange rumour, hitherto unsupported by tangible evidence, reached Egypt, a special correspondent of the *Daily Mail* interviewed prominent Moslems. With one exception these denied all knowledge of the matter. The one—a learned imam whose name I have forgotten, but which may be found in the files of the newspaper in question—admitted that news of this movement had come to him. But, he informed his interviewer, it was confined to members of certain unorthodox sects; therefore he was not in a position to express any opinion regarding it.

This interview must have taken place, I suppose, at about the time that we reached Cairo. It was not prominently featured; but later came a column account by the same correspondent, of a second gathering of Wise Men, numbering not three, but according to his estimate, seventy; and a story of the apparition on the Great Pyramid which closely corresponded to the truth.

Since no other newspaper carried this story, I can only suppose that the correspondent of the *Daily Mail* was staying at Mena House.

Throughout these exacting days I lived in a state of unrelieved suspense. The watch on the Pyramid had had no results; the place was opened again to the public. Rima, who narrowly escaped a serious breakdown, was not fit to be moved for some time. Indeed, during the first forty-eight hours, Dr. Petrie was unable to conceal his anxiety.

The chief remained at Shepheard's awaiting the return of Ali Mahmoud with the heavy baggage; but I had moved to the hotel by the Pyramids in order to be near Rima. She suffered from a strange delusion that I was dead, and my presence was frequently required to reassure her. Later, I learned the origin of this obsession, which at the time puzzled me, as it puzzled Petrie.

Acting partly, I think, upon that one memory which remained to me of the hiatus preceding Rima's abduction, Sir Denis had proceeded in a Royal Air Force plane to Damascus.

The chief during this period was wrapped in one of his most impossible moods. A score of times I tried to discuss the mystery of Fu-Manchu's disappearance; and:

"Your measurements were wrong, Greville," was his invariable conclusion.

Characteristically, he did not question his own!

He referred, of course, to the investigation which we had carried out there, based upon his conviction that there were other chambers in the Great Pyramid. Sceptical as I had been at the time, I was disposed now to believe that Sir Lionel's extraordinary imagination had not misguided him.

Failing the existence of other chambers, and, more astounding still, of another exit, the escape of Dr. Fu-Manchu was susceptible of no material explanation. The later apparition of the Masked Prophet at an inaccessible point on the northern slope, might have been accounted for by daring trickery.

But these were trying days indeed. Knowing, as everyone knows who has spent much time among Orientals, that news travels among them faster than radio can carry it, I killed many idle hours in the native quarter, listening to the talk of shopkeepers, peddlers and mendicants.

In this way, thanks to my knowledge of vernacular Arabic, I kept abreast of the Mokanna movement. Probably I knew, before Nayland Smith and the British intelligence service knew, that the threat of that uprising grew less day by day. It had proved abortive; something had gone wrong. I used to report to the chief such scraps of rumour as reached me. They seemed to afford him matter for amusement.

"We'll sail in the next P. & O., Greville," he said one night. "Rima should be fit enough by then. It's high time we were out of Egypt. I'm only waiting for Ali Mahmoud..."

CHAPTER THIRTY-FOUR

RIMA'S STORY

And then at last came a day when Petrie announced to me privately that Rima was ready, was anxious, to be questioned; to tell her own story.

"Only you and I, Greville," he stipulated. "It remains dangerous ground, and Barton is liable to prove an irritant…"

We had tea with her, Petrie and I, on the balcony of her room overlooking the Pyramids. It was Sunday. The tourist season now was in nearly full flower. Camels with grotesquely poor riders paced up the slope to that little plateau which contains two of the wonders of the world: the Great Pyramid and the Sphinx. There were many cars. In the garden, smart Egyptians and their women occupied the best tables, regarding English, French, and American tourists with thinly veiled amusement.

Rima looked almost ethereal after her strange nervous illness, but so utterly desirable that I felt a savage urge to take her in my arms and stifle her with kisses. But, now that the fear phase had passed, I saw that she regarded me with a queer aloofness.

When her story was told, I understood…

"Of course, Shan, Dr. Petrie has made it all clear to me. You should be grateful to him, dear. I think he has saved me from…

"It was that night when you called for me at Shepheard's—but of course, I'm forgetting; you know nothing about it! You see, Shan, after your disappearance on the evening of our arrival, I was simply in a frenzy. They kept it from me for a long time—Uncle and Sir Denis and the doctor. But at last they had to tell me, of course.

"I didn't know what to do with myself. I began to think that my crazy behaviour was attracting attention—and I rushed up to my room. I hadn't been there more than five minutes when one of the servants bought me a note—from *you*!"

"It was a forgery!" I cried. "It must have been!"

"Don't interrupt, Greville," said Petrie quietly. "These are the *facts*. Remember that they relate to a period during which your own evidence is not available."

Good heavens! it was true. A great part of that night was a blank to me…

"It was from *you*," Rima went on. "You asked me to tell no one, but to come out at once and join you… I couldn't wait for the lift: I simply raced downstairs and out onto the terrace. An Egyptian chauffeur in a blue uniform met me and showed me where you were waiting—"

"I was waiting! Where?"

"Just opposite the hotel, beside a French landaulet. Of course, I ran across to you. Shan! you simply *hauled* me in! You were grim to the nth degree! But I was so utterly happy that at first I thought of nothing except that I had found you again.

"Then, Shan—oh, heavens… Shan!"

"Don't let the memory upset you, Rima," said Petrie. "It's all passed and done with. You know, my dear, he's the third victim, as I have told you. All three of us, Greville, at various times, have had similar experiences at the hands of our Chinese friend."

"I understand," I replied, watching Rima; "I begin to understand. Go on, darling."

"It came to me, my dear, that you were *mad*! I saw, in a flash, what had happened—because something like it had once happened to *me*. I fought with you—oh, my God, how I fought; it was terrible! Then, when I realised it was useless, I tried to *will* you to know what you were doing.

"We passed through Gizeh Village and were out on the causeway to here when the driver pulled up suddenly. A tall man dressed in black was standing in the roadway. He came forward to the right of the car—and I recognized him—

"It was Dr. Fu-Manchu!"

"Rima!"

"I began to collapse. I couldn't stand much more. He spoke to you. I didn't hear the words; but—Shan... you fell back on the seat as though you were—*dead*...

"It was the last straw. I believe I made a fool of myself—or they may have drugged me; but I passed away.

"When I opened my eyes again, after a thousand years of nightmare, I found myself in a strange but delightful room. I was lying on a couch wrapped in a silk dressing gown; and an old negress sat sewing near me...

"It turned out to be part of a suite in a house which must have been right outside Cairo; because all I could see from the little windows in the *mushrabiyeh* screens was miles and miles of desert. I suppose the negress was a servant of Dr. Fu-Manchu, but she was certainly a sweet old thing.

"My first waking thought, Shan, was about you! But the old woman could tell me nothing. She merely said over and over again,

'Don't fret, honey child; it will sure be all right.'

"I spent a whole day in those three small rooms. It was quite impossible to get out, and the old negress never left me. No one else came near us. She did all she could to make me comfortable, but I refused to touch food. I have never passed through such a day in my life. I felt myself to be slowly going mad with suspense. Once, a long way over the desert, I saw some camels; that was towards evening. Otherwise, I saw nothing…

"At sunset the negress lighted the lamps; and she had only just done so when I heard the sound of a gong somewhere in the house below.

"By this time I was in a state of suppressed frenzy, and when I heard that sound I wanted to shriek. The old woman gave me a warning glance, whispered, 'Don't fret, honey child; it will sure be all right,' and went and stood by the door.

"I heard footsteps outside; the door was unlocked—and Dr. Fu-Manchu came in!

"He was dressed as I remembered him in London—but the horrible thing was that he seemed to be much *younger*! I must have been nearer to crashing than I knew at the time; for I can't recall one word that he said to me, except that he made me understand, Shan, that your life depended upon *me*.

"Evidently he saw that I was likely to collapse at any moment. He spoke to the old negress in some language I had never heard—and then forced me to drink a glass of some rather sweet white wine.

"After that I remember him watching me very intently and speaking again. His voice seemed to fade away, and his awful eyes to grow larger and larger—"

"Like a green lake!" I burst in, "which swallowed you up! I know. I know!"

"*How* do you know?" Petrie asked sharply. "When did you derive that curious impression?"

He was studying me keenly: and at once I grasped the significance of my words. They echoed some submerged memory of the hiatus! But, in the moment of uttering them, that memory slipped back again into the limbo of the subconscious.

"No good, Doctor," I said, shaking my head. "You were right—but it's gone! Go on, Rima."

Rima, who seemed intuitively to have seized upon the purpose underlying Petrie's question, looked at me pathetically, and then:

"I *know* you know, Shan dear," she went on. "But you can't remember—nor can I. Because I woke in a gloomy stone chamber, lighted by a round green lamp—"

"The King's Chamber, Greville," Petrie interpolated. "Rima had never seen it before, it seems."

"Dr. Fu-Manchu was sitting by a small table, and there was a big stone sarcophagus just behind him. I was standing in front of him. There was no one else there; and the silence was dreadful.

"'Behind this coffer,' he said, and pointed with an incredibly long finger, 'you will find a mattress and cushions. Lie there, whatever happens, and make no sign—until I clap my hands. Then stand up. Shan Greville's life depends upon you. This is *your* part of the bargain.'

"I heard a gong—somewhere a long way off.

"'To your place,' said Dr. Fu-Manchu in that voice which seems to make every word sound like a command, 'and remember, when I clap my hands…'

"What happened after that, Shan, you know."

CHAPTER THIRTY-FIVE

ORDERED HOME

On the following night Rima returned to Cairo. I remember, as Sir Lionel and I sat in the lounge waiting for her to join us for dinner, that my mind was more nearly at ease than it had been for many days. When presently Rima appeared, although she looked perhaps rather more than normally pale, she had nevertheless contrived to efface any signs of her recent ordeal.

"In the absence of Dr. Petrie," I said, "I prescribe a champagne cocktail."

The patient approved of the prescription.

"What about you, Chief?"

"Whisky and soda," Sir Lionel growled, staring towards the entrance door. "Where the devil's Petrie?"

"A busy medical man," I replied, summoning a waiter, "is always excused social appointments. Isn't he, Chief?"

"Has to be, I suppose."

As I gave the order I found myself thinking about the doctor's earlier days, when, a struggling suburban practitioner in London, he had first found himself involved in the web of Dr. Fu-Manchu.

His published journals of those singular experiences which he had shared with Sir Denis, had created such world-wide interest that today, as I knew, he was independent of the proceeds of his profession. But he was, as someone had said of him, a born healer; and he had the most extensive practice of any English physician in Cairo. Evidently my thoughts were reflected upon my face; for:

"What are you grinning about?" the chief demanded.

"I was wondering," I replied, "if Sir Denis will allow me to publish an account of the story of the Masked Prophet."

"You published an account, as you term it," Rima interrupted, "of what happened in the Tomb of the Black Ape and afterwards. I didn't think it was too flattering to me, but I know you made a lot of money out of it. I don't really think, Uncle—" turning and snuggling up against Sir Lionel—"that it's quite fair, do you? Shouldn't *we* have a share?"

"Yes." The chief stared at me with smothered ferocity. "You've written me up in a painfully frank way, Greville, now I come to think about it... Ah! Here's Petrie!"

As he spoke, I saw the doctor come in from the terrace at a brisk pace. There was urgency in his manner, and when, sighting us, he hurried forward I realised that he was ill at ease.

His first thought, however, was for his patient; and dropping into a chair beside Rima, he looked at her in that encompassing manner which comes to a man who for many years has practised as a physician.

"Quite restored, I see," he said, and glanced critically at the cocktail. "Only one, Rima. Excitants are not desirable... yet."

Seeing me about to call a waiter:

"As I'm rather late, Greville," he went on, "let's go in to dinner; if possible, find a quiet table, as there's something I have to tell you."

"Knew it!" said the chief loudly, watching the speaker. "Got something on your mind, Petrie. What is it?"

"You're right," Petrie admitted, smiling slightly. "I don't quite know what to make of it."

"Nor do I," Sir Lionel replied, "unless you tell me what it is."

"A long message from Smith in Damascus. It was relayed over the telephone. That's what detained me. But don't let us talk about it now."

We stood up and walked along the corridor, which is a miniature jewel bazaar, to the dining room. I had arranged for a quiet table at the farther end, and presently, when we were all seated and the chief, who was host, had given his orders:

"This message is disturbing, in a way," said Petrie. "There's a Dutch steamer of the Rotterdam Lloyd Line, the *Indramatra*, leaving Port Said tomorrow night for Southampton; and Smith insists that, baggage or no baggage, you must all leave in her!"

"What!" Sir Lionel cried so loudly that many heads were turned in our direction. "He must be mad. I won't budge an inch—not one inch—until Ali Mahmoud arrives with the gear."

Dr. Petrie looked grave.

"I have the message here," he continued; "and when I have read it to you, possibly you may change your mind... Dr. Fu-Manchu has been in Damascus. He has disappeared. Smith has every reason to believe that he is on his way here—to Cairo. His mission, Barton is to see *you*!"

CHAPTER THIRTY-SIX

NAYLAND SMITH COMES ABOARD

The *Indramatra* lay off the pontoon, opposite the Custom House at Port Said; and it was a night sailing. Ali Mahmoud had arrived in the nick of time; I could see him now from where I stood, supervising the shipment of the heavy baggage.

That curious sustained murmur, a minor chord made up of human voices, audible whenever cargo is being worked in this odd portal of the East, came to my ears, as I craned out watching the pontoon. I had left Rima, a stewardess, and two coolies busily unpacking trunks; for Rima had something of her uncle's gift for making people work enthusiastically in her interests. Part other personal baggage had been deposited in her cabin, and, having explored the first of her trunks:

There isn't a thing that's fit to wear!" she had declared…

I had considered it prudent to join the chief.

That experienced old traveller had secured a suite with bath, at the Cairo office. Admittedly, the ship was not full, but, nevertheless, someone else had been pencilled in for this accommodation ahead of him. The someone else (a Member of Parliament, he turned out to be) was reduced to an ordinary double cabin, and the purser was having a bad quarter of an hour.

Sir Lionel, armed with a whisky and soda, was sprawling on the little sofa in his sitting room, his feet resting upon a stout wooden chest. He reminded me of an old buccaneer, gloating over ill-gotten treasure; and:

"Has Smith arrived?" he demanded.

"No. I'm just going up to make inquiries, chief…"

And so, now, I found myself craning out and watching the pontoon. It would be nearly an hour before the *Indramatra* sailed, but I could not imagine, since Sir Denis had missed us in Cairo, how he hoped to reach Port Said before we left. Nevertheless, he had advised us to expect him.

I glanced down at Ali Mahmoud, patiently checking the items of our baggage destined for the hold, and experienced a pang of regret in parting from him. Then again I stared towards the shore. I saw the headlights of a car which was being driven rapidly along the waterfront. I saw it pull up just short of the Custom House.

No other steamer was leaving that night, and although, admittedly, this might have been a belated passenger, something told me that it was Nayland Smith.

I was right.

Above the clatter of machinery and minor drone of human voices, with the complementary note of water lapping at the ship's side, a clamour reached me from the shore. There was urgency in the sound. And as I watched, I saw a police launch which had been lying just off the pontoon, run in, in response to a signal. A few moments later, and the little red craft was describing a flattened arc as she headed out rapidly for the *Indramatra*.

One glimpse I had in a momentary glare of the searchlight, of a man seated in the stern, and then I was hurrying down to the lower deck. I had no more than reached the head of the ladder when Nayland Smith came bounding up. As I greeted him:

"Quick!" he snapped and grasped my arm. "The purser's office—where is it? I don't know this ship."

"This way, Sir Denis."

Pushing past groups of passengers, mostly planters and officials from the Dutch East Indies, we went racing across to the purser's office. As I had expected, a number of people were waiting to interview that harassed official, but the curtain was drawn over his door, and I could hear an excited voice within. Sir Denis never hesitated for a moment. He rapped loudly, jerked the curtain aside, and:

"Mr. Purser!" he said, "I regret that I don't know your name—my apologies. But it is vitally urgent that I should see you for a few moments."

The purser, a Sumatra-born Dutchman, stout and normally good-humoured, I judged, at the moment was not in an amiable mood. Mr. John Kennington, M.P., a fussy little man resembling Tweedledee in spectacles, was literally dancing about in his room.

"I say it's an outrage, sir," he was exclaiming, "an outrage. This fellow, Sir Lionel Barton, this travelling mountebank, has almost literally thrown me out of a cabin which I reserved in Cairo. As a British Member of Parliament, I wish to state—"

"I don't know your name, sir," said the purser, looking up wearily at Sir Denis—he spoke excellent English, for the Dutch are first-class linguists; "mine is Voorden: but you can see that I am very much engaged."

"Such a state of affairs," Mr. Kennington continued, extending his rotund person in the manner of a frog about to burst, "such a state of affairs would not be tolerated for a moment in the P. & O."

That, of course, was a slip, and put the purser on our side at once. His growing distaste for the angry passenger was reflected upon normally placid features.

"The P. & O., sir," said Nayland Smith, "is an admirable line, to which I can give you a personal introduction ensuring excellent accommodation."

Mr. Kennington paused, turned, and looked up at the grim face of the speaker; then:

"Possibly, sir, you may know that Members of Parliament, travelling officially, are afforded certain facilities—"

"I do know it, and I feel sure that your complaint is a just one. But since you are a Member of Parliament, you will naturally do everything in your power to assist me. A matter of national urgency demands that I should have two minutes' private conversation with Mr. Voorden."

Mr. Kennington blew himself up again.

"My dear sir," he replied, "I must take this opportunity of pointing out to you that I have certain rights here."

Sir Denis's temper, never of the best, was growing dangerously frayed.

"Mr. Voorden," he said quietly, "I don't know this gentleman's name, but have I your permission to place him in the alleyway until our very urgent business is concluded?"

The purser's broad face broke into a smile. It was a suggestion after his own heart; and:

"May I ask you, Mr Kennington," he said, addressing the outraged M.P., whose features were now assuming a hectic florid hue, "to allow me two minutes with this gentleman? His business, I think, is important."

"Important!" the other exploded. "Important! By heavens, sir,

Rotterdam shall hear of you—Rotterdam shall hear of you!"

He expelled himself from the cabin.

"Here is my card, Mr. Voorden," said Sir Denis, laying a card upon the purser's table: "but in order to save your time and my own, I called upon the Dutch consul on my way to the docks. He was unable to accompany me, but he sends this note."

He laid upon the table a sheet of paper bearing the letterhead of the Dutch consulate in Port Said. The purser put on a pair of horn-rimmed glasses and read the note. Mr Kennington, not far away, might be heard demanding an interview with the captain.

"Sir Denis Nayland Smith," said the purser, standing up, "I am at your service. What can I do for you?"

"Thank you," said Sir Denis, and shook his hand. "Your passenger list, if you please. I want the name of everyone joining the ship at this port."

"Certainly! that is very simple. You will also wish to know, of course, what accommodation they have reserved?"

"Exactly"

A moment later Nayland Smith was bending over a plan of the ship, in close consultation with the purser. I moved to the curtain, drew it aside, and stepped into the alleyway. Mr. Kennington had discovered the second steward and was insisting that that official should conduct him to the captain. I had it in mind to endeavour to pacify the infuriated little man, when the matter was taken out of my hands.

"Sir Lionel Barton is the person's name," shouted Mr. Kennnigton—"who the devil may I ask is Sir Lionel Barton?"

Unfortunately for Mr. Kennington, at that moment Sir Lionel appeared on the scene.

"Does anybody want me?" he inquired in his deep gruff voice.

Mr. Kennington turned and looked up into that sun-baked, truculent mask. He tried bravely to sustain the glare of deep-set eyes beneath tufted brows. But when he spoke, it was with a notable lack of confidence.

"Are you Sir Lionel Barton?"

"I am. Did you want me?"

The second steward escaped, leaving Mr. Kennington to fight his battle alone.

"There seems to be some misunderstanding about our cabins," he said in a tone of gentle melancholy…

CHAPTER THIRTY-SEVEN

THE RELICS OF THE PROPHET

There was some pretty straight talking in the chief's room five minutes later. Rima was not present.

"I have the outline of the thing complete, Barton," said Nayland Smith, puffing furiously at his pipe. "For God's sake, don't interrupt. Just listen. My time is brief. The man Amir Khan blundered onto the location of Mokanna's tomb in some way and up to the time of his disappearance, was undoubtedly acting on his own. I take it you paid him well for his information."

"I did."

Sir Denis nodded.

"He did not belong to that obscure sect, an offshoot of true Mohammedanism, which still holds the tradition of the New Koran. But he knew more than they do, because he knew where the prophet was buried. He was a *thug*; you always knew this. And he deserted because he was recalled by his immediate chief. The laws of *thuggee* (which I don't profess to understand) are very binding upon devotees. His chief learned what had happened; and his chief—"

"Was one of the Fu-Manchu group!" Sir Lionel interrupted. "And so…"

"And so the news reached the doctor. Where he was at the time, we shall probably never know—but he acted swiftly. The possibilities were tremendous. Islam is at least as divided as Christianity. A religious revival is long overdue. The man and the occasion, only, were wanted. Here was the occasion. Dr. Fu-Manchu found the man."

"Whom did he find?"

"I don't know. Listen, and I will tell you all I know. In every religion there are secret sects. I have maintained for many years, in the face of much opposition from learned sources—and from you—that the organisation known as the Si-Fan embodies the greater part of these dissentients—"

"Rot!"

"Such a movement, reinforced by the backing of the Si-Fan, would almost certainly have tipped the scale. This was what Dr. Fu-Manchu saw. The arising of the prophet was staged for him when you blew up that lonely tomb in Khorassan. This he acted upon with the results which we know. Interested parties in the Moslem world were only too ready to receive the new prophet. His material qualities they were prepared to overlook. But it happens—and a memory of Greville's gave me the clue to the truth—that a certain fanatical sect, having representatives at Damascus and also at Mecca, possess or claim to possess copies of the New Koran."

"That's true," said the chief, shifting his feet uneasily, for he was sprawling upon the settee. "I've seen 'em. I knew what I was up against, Smith."

Nayland Smith looked at Sir Lionel with a sort of reluctant admiration.

"You're a remarkable man, Barton," he admitted. "If a modicum of discretion had been added to your outfit, much of this trouble might have been avoided."

"What trouble?" the chief shouted. He kicked at the wooden chest. "Where's the trouble? I've tricked every damned fool among them. And, by heaven! I've tricked Dr. Fu-Manchu himself. You all wondered why I hung on so long in Ispahan—"

He began to laugh loudly; but:

"I know *now*," said Nayland Smith.

And he spoke the words so coldly that the chief's laughter was checked.

"I thought," he went on, "that you were bluffing in Cairo. I know your schoolboy sense of humour. It was a dramatic surprise to me, although I may not have shown it, when your old suitcase was opened before Mr. Aden and I saw the sword, the mask, and the gold plates."

He jumped out of his chair and began to move from foot to foot, since there was no room for him to promenade.

"I carried out my contract with Dr. Fu-Manchu—Rima's life being the price at stake—in what I believed to be all honesty. Don't speak. Barton—let me finish. Dr. Fu-Manchu is the most ghastly menace to our present civilisation which has appeared since Attila the Hun. He is an old man, but, by some miracle which I can only ascribe to his gigantic power, he is as forceful today as he was in the first hour that I ever set eyes on him in a forest of Burma. That's agreed. He has one virtue. According to his admittedly peculiar code—he is a man of honour."

"Stop!"

Sir Lionel was up, now, his strong hands clenched, his eyes glaring upon the speaker.

"Stop, Smith! I won't take it from you or from any man. I may have broken every other commandment, but I have never lied."

"Have I accused you of lying?" Sir Denis's voice was very cool.

"Practically, yes."

"You remained in Ispahan until Solomon Ishak, perhaps the finest craftsman in the East, had duplicated the relics of the prophet. Oh, it was clever work, Barton. But…"

"Well," growled the chief, still glaring at him. "But, what… Didn't the man Aden or Samarkan or whatever his name is—pass the stuff that we showed him in Shepheard's? Did I or did you undertake to deliver up anything else? We had Rima back, and we handed over the duplicates." Furiously he kicked the box. "Ali Mahmoud had the relics. He brought them from old Soloman Ishak back to Cairo, and from Cairo on board here. And there they are!"

He dropped back onto the settee, his mouth working evilly, for he was in murderous humour. But Nayland Smith continued to watch him calmly.

"It would be reviving an ancient libel to say that you argue like a Jesuit, Barton," he remarked coldly.

"Thanks!" snapped the chief. "You have probably said enough."

I think I have never felt more unhappy in my life. The facts now revealed to me were astounding; the ethics of the thing beyond me. But it was ghastly that these two old friends—men of first-rate genius in their separate spheres—should thus be almost at one another's throats.

Loyalty to the chief forbade my siding with Sir Denis, yet in my heart I knew that the latter was right. The price had been Rima's life; and Sir Lionel had played a faked card.

It didn't surprise me; and since he had succeeded, I had it in my heart to forgive him, but:

"You know chief," I said, "I can see what Sir Denis means; so don't boil over. *We* were in the wrong."

I hadn't meant it; I am not clever enough to have thought of it; but that use of "we" rather did the trick. Sir Lionel relaxed and looked at me in an almost kindly way.

"You think so, Greville?" he growled.

"Well, it was the devil of a risk, and Dr. Fu-Manchu," Nayland Smith snapped, "discovered the substitution in Damascus, on the very day, I believe, that I arrived there. By means of what secret knowledge held by certain imams of the Great Mosque he anticipated that the forgery would be detected, I don't know."

He paused—his pipe had gone out, and he struck a match; then:

"*Someone* spoke from the pulpit that evening. The huge mosque was packed to the doors. I have never seen such mass fanaticism in my life."

"Were you there?" asked the chief with sudden boyish enthusiasm.

"I was."

"Good old Smith!"

And in those words I recognized the fact that the storm had blown over.

"The speaker wore a green turban, a green robe, and a thick gold mask."

"It was Fu-Manchu!"

"I am still inclined to doubt it. I don't think I could mistake him. If it were he, then he has thrown off the burden of thirty years. He held his audience in the palm of his hand, as I know Fu-Manchu can do. But the virility of his voice…"

And as he spoke, a sort of half-memory stirred in my brain. It passed—leaving a blank.

"There were doubters there. And that very night, as I believe, the substitution was discovered. The new Mahdi opened brilliantly,

Barton, but he met with a definite check in Damascus. What actually happened I naturally don't profess to know. But—" he pointed to the wooden chest on the floor of the cabin—"are they in there?"

"They are!" said the chief triumphantly.

"The rumour is already spreading—you know how news travels in these parts—that Mokanna is an impostor. I need not add that our Intelligence Department is zealously fostering this. Only one thing could save the situation." He pointed again to the chest. "I don't know where Dr. Fu-Manchu is, but from my knowledge of his methods I should predict that he is not far from Port Said at the present moment."

Those words sent a cold shudder down my spine.

"He's too late," growled Sir Lionel; "we sail in fifteen minutes."

"I know," Nayland Smith returned. "But while I'm aware that I am wasting words, if I were in your shoes, Barton, I should be disposed to send Ali Mahmoud ashore with that crate and sail in comfort."

"You'd do nothing of the sort!" shouted the chief, jumping up again. "You know it as well as I do."

"Very good. I've a few suggestions to make before I go ashore. I can't possibly leave Egypt for at least another week, when I hope that Petrie will be ready to join me."

CHAPTER THIRTY-EIGHT

"THE SWORD OF GOD"

"Bolt the door, Greville," said Sir Lionel.

I did as he directed. His stateroom presented an appearance of untidiness which, even for the chief, touched the phenomenal. He had unpacked the wooden crate, and the floor was littered with straw and paper.

It proved to contain three packages tied up in canvas; one, long and narrow, which enwrapped the sword of the prophet; another, the heaviest, rectangular and perhaps eight inches thick; and a smaller one, which was obviously some kind of box.

"Get busy with the big package," he directed energetically. "Untie the string, but don't cut it. We shall want to use it again."

"Very good," I said resignedly, and set to work.

The *Indramatra* had just pulled out from her berth, Nayland Smith and the Company's agent being the last two visitors to go down the ladder. Rima was in her cabin busily unfolding frocks which had been folded for weeks and about the condition of which she was in complete despair.

What Sir Lionel's object could be in unpacking these treasures, now that at last we had escaped with them, was a problem which defeated me. But mad though he was, there was generally some method in his madness.

"Gad! what a beauty!" he cried.

He had unwrapped the scimitar and was gazing upon it with the eyes of a lover. Indeed I knew, had known for many years, that the chief's heart was wholly in the past. He worshipped these relics of strange men and wild times, although his collections, of which he had one in each of his several houses, must have broken the heart of any museum curator. Priceless pieces were as likely to be found upon the floor, or on the seat of a chair where a careless visitor might sit upon them, as anywhere else. But the fact remained that his enthusiasm was genuine.

"You're a hell of a long time with the plates," he growled.

"These knots want a bit of coping with."

"Give it to me and unpack the mask."

I complied only too willingly.

"Can you see anything lying about, Greville, remotely resembling the Sword of God?—any fitting we could tear down?"

I began to laugh. The purpose of the chief's toil had become evident. He was at his favourite trick again.

"Really," I said, looking up from the floor where I was kneeling untying the box containing the mask, "I don't know what you have in mind, but short of seizing the ship, I can't see how anybody is going to gain access to the purser's safe."

"Can't you?" he growled. "Did you see how anybody was going to gain access to that room in Isphahan? I know more about the methods employed by Dr. Fu-Manchu than you do, Greville. And as I told Smith just now, I think nothing of safes at any time. We shouldn't have the stuff now if I thought as you do."

"True enough," I admitted, and took out a delicate and exquisite mask from the box which held it.

"Gad!" exclaimed Sir Lionel in a low voice—"What a beauty! Unique, Greville, absolutely unique! This one item would make the reputation of any collector."

He paused in his task, stood up, and stared about him. Then from a battered leather hat box he took an old sun helmet, emptied a cigar box onto the bed (it contained quite a dozen cigars) and put the gold mask in their place. Tying the box with a piece of string, he dropped it into the helmet, returning the latter to its leather case. He threw the case on the settee.

"A very clever American," he remarked—"one Edgar Allan Poe—laid it down that the best place to hide a thing was where everyone could see it. Ha! here's what you want, Greville."

An umbrella belonging to Rima had somehow strayed into his cabin, left there in error by a steward, no doubt when the baggage had come aboard. She had bought it in Cairo. It was short, with a fancifully carved handle of glass, representing the Sphinx.

"Wrap it up," he said; "that's splendid."

He laughed, in his loud, boisterous fashion. And something of his crazy humour began to infect me also. His treatment of a menace which had overhung us darkly for so long, which already had cost several lives and had stirred up the beginnings of a promising Arab rising, was stimulating, to say the least.

I wrapped up the umbrella in the canvas packing, tying it with care; and Sir Lionel, having unfastened the gold plates, examined them lingeringly. I knew he would have liked to devote hours to that examination, but the time was not now.

"Where's the Burberry?" he asked.

I pointed to an open door communicating with his bedroom; my old Burberry hung upon a hook there.

He nodded, wrapped the sheets of thin gold in pieces of newspaper, and slipped them into the big pocket of the coat, which contained them quite easily.

"Let me see!" he cried.

I exhibited the parcel I had just completed.

"Not bad," he commented; "I think it will pass. Now, to seal it."

Crossing to a little writing table, and kicking all sorts of litter out of his way as he went, he opened a box containing odds and ends of stationery, and presently found a piece of sealing wax. Lighting many matches and dropping a quantity of wax upon the carpet, he sealed several of the knots, pressing his signet ring upon each of them. Then, holding up the finished product, he laughed like a schoolboy.

"Number one ready!" he cried. "Ah! you have done another. What did you put in the box?"

"Nothing," I replied; "the weight of the mask is negligible."

"Hand me that thin atlas over there," he directed.

From a pile of books thrown carelessly on the floor, I collected the volume to which he referred. It was roughly of about the same size and shape as the fifteen gold plates laid together. It was also very heavy.

"Good enough!" he said, weighing it in his hand. "Hello! Who's this? Don't open, Greville."

Someone was rapping on the cabin door.

"Who's there?" roared Sir Lionel.

"Steward, sir. Miss Barton has asked me to inquire if an umbrella which is missing has been brought in here."

"No," roared the chief, "it hasn't. Never seen it."

"Do you mind if I take a look round, sir?"

"I mind very much. I'm busy. Go away!"

He stood upon the settee, drew the curtain aside, and peered through a porthole.

"We're clear of shore, Greville," he reported. "By heaven! I've tricked him this time!"

A few minutes later we completed the third parcel to his satisfaction, and:

"Cut along to your cabin," he directed; "you haven't far to go. Carry your Burberry over your arm; you can hold the sword underneath it."

"Very good. Where shall I put them?"

"Put the sword under your bed for the time being, and hang the Burberry in the bathroom, or anywhere. I'll come along presently and decide definitely. But first we must see the purser."

Unbolting the door, we sallied forth. I went along to my cabin and then rejoined Sir Lionel. Stewards were still coming and going, carrying stray items of baggage, the ship being in that state of unrest which prevails on leaving port.

"I don't trust these Javanese," the chief whispered. "Every one of them might belong to Dr. Fu-Manchu."

I felt rather disposed to agree with him. But Nayland Smith had been insistent upon our leaving by the first available ship, and failing the *Indramatra*, we should have had to wait for three days.

Passengers were standing about at the foot of the stairs in the neighbourhood of the purser's room, examining notices and making aimless inquiries of almost every European member of the crew who passed. Carrying our strange burdens, we came to the purser's door.

"I simply refuse to occupy a cabin," an excited voice was shouting within, "in which the running water resembles beer. It's scandalous, sir, scandalous!"

"Our friend Kennington," said the chief, unceremoniously jerking the curtain aside and walking in. "Good evening, purser. Sorry to trouble you, but I have some valuables which I wish to leave in your care."

"Very good, Sir Lionel," said the harassed officer, turning in his chair and looking up at us.

"One of them looks a bit bulky for the safe. Perhaps we can manage."

Mr. Kennington, blown up to his full dimensions, was standing at the farther end of the room, glaring. On further examination he was a singular-looking object. His rotundity seemed positively artificial, so suddenly did it develop, and his dark eyes, behind horn-rimmed spectacles, did not seem to belong to his red and choleric face. He had carroty hair, close-cut, and an absurd little moustache.

"I will not be side-tracked in this manner, sir," he cried, as the purser, standing up, turned and unlocked the big safe. "I have already been given accommodation other than that which I reserved, and now…"

"And now," said the chief, looking him up and down in his most truculent and intolerant manner, "you have been given tap water which resembles beer."

"I have, sir. And I will not tolerate it for one moment—not for one moment!"

"Neither should I," said the chief, "if I were a teetotaller. Are you a teetotaller?"

"I am, sir."

"And a member of the Labour party, I take it?"

"Certainly."

"Funny thing, Greville," said Sir Lionel, looking at me, "how these enemies of capital always insist upon the best accommodation. But—"

"By a little readjustment," said the purser, "I can manage your three sealed packages. Sir Lionel."

He reclosed and locked the massive safe.

"And now you will want a receipt for them."

He sat down at his table again.

"I have registered my protests, sir," said Mr. Kennington sternly; "my second protest since I came on board this ship. Since you don't seem to propose to attach any importance to it, I shall make a point of placing the matter before the captain."

He bowed with absurd dignity and went out.

"You know, gentlemen," said Voorden, taking a printed form from a case on his table, "one passenger like that puts years on a ship's purser. According to his passport, Mr. Kennington does not travel much, which perhaps accounts for it. Ah, well!" he sighed wearily, filling in the form, "I suppose it's the sort of thing that the company pays me for. There you are, sir."

Sir Lionel thanked him, folded up the receipt, and placed it in his pocket case. As we went out and were crossing towards the stairs, I heard Mr. Kennington talking to the chief steward.

"I insist upon a table to myself, steward."

"I will do my best, sir."

"It would be pleasant for everybody concerned," said the chief in a loud voice, "if some travellers would insist upon a *ship* to themselves, and stay on board for the rest of their lives."

Whereupon he began to laugh thunderously.

CHAPTER THIRTY-NINE

FLIGHT FROM EGYPT

I stood at the after end of the promenade deck, my arm very tightly about Rima. Together, we watched the lights of Egypt fading in the distance. It was good to be together after that brief but dreadful hiatus in Cairo, but yet, although neither of us spoke, I knew we shared a common regret. It was true we had known sorrow in Egypt, but we had known great happiness there, and the happiness outweighed the sorrow.

It was growing late, and we had the starboard side of the deck to ourselves; a few passengers lingered in the smoke-room, but nearly everybody was in bed. It would have been good to have Nayland Smith with us, but he and Dr. Petrie hoped to be in London in time for the spectacular wedding which Sir Lionel had planned for us.

Personally, I looked forward to that function with the utmost horror. But I was not at all sure that Rima didn't secretly enjoy the prospect. Rima had been a very popular debutante two years before; and I knew the chief would enjoy himself to the top of his bent in circulating paragraphs among gossip writers, and in employing his genius for showmanship to make our wedding a successful public entertainment.

In fact, having few friends of my own in London, and knowing that Rima had many, I felt that those days in the Mediterranean which lay ahead would be the last for a long time during which I should have her to myself.

No words were necessary between us. I just held her very closely, and she nestled against me in perfect contentment, while together we watched the lights of Port Said growing more and more dim upon the horizon.

Only nine passengers had joined the *Indramatra* there, including our own party of three. They had been checked up by Nayland Smith, and not one of them came within the shadow of suspicion. Other than these six first-class passengers and ourselves, no one had come aboard in Egypt, nor had the crew been reinforced. I remembered Sir Denis's parting words: "Unless, which isn't impossible, since we're dealing with Dr. Fu-Manchu, an agent of his has been smuggled aboard disguised as cargo, it would appear, Greville, that, for once in his life, the doctor has misfired."

It was cold comfort, since I had reason to know that the doctor rarely misfired. And I hugged Rima so closely that she demanded a kiss and received many…

When at last, and very reluctantly, I turned in that night, common sense told me that Sir Lionel had pulled off his daring trick and risked Rima's life in the process. But, once in Europe, I believed that we had little to fear on this score, since the religious-political unity of the relics by then would have become nil. Only by their immediate recovery could Dr. Fu-Manchu hope to re-establish the claims of the new prophet, already challenged by reason of their absence. A week would make all the difference.

But, in destroying this daring scheme of the greatest, and most evil man I had ever known, what had we done?

His mentality was incalculable. I believed him too great to waste an hour of his time in so futile a purpose as vengeance. But in this I knew that I might be mistaken. He was a Chinaman, and I knew little of Chinese mentality. He was unscrupulous, valuing human life no more highly than the blades of grass one treads upon. But in this he conformed to his own peculiar code.

No desire for personal aggrandisement inspired him, Nayland Smith had assured me. He aimed to lift China from the mire into which China had fallen. He was, according to his peculiar lights, a great patriot. And, this I knew, according to those same peculiar lights, he was scrupulously honourable.

True, the terms he had extorted upon the strength of the abduction of Rima had been blackmail at its vilest, but blackmail of a kind acceptable to his own code. We had agreed to his terms and had set our names to that agreement. Such implicit trust had he placed in our English honour that he had met us alone—the gesture of a great man if a great villain.

And in all good faith on the part of Nayland Smith and myself we had tricked him! Would he have tricked us in that way? Was it what his inscrutable Chinese conscience would regard as fair warfare, or was it not?

I doubted, and, to be perfectly honest, I feared. I had warned Rima to bolt her door before I said goodnight to her, and now, entering my own cabin, I did the same. I made sure that the sword of God was in my golf bag concealed among the clubs, and the gold plates in the pocket of my Burberry before I began to undress. The wooden chest, nailed up again, stood at the end of a blind alleyway leading to the chief's suite.

The Mediterranean was calm as a great lake, and there was little motion perceptible from stem to stem of the *Indramatra*. My cabin was forward on the port side and only two removed from that occupied by Sir Lionel. These cabins opened on a narrow gallery overlooking the dining saloon, and Rima's was nearly opposite my own.

I had experienced a pang of uneasiness on realising that the stewards were almost exclusively Javanese, some of them of a very Mongolian type: silent, furtive, immobile, squatting like images at the corner of nearly every alleyway—their slippers beside them, their faces expressionless.

Tonight, however, they had all disappeared. The ship was silent, the saloon a dark well. Only faint vibrations from the screw propellers and that creaking of woodwork inseparable from a ship at sea, disturbed the stillness.

I had only partially unpacked, and feeling very wide awake, I began to grope among my baggage for a tin of tobacco which I had bought just before leaving Cairo. I had determined to smoke a final pipe before turning in. A final drink would have been welcome, but I doubted if I could obtain one.

Following some searching, I discovered the tobacco, and I had just raised the lid and begun to fill my pipe when there came a soft rapping upon the door of the cabin…

CHAPTER FORTY

THE SEAPLANE

I confess that I was reluctant to open my door. It was perhaps not surprising after the strain which had been imposed upon me during those past few weeks; but I was conscious of a definite decline of morale. I had many unhappy memories and some dreadful ones: not the least of these that strange lacuna in Cairo, throughout which I had obviously been a passive instrument of the Chinese doctor's will.

The rapping was repeated, rather more insistently, but yet not loudly.

I laid my pipe down on the bed and moved towards the cabin door. Save for that slight creaking of woodwork as the ship rode a barely perceptible swell, there was no sound.

"Who's there?" I said sharply, but without shooting the bolt back.

"Urgent radio message for Mr. Greville."

I heaved a sigh of relief which must have been audible beyond the door, shot the bolt back, and there stood a Marconi operator.

"I shouldn't have disturbed you in the ordinary way," he explained, "but the message was marked 'Immediate delivery'."

"Thanks," I said; "I hadn't turned in." I took the flimsy envelope. "Goodnight," I added.

"Goodnight, sir."

I returned and bolted the door. Then, tearing open the message, I read eagerly.

SOMETHING WILL BE ATTEMPTED TONIGHT STOP
STAY AWAKE AND KEEP A SHARP LOOK-OUT
NAYLAND SMITH

I dropped the message on the bedcover. From what possible source was such an attempt to be looked for? And what should I do?

Lighting my pipe, I stared at the golf bag propped in a corner of the cabin, a strange repository for a relic which already had such a bloody history; but in Sir Lionel's opinion a better one than the purser's safe.

Cudgel my brains as I would—and I was very wide awake now—I could conceive of no plan—even assuming the real whereabouts of the damnable relics to be known to our enemies—whereby they could obtain possession of them, otherwise than by an open raid on my cabin and that of the chief.

It was preposterous! Even if it were admissible that Fu-Manchu had servants among the native members of the crew—what could they do?

Yet, here was the message. What in Heaven's name did it mean?

One thing I determined upon: to obey Nayland Smith's instructions. I would mount guard until daylight, when the normal life of the ship would be resumed. Then, if nothing had occurred, I might safely assume the danger past.

With this laudable object in view, I removed my coat and threw myself on the bed, taking up a booklet issued by the shipping company and illustrated with charts showing the mileage between ports of call.

I read on industriously. Once I thought I detected a faint sound out in the alleyway, but, putting the pamphlet down and listening intently it presently resolved itself into a variation of that endless creaking. I realised that the gentle, soothing motion had become more marked; the swell was slightly increasing.

How long I pursued my reading, I cannot say, for, as often occurs at such times, although I imagined myself to be wide awake, I was actually tired out, and probably no more than a few minutes later I was fast asleep.

I suppose I slept lightly, for there could be little doubt about what awakened me. I know that I sat up with a start, and at first was utterly confused by my surroundings. Ash was on the counterpane where I had dropped my pipe; fortunately, it had not set fire to it. I sat listening.

Above the noise of creaking woodwork and the dim vibration of the shaft, a new sound was perceptible. I glanced at my watch. I had slept for two hours.

Stepping to my cabin door, I shot the bolt, opened, and looked out into the alleyway. Darkness and silence. Nothing moved. I returned and even more plainly, now, could hear this new disturbance.

I had carefully closed the porthole, having painful memories of the acrobatic methods employed by agents of Dr. Fu-Manchu. I unscrewed the bolts and opened it. The sound became much louder; and curiosity grew overpowering. I was as widely awake as ever now, and I determined to go up on deck for a moment.

I had discovered that my cabin door possessed a key—which is unusual in English ships. I locked it, went quietly along the alleyway, and mounted the stairs. Not a soul was about. Both entrances were closed, but the sound had seemed to come from the port side, and therefore I opened the port door and stepped out on deck.

It was a clear, starry night. And as I looked upward and aft my theory was confirmed.

Some kind of heavy aircraft, to judge from the deep drone of her propellers, was flying on a parallel course and rapidly overtaking the *Indramatra*. I went up the ladder to the boat deck, thinking I could obtain a better view. In this I was right.

She was, I thought, a seaplane, but by reason of her position in relation to the ship, and the darkness of the night, I could not be sure of this. I glanced forward to the bridge.

The officer of the watch was out on the port wing, his glasses directed upwards; and I had time to wonder if the rigid discipline of the Dutch Mercantile Marine necessitated his logging the occurrence.

I turned and went back to my cabin. The seaplane, for such I now clearly saw it to be, had passed the ship, and was some little distance ahead of us.

About to pass the alleyway communicating with the chief's suite, I pulled up in doubt. The light was bad, but I could not see the wooden crate which formerly had contained the relics of the prophet.

I tiptoed along, to make sure. Undoubtedly, the crate was gone!

This, of course, might have been accounted for in several ways; yet I was practically certain that the crate had been there when I turned in. I entered my own cabin, and automatically plunged my hand in the golf-bag. The Sword of God was safe. I felt the pendulous pocket of my Burberry in the wardrobe—and the New Creed remained in its hiding place.

I had just slipped into my pyjamas when again came a knocking on the cabin door.

From the jump which I gave, I knew how badly my nerves had suffered.

"Who is it?" I cried.

"Very sorry, Mr. Greville! Marconi again."

I opened the door.

"It's all right," I said, smiling without effort, for frankly I was relieved. "What is it this time?"

"It's another urgent message. It looks as though we had a crook aboard!"

"What!"

I took the radiogram and read:

NO MP NAME OF KENNINGTON IN PRESENT
COMMONS STOP ADVISE PURSER AT ONCE
AND INTERROGATE PASSENGER
NAYLAND SMITH

Looking up, I met the glance of the operator.

"It's queer, isn't it?" he commented. "But I don't see much point in waking the purser at this time of night. Are you by any chance connected with the English police, sir?"

"No. My correspondent is."

"Oh, I see. Well if you want to wake the purser, I can show you his room."

"I'll think it over," I replied. "I know where to find you if I decide to see him."

"Right aft on the boat deck," he said, and turned.

"Goodnight!"

"Goodnight."

I had just reclosed the door, and sitting down was considering

Nayland Smith's second message when there came a sudden lull; a queer stillness. At first, I could not account for it. Then, I knew what had happened.

The engines had been rung off.

CHAPTER FORTY-ONE

A RUBBER BALL

In much the same way, I suppose, as the stopping of a clock will awake a sleeper, the stoppage of the propellers awakened many passengers in the *Indramatra*. As I pulled on a dressing gown and hurried out into the alleyway, voices and movements were audible all about me.

Then, staring across the yawning black gap of the dining saloon, I saw Rima, dishevelled, but adorably dishevelled, endeavouring to adjust a hastily grasped bathrobe. Her glance met mine from the opposite gallery.

"Oh, Shan!" she cried. "What's happened? I didn't get to sleep until about half an hour ago; I thought I heard knocking and voices…"

"I don't know, darling. I'm going to find out."

No sound came from the chief's cabin: doubtless he was fast asleep. Rima and I apparently were the only two passengers sufficiently curious about the stoppage of the engines to have left our rooms. As I joined her at the foot of the staircase the *Indramatra* got under way again but was putting about, as I could plainly detect.

"We're turning back!" exclaimed Rima. "Let's go up and see what's happening."

We went up, and having fought with the fastenings of the starboard door, finally got out on deck. The night was clear enough, and I could see no sign of any craft ahead.

We mounted the ladder to the boat deck. I saw the commander, a seaman of the old school, who, with his fine face and pointed gray beard, might have posed for Vandyck, going forward to the bridge, muffled in a top coat.

Holding Rima tightly as we craned over between two boats, I saw what had happened.

The seaplane floated on an oily swell about three lengths away from us. Assuming her to be in difficulties, the officer of the watch had put the ship about. And now, the *Indramatra*'s searchlight cast a sudden dazzling glare upon the sea; and I saw something else:

An object which looked like a big football was moving in the direction of the seaplane in the wake of a swimmer wearing a life jacket, who, striking out lustily, was apparently towing the ball behind him!

"Whatever's that?" Rima whispered.

From the bridge of the *Indramatra* came a roar through a megaphone; the commander doubtless: but since he spoke in Dutch, I could not follow his words. The engines were rung off again. We lay-to very near the sea-and-air craft; but no reply came from her crew.

The swimmer, towing his singular burden, grasped one of the floats. I saw that a ladder had been thrown down to assist him, and as I watched, he began to clamber up. At which moment:

"Greville!" came a hoarse voice. "What the hell's happening?"

I turned, still holding Rima tightly—and there was the chief, wrapped in his untidy dressing gown.

"I don't know," I replied. "But I'm glad you're here. I have news for you—"

Another challenge came from the bridge—and brought forth no response. The swimmer climbed on board the seaplane. All that I could make out of him was that he wore bathing kit and had a cap upon his head. The light touched him momentarily.

That object which resembled a football was hauled up; and, as we watched, I saw the propellers started. There was some commotion before they cleared away. Men were climbing aboard, clearly visible in the glare of the searchlight. Then the seaplane was off, skimming over the surface of the Mediterranean like a seagull; presently to take to the air, rise, bank sharply and sweep back for the coast of Egypt.

I heard, dimly, a bell, and the engines came to life again. The *Indramatra* was being put back on her course.

CHAPTER FORTY-TWO

THE PURSER'S SAFE

As we regained the main deck, it became evident that something extraordinary was afoot. The purser, in uniform, but wearing a white muffler in lieu of a collar, was standing by the door of his room with the second engineer and another officer. He looked very pale, I thought, and as Sir Lionel came in Voorden fixed a rather wild gaze upon him.

Before he had time to speak, the captain also hastily dressed, appeared from an alleyway and joined the group.

"Something's wrong!" Rima whispered.

A sort of embarrassed hush descended when we came down; then:

"Sir Lionel Barton, I believe?" said the captain, stepping forward. "Your name is well known in my country. But I have not before had the pleasure of meeting you. My name is Vanderhaye."

"How d'you do, Captain," growled the chief, and shook hands. "What's the trouble?"

The captain glanced at the purser and shrugged helplessly.

"I'm afraid, sir," said the latter, addressing Sir Lionel, "that you have suffered a heavy loss."

"What!"

"It is," explained Captain Vanderhaye, his steady blue eyes fixed upon the chief, "a case of minor piracy. Nothing of the kind has ever occurred to me in the forty years I have been at sea. I regret your loss. Sir Lionel, more deeply because it has happened in my ship. But here are the facts: you may judge if I or my officers are to blame."

He stepped to the door of the purser's room, which, as I saw now, was open, and indicated the keyhole with an outstretched finger. The chief, Rima and I, grouped around him, and as I bent forward I saw a really amazing thing.

Where the keyhole had been, as the fitting belonging to a brass flap clearly indicated, was a jagged hole, perhaps an inch and a half in diameter, going clean through the door!

It was sufficiently obvious that such a tunnel must have destroyed the lock, leaving the door at the mercy of any intruder.

"This," said the captain, "is strange enough. How such a thing could be done silently I cannot explain. But be good enough to step inside."

He entered the office. The chief's face was very grim, but, knowing him, I could see that he was stifling a smile. Rima stayed very close to me.

"Look!"

Captain Vanderhaye was pointing to the big safe. The pale-faced purser stood beside him, watching us almost pathetically. And, as I looked, I wondered; looking longer—my wonder grew.

In one hand the commander held a lock, with the other he pointed to a gap, roughly square and some six or seven inches across, in the steel door of the safe.

"This steel," he said, and tapped the lock, "has been cut through like a piece of cheese. No blow lamp could have been used—it would have taken too long and would have aroused some of the people in neighbouring cabins. But see—"

He ran his forefinger along the edge of the cut-out lock. The frayed steel crumbled away like biscuit!

Placing the lock on the purser's table, he shrugged his broad shoulders.

"It is magic!" he declared. "A safebreaker armed with some new thing of science. What can I say? He sprang overboard with his booty and was picked up by that strange seaplane." He swung the door widely open. "Look for yourselves. Nothing has been disturbed, except..."

"Your three sealed parcels, Sir Lionel," said the purser huskily, "which were here, in the bottom of the safe. They are gone!"

CHAPTER FORTY-THREE

THE VOICE IN BRUTON STREET

In the absence of Rima and the chief, the big gloomy house in Bruton Street overpowered me. But with characteristic disregard of my personal wishes Sir Lionel that morning had carried Rima off to Norfolk—true, for two days only. But London, much as I had longed to see it again, can be a lonely spot for a man with few friends.

By common consent, that most singular episode on the high seas had been hushed up as far as possible. It took its place, of course, in the ship's log.

Examination of the cabin occupied by the pseudo-Member of Parliament revealed the fact that two of his three trunks were empty, and that the third contained discarded clothing—and a pneumatic pump. A life jacket was missing from its place; and the crate which had once held the relics (broken open) was discovered in his bathroom. He had taken the precaution of examining this first, thereby exhibiting a knowledge of Sir Lionel's methods!

That the floating ball had contained the sealed packages stolen from the purser's safe was beyond dispute. He had brought this remarkable piece of equipment for that purpose. It was, I suppose, a large rubber bag in two sections which could be hermetically screwed together and then inflated by means of a pump, when, assuming its contents to be not too heavy, it would float.

The method employed in opening the safe, as the captain had said, was a new development in burglary. Later, looking back upon my profound mystification, the genius of Dr. Fu-Manchu has positively awed me; for I know now, although I did not know then, that he himself, with that sardonic humour peculiarly his own, had demonstrated this very process in that untraceable house outside Cairo!

Who was the man posing as "Mr. Kennington"?

Obviously his appearance was due to a cunning disguise. My impression of the swimmer who had climbed into the seaplane was that of a slender, athletic figure. He had been a wonderful actor, too, admirably chosen for his role, since by drawing attention to himself at the outset he had completely lulled everyone's suspicion—even deceiving Nayland Smith...

These queer memories often claimed my mind at the most unlikely moments. We had been absent from England more than a year and had brought back a stack of stuff to be disposed of and catalogued. This tedious business, the chief invariably left to me.

I was three deep in appointments with British Museum authorities, the Royal Society, and others too numerous to mention.

The bloodstained relics of Mokanna occupied a case to themselves in the famous Museum Room at Bruton Street. Sir Lionel had several properties in England, one of which, however, he had recently sold. His collection was distributed among the others, but the gems were in London.

Already, as I had anticipated, he had opened his campaign of publicity for the wedding. With characteristic disregard for the conventions, he had insisted that I must put up at his house. And during the past few days, almost every time I had gone out with Rima I had found our path beset by Press photographers. On more than one occasion I had bolted—to save myself from committing an assault.

Rima and the chief left by an eleven o'clock train for Norfolk, and, a busy day's work now concluded, I looked forward to a dull evening. However, by chance I picked up an old acquaintance at the club; we did a show together and then went on to supper, killing time quite agreeably. For a few hours, at any rate, I forgot my more or less constant longing for Rima.

She was already swamped in appointments with costumiers, hat makers, and others, and had gone to Norfolk to rest, specifying that she would be absent for only two days. She would have refused to go at all, I am sure, under ordinary circumstances; but Mrs. Petrie was meeting her there. Petrie and Sir Denis were already homeward bound, and the chief had planned the return to Norfolk to synchronise with their arrival in London.

If Sir Lionel ever enters paradise, it is beyond doubt that he will reorganise the angels…

I parted from my friend at the top of the Haymarket in the neighbourhood of one o'clock and decided to walk back to Bruton Street. As I set out, going along deserted Piccadilly, a panorama of the recent years unrolled itself before my mind. The giant shadow of Fu-Manchu lay over all my memories.

There had been a time, and this not so distant, when I should have hesitated to walk alone along Piccadilly at one o'clock in the morning; but in some queer fashion my feelings in regard to Dr. Fu-Manchu had undergone a change.

Since that unforgettable interview in the Great Pyramid, I had formed an impression of his greatness which, oddly enough, gave me a sense of security. This may be difficult to understand, but what I mean is that I believed him too big to glance aside at one so insignificant as myself. If ever I stood in his way, he would crush me without hesitation; at the moment he had nothing to gain by intruding upon my humble existence.

So I mused, staring about me as I walked. His resources, I realised, were enormous, apparently inexhaustible, as the daring robbery from the *Indramatra* on the high seas had shown; but the motive which had actuated this could inspire Dr. Fu-Manchu no longer.

There had been a short paragraph in *The Times* that morning (confirming the latest news from Sir Denis) which indicated that the Mokanna rising, or threat of a rising, sometimes referred to as the "Coming of the New Mahdi," had subsided almost as suddenly as it had arisen. The explanation of *The Times* correspondent was that the leader of the movement, whose identity remained unknown, had proved to be an impostor.

There was a fair amount of traffic in Piccadilly, but there were few pedestrians. I lighted my pipe. Crossing to the corner of Bond Street I saw a constable patiently testing the fastenings of shop doors. My thoughts flashed back to the many market streets of the East I had known...

I began to feel pleasantly sleepy. Another busy day was before me; the chief was preparing a paper dealing with Mokanna relics which he would read before the Royal Society. Embodying, as it did, the truth about the abortive rising of the Masked Prophet, it was calculated to create a tremendous sensation, doubtless involving Notes between the Persian Legation and the Foreign Office. This, of course, which any normal man must have wished to avoid, was frankincense and myrrh in the nostrils of Sir Lionel.

At eleven o'clock four famous experts had been invited to examine the relics: Hall-Ramsden of the British Museum; Dr. Brieux of Paris; Professor Max Eisner—Germany's greatest Orientalist; and Sir Wallace Syms of the Royal Society.

I think the chief's hasty departure had something to do with this engagement. He avoided his distinguished contemporaries as one avoids a pestilence. I had rarely known such a meeting which had not developed into a fight.

"Better wait for the Royal Society night, Greville," he had said. "Then I can go for the lot of 'em together!"

Turning into Bruton Street, I saw it deserted as far as Berkeley Square. Sir Lionel's house was one of the few not converted to commercial use; for this once favoured residential district is being rapidly absorbed into the shopping zone. He had had tempting offers for the property; but the mere fact that others were so anxious to buy was sufficient to ensure his refusal to sell. The gloomy old mansion, which he rarely occupied, but where a staff of servants was maintained, cost him somewhere in the neighbourhood of two thousand a year to keep empty.

I was in sight of the entrance, guarded by two miniature obelisks, and was already fumbling for my key when an odd thing occurred.

The adjoining house had been up for sale ever since I could remember. It was unoccupied and plastered all over with auctioneers' boards—a pathetically frequent sight in Mayfair. And as I passed the iron railing guarding the area of the basement—indeed, had my foot on Sir Lionel's steps—a voice called me by name…

"Shan!"

The voice came from the basement of the empty house!

It was a woman's voice; not loud, but appealing. My heart leapt wildly. In tone it was not unlike the voice of Rima!

I turned back, staring down into the darkness below. An illusion, I thought. Yet I could have sworn it was a human voice. And as I stood there looking down:

"Shan!" it came again, more faintly.

It chilled me! It was uncanny—but investigate I must. I looked up and down the street; not a soul was in sight. Then, pushing open the iron gate, I descended the steps to the little sunken forecourt.

There was no repetition of the sound, and it was very dark down there in the area. But I could see that a window of the empty house had been taken out, and it occurred to me that the call had come from someone inside. Standing by the frameless window:

"Who's there?" I cried.

There was no reply.

Yet I knew that a second time I could not have been mistaken.

Someone had called my name. I must learn the truth. My pipe gripped firmly between my teeth, and, ignoring accumulated dust on the ledge, I climbed over a low sill and dropped into the gloom of the deserted house. I put my hand into my topcoat pocket in search of matches.

CHAPTER FORTY-FOUR

"THIS WAS THE ONLY WAY..."

A paralysing grip seized my ankles; my arms were pinioned behind me, and an impalpable something was pressed over my mouth! I experienced a sudden sharp pain in my arm, as though something had seared the flesh. Then... I realised that, struggle as I might, I was helpless—helpless as a child!

That I had walked into a trap laid by common footpads was the thought that flashed across my mind. But the presence of a woman, of a woman who knew my name, promptly banished it. I had walked into a trap—yes! But the identity of the one who had baited that trap suddenly forced itself upon my brain with all the reality of a vision: long, narrow, brilliantly green eyes seemed to be looking into mine out of the darkness...

I was spurred to a great effort for safety. I exerted every nerve and sinew in a violent bid for liberty.

Good heavens! *what* was it that had me at its mercy! Surely no human hands gripped my ankles; no arms of flesh and blood could hold a struggling, muscular man, immovable!

Yet, so I was held—immovable! My strivings were utterly futile:

no sound of quickened breathing, nothing to show that my struggles inconvenienced these unseen captors. No flinching; no perceptible tremor of the hands—if hands they were—that had locked themselves about me.

I swore in an agony of furious impotence. But only a groan escaped from the pad held over my mouth. Then, I stood still— tensed nervously... The crowning strangeness of the thing had suddenly been borne home to me.

Held captive though I was, no attempt had been made on my personal possessions, no word had been spoken! Nothing had moved—nothing breathed. Indeed, although I stood but a few yards from a Mayfair street, there was something, awful in the stillness— something uncanny in the silent strength which held me. Doubts were dispelled; the cold water of nervous fear trickled down my spine. For what is more fearful than utter helplessness in the face of an enemy? I was afraid—grimly, dreadfully afraid.

I felt chilled, too, as though by the near presence of ice. The pad was not pressed so tightly over my mouth as to be stifling, but nevertheless I held my breath, listening. Save for the thumping of my heart, not a sound could I hear.

Then, from afar off, as though from a remote room of the empty house, came a voice—a wonderful and a strange voice, penetrating, sweet, and low; the voice of a woman. Although the speaker seemed to be far away—very far away—the impression was not as that of a loud voice heard in the distance; it was that of a soft, caressing voice which carried clearly every word to my ear, from some other place; almost from some other world.

"You have nothing to fear, Shan," it said. "No harm shall come to you. This was the only way."

The voice ceased... and then, I was free!

For several seconds, an unfamiliar numbness, the spell of the hidden speaker, lay upon me. I stood stock still, questioning my sanity. Then natural instincts reasserted themselves. I lashed out right and left, with hand and foot, might and main!

A gashed knuckle was my only reward—caused by a window casement. With fingers far from steady, at last I found the matches, struck one and looked quickly about me. I was alone!

The unsatisfactory light showed a large kitchen, practically stripped; a big, dirty cooking range at one end, torn wall paper, and general odds and ends upon the floor; an old whitewash pail in a corner—my pipe lying at my feet. Absolutely nothing else. I ran to the only door which I could see.

It was locked.

The cupboards!… both were empty!

My fourth match smouldered down to my fingers, and, as a man in a dream, I climbed out again into the well of the area, looking up at dirty vacant windows, plastered over with house agents' bills.

"What the devil!" I said aloud.

A voice answered from immediately above me.

"Hello, there!"

I turned with a start. It was a policeman—a real substantial constable; the same, I thought, whom I had seen examining shop doors in Bond Street.

"What's your game, eh?"

He was standing by the iron gate, looking down at me. My first impulse was to tell him the truth. I was conscious of a crying necessity for someone to confide in. Then, the thought of the question which had already flashed through my own mind restrained me: such a tale would be discredited by any, and by every policeman in the force.

"It's all right, constable," I said, going up the steps. "I thought I heard a row in this house, so I went in to investigate. But there seems to be no one there."

The man's attitude of suspicion relaxed when he had had a good look at me.

"I live next door," I went on, "and was just about to go in when I heard it."

"What sort of a row, sir?"

"Don't know exactly," I replied—"scuffling sounds."

The officer looked surprised.

"Can't be rats, can it?" he mused. "Been inside?"

"I looked in through that broken kitchen window."

"Nobody there?"

"No, nobody."

"Think I'll take a look round."

He went down the steps, shot a light into the broken window, and finally climbed over, as I had done. He examined the kitchen, trying the door which I knew to be locked; then:

"Must have been mistaken, sir," he said; "the place has been empty for years. But I believe it's been sold recently and is going to be converted into flats."

He walked up the steps and approached the front entrance, directing his light through the glass panels into an empty hallway, at the same time ringing the bell, though with what idea I was unable to conjecture.

"Nobody here," he concluded. "Nothing to make it worth anybody's while, is there?"

"I shouldn't think so," I agreed; and, entirely contrary to regulations, slipped a ten-shilling note into his hand. "Sorry I have been unable to find you a case, though."

"Right-ho!" the constable grinned; "better luck next time. Goodnight, sir."

"Goodnight," I said, taking out my key and opening Sir Lionel's door.

As I hung up my hat and coat I stood in the lobby trying to get my ideas into some kind of order. What, exactly, had happened?

Had I fallen victim to a delusion?—was my brain slightly out of gear? And if so, where had delusion ceased and actuality commenced? I had spoken to the constable; this was beyond dispute. But had I ever heard that strange voice? Had I ever been gripped as in a vice and listened to those words? And if I had, what did it all mean? Who could profit by it?

If, as I suspected—and the suspicion was abominable—we had blown the trumpet of triumph too soon, why should Fu-Manchu, or anyone associated with him, stoop to a meaningless practical joke?

I stared about the lobby with its curious decorations, and up the fine old staircase to where a row of Saracen armour stood on guard. The servants had long since retired, and there was not a sound to be heard in the house. Pushing open the dining-room door, I turned up one of the lights.

There was cold supper on the buffet, which Betts invariably placed there. I helped myself to a stiff whisky and soda, extinguished the light, and went upstairs.

Needless to say that I was badly shaken, mystified, utterly astounded. Aimlessly I opened the door of the Museum Room, turning up all the lamps.

Walking in, I dropped into one of the big settees, took a cigarette from a box which lay there, lighting it and staring about me. I was surrounded by the finest private collection of its kind in Great Britain. Sir Lionel's many donations to public institutions contained treasures enough, but here was the cream of a lifetime of research.

Directly facing me where I sat, in a small case which had been stripped for the purpose, were the fifteen gold plates of the New Koran mounted on little wooden easels; the mask above them, and the magnificent Sword of God suspended below. A table with paper, writing material, lenses, and other conveniences, was set not far away, in preparation for the visit of the experts in the morning.

And I sat, dully gazing at all this for fully five minutes—or so I estimated at the time.

As a matter of fact, I may have remained there longer; I have no recollection of going upstairs, but it is certain that I did not fall asleep in the Museum Room. I remember that a welcome drowsiness claimed me as I sat there, and I remember extinguishing my cigarette in an ashtray.

Of my movements from that point onward I retain no memory whatever!

CHAPTER FORTY-FIVE

MEMORY RETURNS

My next impression was of acute pain in both ankles. My head was swimming as after a wild night, and my eyelids seemed to be weighted with lead. I raised them, however, by what I felt to be a definite muscular effort. And, curious circumstances—very curious indeed, as I came to realise later—my brain immediately began to function from the last waking moment I have recorded; namely, from the moment when, seated in the Museum Room, I began to feel very drowsy.

My first thought now was that I had fallen asleep on the settee in some unnatural position, which might account for the pain in my ankles. I looked about me…

I was certainly lying on a divan, as I had supposed; but my ankles were fastened together by a single strand of that dull, yellowish-gray material resembling catgut, and no thicker than a violin string, which had played a part in the death of poor Dr. Van Berg in Ispahan!

My fragile bonds were fastened so tightly as to be painful, and I struggled to my feet. Wedging one foot firmly against the floor, I kicked forward with the other, supposing that the slender link would snap.

The result was that I kicked myself backwards!

I fell among the cushions of the divan, aware that I had badly strained a tendon. Helpless, bewildered, struggling with some memory ever growing, I lay where I had fallen, looking about me. And this was what I saw:

A long, low salon—that, I thought, of an old Egyptian house; parts of the walls were tiled, and a large *mushrabiyeh* window formed a recess at one end. there were some rugs upon the floor, and the room was lighted by a number of lamps having shades of a Chinese pattern which swung from the wooden ceiling. The furniture, scanty, was of mixed Arab and Chinese character. There were deep bookcases laden with volumes in most unfamiliar bindings as well as a number of glass cabinets containing most singular objects.

In one was something which at first I took to be a human head, that of a woman. But, focusing my gaze upon it, I realised that it was an unusually perfect mummy head. In another were some small green snakes, alive. I saw a human skeleton; and in a kind of miniature conservatory which occupied the recess formed by the *mushrabiyeh* window, queer-looking orchids, livid and ugly, were growing.

A definite conviction claimed my mind that I had been in this room before. But—perhaps the most remarkable feature of the experience—it reached my brain in just the same way that such impressions reach us in everyday life. I thought, "This has all happened before." The only difference was that my prophetic anticipations lasted much longer than is normally the case.

Upon a long, wooden table, resembling a monkish refectory table, lay a number of open volumes among test tubes and other scientific paraphernalia. Standing up, I saw that the table was covered with glass.

Then, turning around, I realised that in many other cabinets hitherto invisible were rows of chemical bottles and apparatus. I was, then, in a room which was at least partly a laboratory; for in one corner I saw a working bench with electrical fittings. There were three doors to the room, of old, bleached teak. They possessed some peculiarity which puzzled me, until I recognized wherein it lay:

These doors had neither latches, handles, nor keyholes. And as I grasped this curious fact, one of them slipped noiselessly open.

And Dr. Fu-Manchu came in…

All who have followed my attempts to record the strange and tragic events which followed upon Sir Lionel Barton's discovery of the tomb of El Mokanna, will recognise at this point something which I was totally unable to recognise at the time:

I was living again through that hiatus in Cairo; bridging the gap which led to the loss of Rima! That everything in the room, every word spoken by the Chinese doctor, seemed familiar, was natural enough; since I had seen those things and heard those words before.

Again that compelling glance absorbed me. The green, globular lamp upon a silver pedestal was lighted on the long table. And I watched the Chinaman, with long, flexible, bony fingers, examining the progress of some chemical experiment in which he had evidently been engaged at the time of quitting the room.

He spoke to me of this experiment and of others; of the new anaesthetic prepared from mimosa; of the fabrication of spider web—a substance stronger than any known to commerce. He discussed his daughter, Nayland Smith, and Dr. Petrie; and he spoke of the essential oil of a rare orchid found in Burma, which for twenty-five years he had studied in quest of what the old philosophers called the elixir of life.

And I knew, watching him, that he had thrown off the burden of many years, had cheated man's chiefest enemy—Time.

He went on to criticise the chief, stripping him bare of all his glamour, placing his good qualities in the scale against the colossal egoism of the man. "You love a shell," he said, "an accomplishment, a genius, if you like, but a phantom, a hollow thing, having no real existence."

So it went on to the point where I was forced to submit to an injection of that strange new drug in which the Chinese doctor evidently took such pride.

I experienced a sudden and unfamiliar glow throughout my entire body. I became exhilarated; some added clarity of vision came to me. And presently I took my orders from Dr. Fu-Manchu as a keen subaltern takes orders from his colonel.

Exulting in the knowledge that by reason of my association with the great Chinese physician, I was above the trivialities of common humanity, god-like, superior, all-embracing, I set out for Shepheard's—intent only upon bringing Rima within the fold of this all-powerful genius.

When we pulled up opposite the hotel, and the driver had run across with my note, I knew a fever of impatience—I could scarcely contain myself. But at last I saw her come out, my letter in her hand, saw her run down the steps.

Then, we were together, and my heart was singing with gladness... I was taking her to Dr. Fu-Manchu!

She could not understand; I knew that she could never understand until she had stood face to face with that great and wonderful man, as I had done.

And at first I tried to pacify her, holding her very close. She fought with me, and even endeavoured to attract the attention of a British policeman. But at last she lay passive in my arms, watching me. And I grew very uneasy.

I was assailed by odd doubts. We were far out on the road to Gizeh when suddenly the car pulled up. I saw Dr. Fu-Manchu standing beside me.

"You have done well," he said; "you may rest now…"

CHAPTER FORTY-SIX

FAH LO SUEE

"Shan, dear, I know you are very sleepy, but it's getting cold and late, too."

I stirred lazily, opening my eyes. I was pillowed on a warm shoulder, a bare arm encircling my neck. That silvery voice had awakened me. A long jade earring touched my cheek coldly, and caressing fingers stroked my hair.

Yes! I was with Fah Lo Suee, somewhere on the banks of the Nile. And I was content—utterly, rapturously content.

"Love dreams are bitter-sweet, Shan, because we know we are dreaming…"

I could see a long reach of the river, silver under the moon, dahabeahs moored against the left bank, where groups of palms formed a background for their slender, graceful masts.

"I think someone has been watching, Shan; I am going to drive you back to Shepheard's now."

And as she drove, I watched the delicate profile of the driver. She was very beautiful, I thought. How wonderful to have won the love of such a woman. She linked her arms about me and crushed her lips against mine, her long, narrow eyes closed.

In the complete surrender of that embrace I experienced a mad triumph, in which Rima, Nayland Smith, the chief, all, were forgotten.

CHAPTER FORTY-SEVEN

IVORY HANDS

I closed my eyes again, pressing my face against that satin pillow. I felt I could have stayed there forever.

"You know, Shan," Fah Lo Suee's voice went on—that silvery voice in which I seemed to hear the note of a bell—"you have often hated me and you will hate me again."

"I could never hate you," I said drowsily.

"I have tricked you many times; for, although I love you, Shan, you are really not very clever."

"Cleverer men than I would give all for your kisses," I whispered.

"That is true," she replied, without vanity; for with much of his powerful brain she had also inherited from the Chinese doctor a philosophy by virtue of which she judged herself equally with others. "But I find hatred hard to accept."

I kept my eyes obstinately closed. Some vague idea was stirring in my brain that when I opened them that act would herald the end of this delicious interlude.

She was so slender—so exquisite—her personality enveloped me like a perfume.

"I have given you back the memory of forgotten hours, Shan. There is no disloyalty in what I have done. Your memories can only tell you again what you know already: that my father is the greatest genius the world has ever known. The old house at Gizeh is deserted again, even if you could find it. Your other memories are of me."

I clutched her tightly.

"Why should you leave me?"

She clung to me for a moment, and I could hear her heart beating; then:

"Because the false is valueless to me, and the true I can never have."

The words were so strangely spoken, in so strange a voice, that at last I opened my eyes again... and, astounded, broke free from Fah Lo Suee's clinging arms and stared about me. I was in the Museum Room in Bruton Street!

A silk dressing gown I had over my pyjamas; a pair of Arab slippers were on my feet. Fah Lo Suee, in a pale green frock which did full justice to her perfect back and shoulders, was lying among the cushions beside me, her fur coat on the floor near by.

She was watching me under half-lowered lashes—doubting me, it would seem. There was more of appeal than command in those emerald green, long, wonderful eyes. Staring about the room, I saw everything was as I had left it; and:

"Well?" Fah Lo Suee murmured, continuing to watch me.

I turned and looked down at her where she lay.

And, as her glance met mine, I was claimed, submerged, swept away by such a wave of desire for this woman as I had never known for anyone in the whole of my life. I dropped to the floor, clasping her knees.

"You cannot—you must not—you dare not go!"

Her lips rippled in a smile—those perfect lips which I realised I adored; and then very wistfully:

"If only that were true!" she murmured.

"But it is!" I knelt upon the settee, grasping her fiercely, and looking into those eyes which beckoned to me—beckoned to me... "Why do you say that? How can you doubt it?"

But she continued to smile.

And then, as I stooped to kiss her, she thrust her hands, slender, exquisite ivory hands against me, and pushed me back. I would have resisted—

"*Shan!*" she said.

And although the word was spoken as an appeal, yet it was a command; and a command which I obeyed. Yes, she was right. There was some reason—some reason, which escaped me—why we must part. I clutched my head feverishly, thinking—thinking. What could that reason be?

"I am going, dear. You mustn't come down to the door—I know my way."

But I sprang up. She had stooped and was taking up her cloak. Mechanically, I slipped it about her shoulders. She leaned back as I did so and submitted to my frenzied kisses. At last, releasing herself, and pulling the cloak about her slim body:

"Goodbye, Shan dear," she said, brokenly, but with a determination which I knew I had no power to weaken. "Please go back to bed—and go to sleep."

Hot tears burned behind my eyes. I felt that life had nothing left for me. But—I obeyed.

Passing out onto the landing where suits of Saracen armour stood on guard, I watched Fah Lo Suee descend the broad staircase. A light burned in the lobby, as was customary, and, reaching the foot of the stairs, she turned.

With one slender, unforgettable, indolent hand, she beckoned to me imperiously.

I obeyed her order—I moved towards the staircase leading to the floor above. I had begun to go up when I heard the street door close…

CHAPTER FORTY-EIGHT

I REALLY AWAKEN

"Nine o'clock, sir. Are you ready for your tea?"

I opened my eyes and stared into the face of Betts. Upon a salver he carried the morning papers and a pile of correspondence. Placing them upon the table, he crossed and drew back the curtains before the windows.

"A beautiful morning again, sir," he went on; I hope this will continue until the happy day."

I sat up.

"Shall I bring your tea, sir?"

"Yes, please do."

As that venerable old scoundrel, whose job was one of those which every butler is looking for, went out of the room, I stared about me in search of my dressing gown.

There it was, thrown over the back of an armchair—upon which also I saw my dress clothes. I jumped out of bed, put on the old Arab slippers, and then the dressing gown.

Never in my life had I been visited by so singular, so vivid a dream… a dream? Where had dreaming left off? I must make notes while the facts were clear in my memory.

I went out and down to the library; grabbed a writing pad and a pencil. I was on the point of returning upstairs when that query, "Where had dreaming left off?" presented itself in a new aspect.

Dropping pad and pencil, I hurried along the gallery and into the Museum Room...

I could not forget that Petrie, that man of scientific mind, had once endeavoured to shoot his oldest friend, Sir Denis, under some damnable influence controlled by Dr. Fu-Manchu. And had I not myself seen Rima, actuated by the same unholy power, obeying the deathly orders of Fah Lo Suee?

The Museum Room looked exactly as I had left it—except that Betts, or one of the maids, had cleaned the ash tray in which I remembered having placed the stub of a cigarette. The table prepared for my eleven o'clock appointment was in order. Everything was in order.

And—that which above all engaged my particular attention—the small case containing the relics of Mokanna showed no signs of disturbance. There were the mask, the plates, and the sword.

I returned to the library for pencil and writing pad. If I had dreamed, it had been a clairvoyant dream, vivid as an actual experience. It had given me certain knowledge which might prove invaluable to Nayland Smith.

Perhaps analysis of that piece of slender twine which I knew was in Sir Denis's possession would show it to be indeed composed of spider web. I wondered if the mystery of the forcing of the safe on the *Indramatra* had been solved for me. And I wondered if the liquid smelling strongly of mimosa which still remained in that spray found upon the dead Negro in Ispahan would respond to any test known to science?

Strangest fact of all, I loathed the memory of Fah Lo Suee!

I was ashamed, humiliated, utterly overcome by those dream recollections. I had desired her, adored her, covered her with kisses. While now—my true, waking self—I knew that there was only one woman in all the world for me... and that woman was Rima!

CHAPTER FORTY-NINE

A COMMITTEE OF EXPERTS

Professor Eisner was the first of the experts to arrive. I knew his name, of course, but he himself proved something of a surprise. He had iron-gray hair cut close to a very fine skull, and wore a small monocle. He was otherwise clean-shaven, presenting in his walk, his build, his manner, an Englishman's conception of the typical Prussian cavalry officer.

He was shown into the big Syrian room on the ground floor, where suitable refreshments had been prepared by Betts, and proved on acquaintance to be a charming as well as a clever man.

Then came the Frenchman, Dr. Brieux, a very different type. He wore a caped overcoat and a large black soft hat. I saw him approaching from the window, as a matter of fact, and predicted to myself that he would stop at the door and ring the bell. I was right. Here was the traditional scholar—stooping, with high, bald brow, scanty white hair and beard, and large, horn-rimmed glasses.

He greeted Professor Eisner very coldly. I didn't know it at the time, but they held directly opposite views regarding the date when the Khuld Palace in Old Baghdad was deserted in favour of the

Palace of the Golden Gate. A heated controversy had raged in the learned journals between these two distinguished Orientalists. I fear I had overlooked this.

I know and love the Near East and its peoples; their arts and crafts, and the details of their domestic life. But this hair-splitting on a matter of dates is something quite outside my province.

The learned Englishmen were late: they arrived together; and I was glad of their arrival. Professor Eisner was sipping a glass of the chief's magnificent old sherry and nibbling some sort of savoury provided by Betts; Dr. Brieux, hands behind him, was staring out of the window, his back ostentatiously turned to his German confrère.

When Mr. Hall-Ramsden of the British Museum and Sir Wallace Syms of the Royal Society had chatted for a time with the distinguished visitors, I led the way upstairs to the Museum Room.

As I have mentioned I had prepared everything early the night before. My notes, a map of our route, a diary covering the period we had spent in the Place of the Great Magician, and one or two minor objects discovered in the tomb of the prophet, were ready upon the table.

At all costs (such were the chief's instructions) I had to avoid giving away any of the dramatic points—he had made a list of them—which he proposed to spring upon the Royal Society.

This was not in the remotest degree my kind of job. I hated it from the word Go! The dream or vision which had disturbed my sleep during the night continued to haunt me. I was uncertain of myself—uncertain that the whole episode was not some damnable aftermath to that drug which had taken toll of several hours of my life in Cairo.

At the best of times I should have been ill at ease, but on this occasion I was doubly so. However, I attacked the business.

Removing the mask, the plates, and the sword from the cabinet in which they rested, I placed them upon the big table.

Professor Eisner claimed the gold plates with a motion resembling that of a hawk swooping upon its prey. Dr. Brieux took up the mask between delicate, nervous fingers, and peered at it closely through the powerful lenses of his spectacles. Hall-Ramsden and Sir Wallace Syms bent over the Sword of God.

I glanced at my notes, and, realising that nobody was listening to me, intoned the situation, condition, external appearance, and so forth, of the half-buried ruin which had been the tomb of the Mokanna. Finally:

"Here are the photographs to which I have referred, gentlemen," I said, opening a portfolio containing more than three hundred photographs taken by Rima. "If any questions occur to you, I shall be glad in Sir Lionel's absence to answer them to the best of my ability."

I had gone through this painful duty quite automatically. Now, I had time to observe the four specialists. And looking at them where they sat around the big table, I sensed at once a queer atmosphere.

Mr. Hall-Ramsden glanced at me furtively, but catching my eye resumed a muttered colloquy with Sir Wallace Syms. Professor Eisner and Dr. Brieux seemed to have discovered common ground. The doctor, holding up the mask, was talking with tremendous rapidity, and the professor, alternately tapping the plates and pointing to the sword seemed to be agreeing, judging from his short ejaculations of "*Ja, ja!*"

"Can I assist you in any way, gentlemen?" I asked somewhat irritably.

As the chief officer of the expedition which had discovered the relics, I felt that I was receiving scant courtesy. But, as I spoke, four pairs of eyes were turned upon me.

There came a moment of silence, as I looked from face to face; and then it was the German professor who spoke:

"Mr. Greville," he said, "I understand that you were present when Sir Lionel Barton opened the tomb of El Mokanna?"

"Certainly I was present, Professor."

"This was what I understood." He nodded slowly. "Were you actually present at the time that these relics were unearthed?"

His inquiry was made in a way kindly enough, but it jagged me horribly. I looked from face to face, meeting with nothing but unfathomable glances.

"Your question is a strange one," I replied slowly. "Ali Mahmoud, the headman in charge of our party, was actually first among us to see anything of the relics: he saw a corner of one of those gold plates. I was the first to see an entire plate (I think it was ninth in the series, as a matter of fact). Sir Lionel, and Rima, his niece, as well as the late Dr. Van Berg, were present when the treasure was brought to light."

Professor Eisner had a habit of closing his left eye; betokening concentration, no doubt; and, now, his right eye—a cold blue eye—focused upon me through the little monocle, registered something between incredulity, amusement and pity.

Sir Wallace I knew for an avowed enemy of the chief. Regarding Hall-Ramsden's attitude, I knew nothing. Of Professor Eisner Sir Lionel had always spoken favourably, but I was aware that he regarded Dr. Brieux as a mere impostor.

But now, under the gaze of that magnified blue eye, I realised that the authenticity of these treasures, which had nearly led to a Holy War in the East, was being questioned by the four men seated about the table!

Instantly I pictured the scene if Sir Lionel had been present! Hall-

Ramsden might have put up a show, and the German looked like a man of his hands: but as for the other two, I was confident that they would have been thrown bodily downstairs...

"Gentlemen," I said, "you seem to share some common opinion about the relics of El Mokanna. I should be glad to know your views."

A further exchange of glances followed. I realised that in some way my words had created embarrassment. Finally, having cleared his throat, it was Hall-Ramsden who answered me.

"Mr. Greville," he said, "I have heard you well spoken of, and, personally, I should not think of doubting your integrity. Sir Lionel Barton—" he cleared his throat again—"as an Orientalist of international reputation, is naturally above suspicion."

Dr. Brieux blew his nose.

"Since it has been arranged for Sir Lionel to address the Royal Society next Thursday on the subject"—he extended his hand towards the objects on the table—"of these relics, I recognise, of course—we all recognise—that there must be some strange mistake, or else..."

He hesitated, glancing about as if to seek help from one of his confrères.

"That Barton," Sir Wallace Syms continued—"whose sense of humour sometimes betrays him—has seen fit to play a joke upon us!"

By this time I was thoroughly angry.

"What the devil do you mean. Sir Wallace?" I asked.

My anger had one immediate effect. Professor Eisner stood up and approached me, putting his arm about my shoulders.

"My young friend," he explained, "something has gone wrong. It will all be explained, no doubt. But be calm."

His manner quietened me. I recognized its sincerity. And, giving me a kind of final reassuring hug:

"I shall not be surprised to hear," he went on, "that you have not examined these relics recently. Eh?"

"Not," I admitted, "since they were put in the case."

"Since you placed them in the case, eh? Now, you have already a considerable reputation, Mr. Greville. I have talked with you, and you know your subject. Before we say any more, please to look at this sword."

He stepped to the table, took up the Sword of God, returned, and handed it to me. My anger was still simmering as I took the thing up and glanced at it. Having done so:

"Well," I replied, "I have looked. What do you expect me to say?"

"To say nothing—yet." Again that reassuring arm was around my shoulders. "But to look, examine carefully—"

"It's simply absurd!" came the voice of Dr. Brieux.

"If you please!" snapped the Professor sharply—"if you please! What you have to say, Doctor can wait for a moment."

Amid a silence which vibrated with hostility, I examined the blade in my hand. And I suppose, as I did so, my expression changed.

"Ah! you see, eh?" said the German.

And while I stared with horrified eyes at the blade, the inlay, the hilt, he had darted to the table, almost immediately to return with one of the gold plates. Relieving me of the sword, he placed the inscribed tablet in my hands.

"It is beautifully done!" He almost whispered the words, very close to my ear; "and rubbed down very fine. But look…"

He held a glass before my eye—one of those which I had provided for this very purpose.

I looked—and I knew!

Tossing the plate down, I faced the three men around the table. Professor Eisner remained beside me.

"Gentlemen," I said—"my apologies. I can only ask you to remain silent until this mystery has been cleared up. I will try, to the best of my ability, to explain."

The sword, the plates, and the mask, which I had exhibited to these four experts, were, beyond any shadow of doubt, *the duplicates made by Solomon Ishak...*

CHAPTER FIFTY

DR. FU-MANCHU TRIUMPHS

Thanks to Rima's photographs, I proved my case. The blade of the sword, as I realised, had been provided by Soloman Ishak. It closely resembled the sword of the prophet, but differed in several essential particulars.

The stones in the hilt (the hilt had been reproduced exactly) were genuine and must have cost the chief some hundreds of pounds; but they were much smaller than those shown in the photograph; and some of them badly flawed.

Under a powerful lens the plates shrieked forgery aloud. I learned later that they had been photographed from Rima's negatives onto the gold and then engraved by Solomon's workmen. Closely examined, the newly cut gold betrayed the secret.

The mask was the most perfect duplicate I have ever handled; but the two large jewels were reconstructed; and the delicate engravery, magnified, betrayed itself in the same way as that upon the plates.

However, a friendly atmosphere was re-established before the party broke up. I had admitted—could see no alternative—that Sir Lionel had a duplicate set made in Persia. And it was obvious that this was the set which now lay upon the table.

When and where the substitution had taken place, I left to the imagination of my visitors. They were sympathetic in a way, but the Englishmen were laughing at me; and the Frenchman, who had come from Paris especially to view the relics, was very plainly annoyed.

Professor Eisner alone seemed to understand and to sympathise. He was the last to leave, and:

"Mr. Greville," he said in parting, "Sir Lionel Barton has touched deep, secret influences in this matter. He has been clever—very clever; but they have been more clever still. Eh? You will find out one day when this trick was done."

But as from the window I watched him swinging down Bruton Street with the walk of a dragoon, I knew that I had nothing to find out. I already knew where dreaming had ended and reality had begun. And I knew why Fah Lo Suee had whispered: "You will live to hate me…"

I was still trying to get a call through to the chief, whose Norfolk number was a private extension, when Betts came in and announced:

"Sir Denis Nayland Smith and Dr. Petrie, sir."

I hung up the receiver and positively sprang to meet them. They were waiting for me in the room on the left of the lobby, the room in which I had received my learned visitors that morning. I suppose my expression must have betrayed me, for I saw, as I ran in, that both had sensed the fact that there was something wrong.

"What is it, Greville?" snapped Nayland Smith—"Barton? Rima?"

"Both safe," I replied. "This is a delightful surprise! You are a whole day ahead of your schedule!"

"Flew from Marseilles," said Sir Denis.

"But something is wrong with you," Dr. Petrie declared, holding onto my hand and looking at me searchingly.

I nodded, smiling, although I was far from mirthful.

"Suppose you prescribe a drink, Doctor!" I suggested; "I feel badly shot away. Then I will try to explain the position."

It occupied me longer than I could have supposed; involving as it did an account of what had happened since I had parted from my friend on the previous night, right up to my recent interview with the four experts.

Long before I had reached the end of it, Nayland Smith was pacing up and down the room in his restless fashion, having relighted his pipe three or four times. But at last, when that strange story was ended:

"Amazing," he snapped, "but ghastly." He turned to Petrie. "I told you that Fu-Manchu would be in England ahead of us."

"You did," the doctor agreed.

"He is here?" I exclaimed.

"Undoubtedly, Greville. He keeps a close watch upon his beautiful daughter! Your dream, as it seemed to you, was of course no dream at all. You were subjected last night, in the basement of the adjoining house, to the treatment referred to by Dr. Fu-Manchu; an injection in your arm. Petrie can probably discover the mark. Eh, Petrie?"

"Possibly," the doctor replied guardedly. "But I can make an examination later, Smith. Please carry on."

"Very well. Later, you were given that 'simple antidote' which he mentioned. You remember now those lost hours in Cairo. And some of your memories, Greville, are most illuminating. I can see Hewlett and myself searching the Sukkariya quarter, when actually the house for which we were looking was somewhere out at Gizeh!

"The drug used by Fu-Manchu (obviously that mentioned by McGovem) renders the subject peculiarly susceptible to suggestion. I suppose you appreciate that you had your instructions from Fah Lo

Suee, who was awaiting your return in the adjoining empty house, to open the door for her at a specified time?"

"I *must* have opened it," I returned blankly; "for, otherwise, how did she get in?"

"You certainly *did* open it; just as certainly as you once aided in the abduction of Rima from Shepheard's in Cairo!

"She substituted the duplicates, which of course she had brought with her, for the real relics, and presumably handed the latter to an accomplice in waiting. The phase which followed, Greville—" he smiled that inimitable smile—"is one which I prefer to forget."

"Let's all agree to forget it," said Petrie.

"Dr. Fu-Manchu is the greatest master of drugs this old world of ours has ever known. His daughter is an apt pupil. I believe she has a sincere affection for you, Greville—God knows why! But, since you did not dream, we have the word of Fu-Manchu that no harm will come to you. Frankly, I think Barton has got off lightly—"

"So do I!" Petrie interrupted again.

"After all, even in this stage of laxity, there are things which are not done. The word of a prison governor to a convict is as sacred as any man's word to any other man; and according to my view, which may be peculiar, Barton doubled on Dr. Fu-Manchu. I believe that super-devil to be too great a character to waste a moment upon revenge. But in the circumstances, Greville, if you don't mind, I should like to get through to Sir Lionel—and there's someone there whom Petrie is dying to speak to…"

CHAPTER FIFTY-ONE

WEDDING MORNING

U pon the events of the next few days I prefer not to dwell. At my first interview with Sir Lionel following the loss of the relics of the Masked Prophet, I believed for one hectic moment that he would attempt to strangle me with his own hands.

Perhaps it was the presence of Nayland Smith, alone, which prevented him from making an assault. I can see him now, pacing up and down the Museum Room, clenching and relaxing his big fists, and looking murder from underneath tufted eyebrows.

"No possible blame attaches to Greville," said Sir Denis.

The chief growled inarticulately.

"And I would remind you that in somewhat similar circumstances, and not long ago, you personally assisted the same lady to open the Tomb of the Black Ape, in the Valley of the Kings, and to walk away with its contents. Rather a good parallel, I think?"

Sir Lionel stood still, staring hard at the speaker, then:

"Damn it!" he admitted—"you're right!"

He transferred his stare to Petrie, and finally to me.

"Forget my somewhat harsh criticisms, Greville," he said.

"Unlike Smith, I often say more than I mean. But this cancellation of my address to the Royal Society is going to set poisoned tongues wagging."

This was true enough. Not only had he been deprived of that hour of triumph in anticipation of which he had lived for many months past, but unpleasant whispers were going around the more scholarly clubs. Scotland Yard, working secretly, had put its vast machinery in motion in an endeavour to trace Fah Lo Suee.

They failed, as indeed we all knew they must fail. Servants of Dr. Fu-Manchu perused secret avenues of travel upon which the Customs and the police apparently had no check. There was theory held at Scotland Yard, and shared, I believe, by our old friend Weymouth, that the Chinese doctor worked in concert with what is known as the "underworld".

This theory Nayland Smith declined to entertain.

"His organisation is infinitely superior to anything established among the criminal classes," he declared. "He would not stoop to use such instruments."

However, the chief's resiliency of character was not the least amazing of his attributes; and within forty-eight hours he was deep in a book dealing with the Masked Prophet, of which he designed to publish a limited edition, illustrated by selected photographs of Rima's.

"I don't know why I allow you to issue your rotten accounts of my expeditions, Greville!" he shouted one day, when I entered the library and found him at work.

He was surrounded by masses of records and untidy heaps of manuscript notes, portfolios, and what-not. Two shorthand typists were in attendance.

"Their scientific value is nil, and they depict me personally as a cross between a large ape and a human half-wit…"

In the meantime he had relaxed no jot of his publicity campaign upon my wedding, to which an added piquancy was given by what happened at the Athenaeum Club.

Following a heated argument there with Sir Wallace Syms, the chief challenged him to a duel within hearing of fully twelve members!

This resulted in a crop of spicy paragraphs, practically all of which included a reference to the forthcoming ceremony at St. Margaret's. My horror of this ceremony grew with almost every passing hour.

I had been pestered by interviewers and gossip writers for particulars of my family history, my interests in sport, and other purely personal matters, until I was reduced to a state of nerves as bad as anything I had known in the most evil times of the past.

A popular debutante two years before, Rima had spent one hectic season in London under the wing of Lady Ettrington, Sir Lionel's younger sister and a chip of the old block whom I wholeheartedly detested.

Rima's decision to abandon society and to join her eccentric uncle in the capacity of photographer had bought down upon her head the wrath of Lady Ettrington. Her later decision to marry me, instead of some society idler, had resulted in my name being written in large letters in her ladyship's Black Book.

The apartment once known as the breakfast room at Bruton Street, but which the chief had had converted into a sort of overflow library, was rapidly filling up with wedding presents. Rima's waking hours were distributed between hat shops, hairdressing establishments, and modistes.

Sometimes she would meet me for lunch, at other times she was too busy. Women, however, never seem to tire under this particular kind of stress. One such day would have exhausted me. Of presents to the bridegroom there were notably few. Such friends as I had were distributed all over the world.

Among all this fuss and bother and the twittering of Rima's bridesmaids (only two of whom I had ever met before), I felt a good deal of an outsider. To me the whole thing was unspeakably idiotic—a waste of time and as utterly undignified an exhibition as only a spectacular wedding can offer.

The chief, however, was enjoying himself to the top of his bent, sparing no expense to make the entertainment a popular one. The number of people who had accepted invitations appalled me.

I knew many of them by name, but few of them personally; and in cold print it appeared that the bridegroom would be the least distinguished person present at the church.

In many respects those days were the worst I have ever lived through...

But I moved under a cloud. Since the loss of the relics I had felt in some indefinable way that of actual danger from Dr. Fu-Manchu there was none. His last project had failed; but I was convinced that failure and success alike left him unmoved. Over and over again I discussed the matter with Nayland Smith and Petrie, and with Superintendent Weymouth, who had been staying somewhere in the Midlands but who was now back in London prior to returning to Cairo.

"In the old days," he said on one occasion, "Fu-Manchu was operating under cover, and he stuck at nothing to get rid of those who picked up any clue to his plans. From what you tell me now it appears that in this last job he had nothing to hide."

This, then, was not the shadow which haunted me: it was the memory of Fah Lo Suee...

To what extent aided by those strange drugs of which her father alone possessed the secret I was unable to decide, but definitely she had power to throw some sort of spell upon me, under which I became her helpless slave. Rima knew something, but not all, of the truth.

She knew that I had followed Fah Lo Suee from Shepheard's that night in Cairo, but of what had happened later she knew nothing; nor of what had happened in Bruton Street.

But something there was which she knew and had known from the first: that Fah Lo Suee possessed a snake-like fascination to which I, perhaps any man, was liable to succumb. And she knew that this incalculable woman experienced a kind of feline passion for me.

Often, when we had been separated, I surprised a question in her eyes. Perhaps she knew that I dreaded meeting Fu-Manchu's daughter as greatly as she dreaded it herself.

And all the time, while I looked on, feeling like a complete stranger, arrangements for the wedding proceeded. Sir Lionel dictated chapter after chapter of his book, and at the same time several papers to scientific publications which he occasionally favoured with contributions; interviewed representatives of the Press, quarrelled with the caterers responsible for the reception; wrote insulting letters to *The Times*; in short, thoroughly enjoyed himself.

I pointed out to him, one day, that since Rima and I would have to live upon my comparatively slender income, our married life would be something of an anti-climax to our wedding.

"You've got a good job!" he shouted. "Damn it! I pay you a thousand a year!—and you must make something out of your ridiculous books!"

The discussion was not carried any further. I realised that it was one I should never have begun.

I had his sister Lady Ettrington to cope with, also. She issued an ultimatum to the effect that she would not be present in the church unless it was arranged that I took up my residence elsewhere than under the same roof as her niece Rima.

This led to a tremendous row between brother and sister. It took place in the room where the presents were assembled: a draw, in which both parties exhibited the celebrated Barton temperament in its most lurid form.

"You can go to the devil!" was Sir Lionel's final politeness. "As to being in the church, personally I don't remember having invited you..."

It had all blown over, however, which was the way with storms in this peculiar family; and being awakened by Betts one morning, that privileged old idiot opened the curtains and announced:

"The happy day has arrived, sir..."

CHAPTER FIFTY-TWO

DR. FU-MANCHU BOWS

Not being a society reporter, the wedding at St. Margaret's must be taken for granted in this account. Suffice to say that it duly took place.

My best man was first rate, and Rima looked so lovely that I was almost reconciled to this dreadful occasion. The crowd inside the church was small in comparison with the crowd outside. Sir Lionel's gift of showmanship would have put C.B. Cochran out of business, had the chief decided to plunge into the theatrical sphere.

He sailed into the church through a solid avenue of humanity with that dainty bride on his arm, smiling cheerfully, right and left, as who should say, "What did I tell you? Isn't she a beauty?"

My own entrance took place in a sort of merciful haze, out of which, dimly, I heard reassuring words from my best man. The ceremony itself stunned me.

I am no believer in the marriage service, and neither is Sir Lionel. He would not for the price of a kingdom have taken those awful vows demanded by the priest, but he thoroughly enjoyed hearing me commit myself to that which he would never have undertaken.

When we came out again into the sunshine (as the sentimental Betts had prayed this was a glorious day) a battery of cameras awaited us.

We escaped finally in a Rolls two-seater—one of Sir Lionel's presents to the bride—in which he had insisted we must drive away, although frankly I was in no fit condition for the job.

However, I managed it without mishap—to find a second camera battery awaiting us in Bruton Street...

Inside the house I found myself lost in a maze of unfamiliar faces. It was like a first night at a London theatre. Even the servants were strangers, many of them, although Sir Lionel had reinforcements there from other of his establishments.

One fleeting glimpse I had of Petrie's beautiful wife. She waved to me from a distant corner and then disappeared before I could reach her. A queer situation: I was the cause, the centre, of this gathering—and I didn't seem to know a soul!

The room containing the wedding presents looked promising. I saw Betts there presiding over a sort of extemporised snack-bar. I also saw a detective whom I had chanced to meet in London two years before. He winked at me solemnly—the first man I had recognized at my own wedding reception.

It was one of the queerest experiences of my life. And, owing to my association with Sir Lionel, my days had been far from humdrum.

Exactly what occurred in the interval preceding that strange intrusion which must form the end of this chronicle I cannot definitely state. At one moment I was with Rima; in the next I had lost her... I exchanged greetings with Nayland Smith—and then found myself talking to a perfect stranger... Petrie expressed a wish to drink my health... and we were separated on our way to the buffet...

Over the heads of a group of perfect strangers I presently caught the eye of Betts. He signaled to me.

I extricated myself from the crowd and joined him.

"A somewhat belated visitor, sir, wishes to add his congratulations on this happy day."

"Who is he, Betts?"

Betts extended a salver, with a perfect gesture. Jostled on all sides, I took up a card, and read:

Dr. Fu-Manchu

There was no address; just those three words.

I became suddenly unaware of everything, and of everybody about me, except Betts and the card of Dr. Fu-Manchu. I spoke—and my voice seemed to come from far away.

"Did you—*see* the visitor?"

"I showed him up to the Museum Room, sir, which, having been locked, is the only suitable room in the house today. He expressed a wish to see you *alone*, sir."

"Is *he* alone?"

"Yes, sir…"

A band had started playing somewhere.

People spoke to me on my way: I don't know who they were. One idea, one idea only was burning in my brain: this was a trap, a trap into which the doctor expected that all his enemies assembled in that house would fall!

A final question I threw at Betts:

"He's a tall man?"

"Very tall, sir, and distinguished; Chinese, I believe…"

I battled my way to the staircase. Couples were seated upon it fully halfway up. I heard the chief's loud laugh and had a hazy impression that Nayland Smith formed one of the group in the lobby.

They were the two for whom this trap had been laid!

While disavowing any claims to heroism, I must state here that I mounted those stairs to the Museum Room fully expecting to meet destruction. I was determined to meet it alone. The plan should fail. With moderate luck, I might escape; but, even if I crashed, the Chinese doctor would have been foiled.

Sounds of voices, laughter, music, followed me as I threw open the door guarded left and right by phantoms clothed in Saracen armour.

The Museum Room was empty!

For a moment I doubted the evidence of my senses. After all, was it credible that Fu-Manchu should have presented himself at Sir Lionel's house? Was it possible that he could have crossed the lobby without being recognized by one of the many present who knew him?

I was aware, of course, that the room had three doors; but, even so, escape to the street without detection was next to impossible.

But definitely there was no one there!

Then, on the table, that memorable table which I had prepared for the private view of the relics, I saw that a small parcel lay.

A dimmed clamour of voices and music reached me, with which mingled the traffic hum of Bruton Street.

Neatly wrapped and sealed it lay before me; that package which I believed to contain—death.

The motives which actuated me I realise now, looking back, were obscure; but I opened the parcel and found it to consist of a small casket apparently of crystal, carved (as I supposed at the time) in a pattern of regular prisms which glittered brightly in the sunlight.

An ebony box was inside the casket. A sheet of thick, yellow notepaper, folded, lay on the lid of the box. I opened the box.

It was lined with velvet; and, resting upon the velvet, I saw a string of pink pearls coiled around a scarab ring.

My brain performed a somersault. Someone was calling my name, but I didn't heed the interruption. I was unfolding the sheet of thick, yellow notepaper. It was neither headed nor dated. In jet-black, cramped writing it contained these words:

To Mr. Shan Greville.

Greeting.

You have suffered at my hands, because unwittingly you have sometimes obstructed me. I bear you no ill will. Indeed, I respect you—for you are an honourable man; and I wish you every happiness.

The pearls are for your bride. They are the only perfectly matched set of a hundred pink pearls in the world. The casket is also for her. She is beautiful, brave, and virtuous, a combination of qualities so rare that the woman possessing them is a jewel above price. It is set with eighty flawless diamonds and was made to the order of Catherine of Russia—who was brave, but neither beautiful nor virtuous.

The ebony box is for you. It will interest Sir Lionel Barton. It bears engraved upon it the seal of King Solomon and came from his temple. The ring, also, I request you to accept. It is the signet ring of Khufu—supposed builder of the Great Pyramid.

Commend me to Sir Denis Nayland Smith, to Dr. Petrie, and to Karamenfeh, his wife, and convey my good wishes to Superintendent Weymouth.

I desire you every good fortune.

Greeting and Farewell.
Fu-Manchu.

ABOUT THE AUTHOR

Sax Rohmer was born Arthur Henry Ward in 1883, in Birmingham, England, adding "Sarsfield" to his name in 1901. He was four years old when Sherlock Holmes appeared in print, five when the Jack the Ripper murders began, and sixteen when H.G. Wells' Martians invaded.

Initially pursuing a career as a civil servant, he turned to writing as a journalist, poet, comedy sketch writer, and songwriter in British music halls. At age twenty he submitted the short story "The Mysterious Mummy" to *Pearson's* magazine and "The Leopard-Couch" to *Chamber's Journal*. Both were published under the byline "A. Sarsfield Ward."

Ward's Bohemian associates Cumper, Bailey, and Dodgson gave him the nickname "Digger," which he used as his byline on several serialized stories. Then, in 1908, the song "Bang Went the Chance of a Lifetime" appeared under the byline "Sax Rohmer." Becoming immersed in theosophy, alchemy, and mysticism, Ward decided the name was appropriate to his writing, so when "The Zayat Kiss" first appeared in *The Story-Teller* magazine in October,

1912, it was credited to Sax Rohmer.

That was the first story featuring Fu-Manchu, and the first portion of the novel *The Mystery of Dr. Fu-Manchu*. Novels such as *The Yellow Claw*, *Tales of Secret Egypt*, *Dope*, *The Dream Detective*, *The Green Eyes of Bast*, and *Tales of Chinatown* made Rohmer one of the most successful novelists of the 1920s and 1930s.

There are fourteen Fu-Manchu novels, and the character has been featured in radio, television, comic strips, and comic books. He first appeared in film in 1923, and has been portrayed by such actors as Boris Karloff, Christopher Lee, John Carradine, Peter Sellers, and Nicolas Cage.

Rohmer died in 1959, a victim of an outbreak of the type A influenza known as the Asian flu.

APPRECIATING DR. FU-MANCHU

BY LESLIE S. KLINGER

The "yellow peril"—that stereotypical threat of Asian conquest—seized the public imagination in the late nineteenth century, in political diatribes and in fiction. While several authors exploited this fear, the work of Arthur Henry Sarsfield Ward, better known as Sax Rohmer, stood out.

Dr. Fu-Manchu was born in Rohmer's short story "The Zayat Kiss," which first appeared in a British magazine in 1912. Nine more stories quickly appeared and, in 1913, the tales were collected as *The Mystery of Dr. Fu-Manchu* (*The Insidious Dr. Fu-Manchu* in America). The Doctor appeared in two more series before the end of the Great War, collected as *The Devil Doctor* (*The Return of Dr. Fu-Manchu*) and *The Si-Fan Mysteries* (*The Hand of Fu-Manchu*).

After a fourteen-year absence, the Doctor reappeared in 1931, in *The Daughter of Fu-Manchu*. There were nine more novels, continuing until Rohmer's death in 1959, when *Emperor Fu-Manchu* was published. Four stories, which had previously appeared only in magazines, were published in 1973 as *The Wrath of Fu-Manchu*.

The Fu-Manchu stories also have been the basis of numerous

motion pictures, most famously the 1932 MGM film *The Mask of Fu Manchu*, featuring Boris Karloff as the Doctor.

In the early stories, Fu-Manchu and his cohorts are the "yellow menace," whose aim is to establish domination of the Asian races. In the 1930s Fu-Manchu foments political dissension among the working classes. By the 1940s, as the wars in Europe and Asia threaten terrible destruction, Fu-Manchu works to depose other world leaders and defeat the Communists in Russia and China.

Rohmer undoubtedly read the works of Conan Doyle, and there is a strong resemblance between Nayland Smith and Holmes. There are also marked parallels between the four doctors, Petrie and Watson as the narrator-comrades, and Dr. Fu-Manchu and Professor Moriarty as the arch-villains.

The emphasis is on fast-paced action set in exotic locations, evocatively described in luxuriant detail, with countless thrills occurring to the unrelenting ticking of a tightly-wound clock. Strong romantic elements and sensually described, sexually attractive women appear throughout the tales, but ultimately it is the *fantastic* nature of the adventures that appeal.

This is the continuing appeal of Dr. Fu-Manchu, for despite his occasional tactic of alliance with the West, he unrelentingly pursued his own agenda of world domination. In the long run, Rohmer's depiction of Fu-Manchu rose above the fears and prejudices that may have created him to become a picture of a timeless and implacable creature of menace.

A complete version of this essay can be found in *The Mystery of Dr. Fu-Manchu*, also available from Titan Books